GUNZ AND ROSES

GUNZ AND ROSES

KEISHA ERVIN

www.urbanbooks.net

Urban Books, LLC
78 East Industry Court
Deer Park, NY 11729

Gunz and Roses Copyright © 2009 Keisha Ervin

ISBN 13: 978-1-60162-446-8
ISBN 10: 1-60162-446-8

First Mass Market Printing April 2011
First Trade Paperback Printing September 2009
Printed in the United States of America

10 9 8 7 6 5 4 3 2 1

This is a work of fiction. Any references or similarities to actual events, real people, living, or dead, or to real locales are intended to give the novel a sense of reality. Any similarity in other names, characters, places, and incidents is entirely coincidental.

Distributed by Kensington Publishing Corp.
Submit Wholesale Orders to:
Kensington Publishing Corp.
C/O Penguin Group (USA) Inc.
Attention: Order Processing
405 Murray Hill Parkway
East Rutherford, NJ 07073-2316
Phone: 1-800-526-0275
Fax: 1-800-227-9604

Dedication

I dedicate this book to the strong women in my life who have helped, guided, and loved me unconditionally this past year. Mama, Locia, Joan and Slyvette Bassett, TuShonda and last but not least, Brenda Hampton. If it weren't for you ladies I don't know what I would've done or where or I would be. I thank you from the bottom of my heart.

The one who loves least controls the relationship . . .

Source Unknown

Acknowledgments

Lord, people just don't know how much I've prayed and gave just to be where I am right now. I wish that I could say that this journey has been easy but it hasn't. Along the way I have dodged and jumped over many hurdles. I've been lied to, misused, taken for granted, and taken advantage of. My fans and people on the street think that I have it going on and think that I have it made because of the number of books I have on the shelf, the clothes I wear, and the way I rock my hair. What they don't know is that so many nights have passed where I have cried until my eyes were swollen and my throat was sore because of all the problems and obstacles I've faced, some great and some small. But You being God delivered me from them all. You have been my comfort, my shelter and my confidante. It is another day's journey and all I can say Lord is that I'm glad to be here.

Dear Kyrese,

My gosh!!! You're nine years old now which means that with each day I'm getting older. Lol. Words cannot explain how much I love you. My heart melts every time I look into your eyes. I am so proud of you. You are growing up to be a very bright, charismatic, handsome, and intelligent young man. I cannot wait to see what the future holds for you.

Loving you with all of my heart,
Mom

I have to say thank you and I love you to my mother Pat, my father Carl, my brother Keon, my boyfriend Jay, Locia, Sharissa, Monique, Dee, Tu-Shonda, Ashley, the entire Ervin, Poe and Bassett families!!!

Also I have to give a special thank you to Brenda my new agent. YAY!!!! Thank you for helping me get out of a bad situation with the previous company I was with and into a good one. You have come to be an awesome friend and a damn good agent. The sky is the limit for us and I know with you by my side we can touch the stars. I love you.

And to Carl Weber and the entire Urban family staff, I thank you all from the bottom of heart. Working with you all has been such a pleasure. Carl thanks for opening your arms and welcoming me into your world. I promise not to let you down.

For all you readers out there who have enjoyed my work and wrote to me giving me words of encouragement know that I don't take any of it for granted. Without you all I wouldn't be here so thank you and if you would like to email me with any questions or feedback please contact me at keisha_ervin2002@yahoo.com or www.myspace.com/keishaervin.

GUNZ AND ROSES

I'll do whateva u like . . .

Nicole Sherzinger, "Whatever U Like"

Chapter One

There she was, posted by the bar, chilling, sipping on her third Long Island Iced Tea. when she noticed him. The club was packed and overflowing with people, but somehow their eyes still met. Gray, with her pouty pink lips wrapped around the thin red straw in her drink, watched as he and his mans came bouncing through the door and took over the spot. Everybody in the club, even the most well-known players and hustlers, wanted to show them love.

The whole squad was donned in white tees, hoodies, and designer baggy jeans. From the dip in their walk to the killer instinct in their eyes, Gray could tell they were some trap-by-day, play-all-night, go-gettin'-ass niggas. But out of the whole crew, one stood out the most. There was a quiet confidence about him that reminded her of the actor Idris Elba. She could tell by the swagger in his walk that he knew he was hot. Hell, she couldn't even front; homeboy had her open on sight.

He reminded her of a six foot three West African

god. His skin was the shade of rich black Hawaiian sand, but his eyes were what drew her to him the most. They were shaped like diamonds and somewhat intimidating. A trimmed goatee outlined his full lips, which were begging to be licked. Smooth, spinning waves with a lining so precise it resembled a work of art caused the lips of her pussy to coat with cream.

Gray wanted to be put on in the worst way. Like Brandy, she wanted to be down. She didn't know his name, if he had a girl, or what part of The Lou he was from, but he had to be the most handsome man she had ever seen. This dude was most definitely the truth. On sight he could get it how he wanted, but there was something behind his mesmerizing eyes that screamed *RUN!*

"Gray . . . Gray!" Kema, one of her best friends, shook her arm, bringing her out of a daze. "C'mon, girl, they playin' our song!"

Gray was so transfixed on the chocolate-colored cutie that she didn't even hear her jam thumpin'. "Whatever U Like" by Nicole Scherzinger was spilling through the speakers, causing the wooden floor underneath her feet to vibrate all the way to her soul. As if they'd rehearsed it, she and her girls Kema, Heidi, and Tee-Tee formed a semicircle in the middle of the dance floor and started doing their thing. The neon lights up above served as their spotlight. Lost in the music, Gray's body became one with the beat.

She'd just been hired to work at one of the nation's top style magazines, and all of the pumped-up energy inside her was dying to be released. As soon as her stilettos hit the floor, her lower half began to pop, lock, and drop. She was killin' it, and everybody in the club was taking notice. Seductively she wound her hips when she felt the sensation of two strong hands wrap around her waist. She hoped that it was the guy she'd been checkin', but it wasn't. This dude was a baby.

Poor thing had no idea what he was getting himself into. Gray had something to prove. It was either her or him; one of them was about to get bodied on the dance floor. With the confidence of an exotic dancer, she walked up on him, spun around, and dipped down low. Gray was so far down that her ass was almost sweeping the floor. Totally feeling herself, she wound her hips while still bent low. Slithering her body like a snake, she made her way back up and massaged her ample butt cheeks into his hardened dick.

All the guy could utter was, "Damn."

Gray simply ignored him and continued to do her thing. Tipsy and uninhibited, she leaned over and enticingly made her booty shake. Locking eyes with the black knight from across the room, she ran her hands through her hair and mouthed the words, *Something 'bout that cocky thing you got make me wanna see what's really going on*. It seemed like he enjoyed watching her put on a show, so Gray put even more energy into her erotic dance moves while singing the words to the song: "I'll do whatever you like, I'll do whatever you like, I can do, I can do, I'll do, I'll do, whatever you like."

Having his full attention, she then bit down onto her lower lip and smiled. Even though she was dancing with another man, Gray was the coffee-colored don's private dancer. She could tell that the chocolate thug liked what he saw when he hit her with a sexy grin and winked his eye in approval. Gray knew just the right moves to make him want to taste it. The way she worked her hips and thighs had him hypnotized.

There was no denying it. Gray was one of the coldest chicks in the club. She wasn't model thin or outrageously plump; Gray was a confident size fourteen and loving it. That night she rocked the hell out of a mint green, plunging V-neck, tunic mini-dress and gold YSL heels. Her long black hair was set in full, wavy curls, emphasizing the golden hue in her caramel skin.

She possessed catlike ocean blue eyes that seemed to put anyone in her presence in a trance, dangerously high cheek bones, bunny nose, and succulent full pink lips. All of her Korean and African American assets were on full display that night. In so many words, homegirl had it going on. You couldn't tell her she wasn't the shit. Beyoncé, Ciara, or any of them R&B bitches didn't have a thing on her.

With the clock striking 2:30 AM, the club lights went from dim to bright, letting everyone know it was time to head home. As she picked up her gold Louis Vuitton Miroir bag, the guy Gray had been dancing with tried to push up, but she wasn't having it. Only one man had her attention that night, so she searched the club, only to find that he was already gone. "Shit," she whispered underneath her breath.

"Where we going now?" Gray asked as she and

her girls exited club Dolce's door and welcomed the cool spring air. "'Cause y'all know we gots ta kick it. A week from now I start my new job, so all this shaking my ass in the club shit every night has got to stop."

"On the Eastside," Kema said while smiling and blowing kisses at different men as they strode by. "But first let me go holla at one of my tenders," she announced before disappearing in the crowd.

"Oh, hell no," Gray groaned with her arms folded across her chest. Her feet were killing her

"What's wrong wit' you?" Heidi asked.

"My feet hurt and this bitch gon' be all day. You know she got the keys."

"Damn, she do," her other friend, Tee-Tee, joined in. "Shit, you right. She better hurry up 'cause I gots to get home to my boo." He smiled devilishly as he thought about all the freaky things he wanted to do.

"Oh my God. Is that all you two think about?" Gray rolled her eyes to the sky.

"Eww, don't hate 'cause you ain't gettin' no dick. You the crazy muthafucka. Personally, I don't know how you do it. I couldn't imagine going a year and a half without gettin' some dick. On everything I love, I swear to God I would be somewhere hemmed up in a corner shaking."

"Yo' ass is stupid, and besides, it ain't my fault that I haven't met anybody worth giving it to."

"Whateva." He sucked his teeth. "Better you than me 'cause personally, I couldn't do it. I get sick just thinking about it."

While Gray tried her best to ignore the fact that

she hadn't been kissed, held, or touched in over a
year, she noticed that the street, Broadway, had somehow magically morphed into an outdoor night club.
The atmosphere was live. Nobody seemed to be
going home. There had to be about a hundred cars
ranging from tricked-out old schools to Benzes and
Hummers riding up and down the street. Hoochies
of all different shapes and sizes were going hard for a
shot at being the next hustler's wife. Gray, on the
other hand, wasn't fazed a bit by the iced-out medal-
lions and hundred thousand–dollar cars. After college, she'd landed a job writing for *Alive* magazine.
Gray had her own dough, so how fat a nigga's pockets were didn't turn her on at all.

"Who . . . is . . . that . . . li'l daddy?" Tee-Tee
stressed in great amazement.

Gray glanced to her right and noticed that the
dude she'd been eye-fuckin' from afar had pulled
up directly in front of her in a silver '09 Murciélago.
She had never seen anything like it. The car was
stunningly breathtaking, and when the suicide doors
came up, she really bugged out.

"He is most definitely a winner," Tee-Tee whispered underneath his breath as the guy stepped out
of his ride and leaned up against the hood.

And Tee-Tee was absolutely right. This dude was
the type of man you wanted to sink your teeth into.
He looked like he had the technique to freak a girl
inside out. His entire being reminded her of a sexual chocolate bar, and his outfit only made him
look fresher. Even though it was your typical hood-
boy attire, he was still the hottest dude within
miles. His tall, muscular frame was draped in a ther-

mal, fitted but still a little baggy embroidered Rich Yung jeans, and Tims. This dude could most definitely get it. Instantly, he had Gray's vote.

"Yo, come here. Let me holla at you for a second." He looked her square in the eyes.

"Who, me?" Gray's eyes grew wide as she pointed to her chest.

"Yeah, you. Who else you think I'm talkin' to? Come here."

Gray's right eyebrow instantly sprouted into an arch. She wanted to ask him who he was talking to but thought against it. There was something about his demeanor that told her that this man didn't fuck around or play games, so instead of getting smart, she placed her shoulders back and strutted over to him. Sheer appreciation was written all over his face. She had the meanest walk that he'd ever been blessed to see.

"Okay, I'm here. Now what?"

"What you mean, now what?" He gripped her waist and pulled her close. "You been fuckin' wit' my ass all night; now you wanna act shy."

"First of all, I'm far from shy. And why are your hands on me?"

"Correction: they're wrapped around you, and that's where they're supposed to be."

"Oh, really?" Gray nervously grinned.

"Don't front, ma. You know you like it." He pulled her even farther in between his legs, his hard dick now poking her thigh.

"What's your name?"

"Gunz."

"Gunz," she repeated, shocked.

"Yeah." He massaged her hips. "What, you got a problem with my name?"

"No."

"Bet not," he whispered into her ear.

"Whateva." Gray laughed.

"You know I like 'em thick." He ignored her and admired her frame.

"Okay, you are officially a mess."

"What's your name?"

"Gray, but you can call me G."

"How about I call you my girl?"

Gray's lungs had officially deflated and she couldn't breathe. This dude had her heart in the palm of his hand and didn't even know it. For a minute they just stood gazing into each other's eyes, each wondering what the other was thinking, when a cool breeze swept over each of their bodies.

"Ooh." She hugged herself tight.

"You a'ight?" Gunz gently began caressing her goose bump–covered arms.

"Just a little cold."

"We can take care of that." He stood up. Her breasts were now pressed up against his broad chest. "C'mon."

Gunz took Gray's hand and led her over to the passenger side door of his car. Before she got in, Gray looked around for Heidi and Tee-Tee, but noticed that they, too, had disappeared. Figuring she would look for her friends in a minute, she hopped inside Gunz's car. Once in, she sat comfortably in the custom made, butter-soft leather seats while Gunz talked on his cell phone. Common's "I Want You" played as she sat quietly, thinking, *What in the hell have I gotten myself into?*

"My bad. That was my pot'nah from out of town," he let her know as he flipped his phone shut.

"No problem."

"Yo, I'm feelin' crazy nice right now." He laughed, running his hands down his face. Gunz had drunk five glasses of Hennessy neat.

"I see."

"So, what's good wit' you, Gray?" he asked, pulling a blunt and two thick wads of cash out of his pocket at the same time.

"You tell me." She arched one eyebrow, wondering if she was supposed to be impressed.

"At the moment, you."

"Is that right?" She laughed.

"Yeah, and my bad; you smoke?" He attempted to pass her the blunt.

"Nah, you good." She pushed his hand back toward him.

"So this y'all li'l spot?"

"Nah," she replied, remembering her friends. "What, you come here a lot?"

"Nah, shorty, a nigga like me always on the move. As a matter of fact, I just got back into town today."

"From where?"

"Vegas."

"What were you there for?"

"I went to see the fight."

"The Sugar Shane Mosley fight?"

"Yeah, I had some money on that shit."

"I wanted to go see that fight. Did you win?"

"C'mon, ma." He twisted up his face like she was crazy. "Ya boy here never loses. I always play to win."

"Oh, word?"

"Word. And don't think I forgot." He placed his head down and gave her his infamous crooked grin.

"Forgot what?"

"How you was throwing that ass all up on that nigga in the club. What, you was try'na make me jealous?" Gunz eyed her shimmering bronze legs and wondered how they would feel up on his shoulders.

Following his eyes, Gray came to the conclusion that he was peepin' her frame, but she played it cool. She couldn't let him know that his gaze alone made her want to jump on his dick and ride it all the way until the sun came up.

"How could I possibly make you jealous? I don't even know you."

"Gray,"—he scooted closer—"so you try'na tell me that show wasn't for me?"

"Gunz," she countered back, "stop asking me questions you already know the answers to."

"So I guess your evil plan worked." He moved his face closer to hers, his lips barely inches away from her wanting mouth.

"What evil plan?" Her lips nervously brushed up against his.

"To make my dick hard." He took her hand and placed it on his growing manhood. Gray's eyes immediately grew wide with surprise. Gunz's dick stretched halfway down his thigh. "You feel how hard that is? You know you did that, right?"

"It's so big." She absently purred, massaging him through his pants. The effects of the Long Island Iced Tea had officially kicked in.

"Keep it up and I'ma have to punish you." He softly kissed her lips.

"Well, all right."

"So what's the deal, shorty? You gon' kick it wit' a nigga tonight or what?"

"Are you askin' me or tellin' me?" She shot him a sexy grin, allowing her smile to glow in the moonlight.

"Stop wit' the cat and mouse game, Gray. You and I both know you coming home wit' me tonight." He kissed her again.

Gray was so into the feel of his lips on hers that she didn't even notice his hand slip underneath her dress and between her thighs. Lightly, he began to thumb her stiff clit. She didn't intend to release a moan, but the tingling sensation that was building in her pussy was too much to bear. Caressing the side of his face, Gray became overwhelmed by the tip of his tongue as she moved his hand away. Gunz respected her choice, and instead decided to relish in the movement of their tongues slow dancing with one another.

"I knew you was wet." He opened his eyes then pecked her lips once more before falling back.

Gray's mouth couldn't come up with the right words to say, she was so turned on. Gunz's captivating voodoo had completely taken over. Usually, she wouldn't let things go this far, but there was something about the gorgeous creature sitting before her that had her acting totally out of character. For some reason, she couldn't compose herself. Gunz looked good as hell slumped back in the driver's seat. His eyes were at half mast, as clouds of weed smoke drew pictures in front of his face.

"Look, this was fun, but I gotta go." She opened the door, knowing it was past time for her to leave. With one foot on the pavement, she felt Gunz grab her hand and gently pull her back.

"Where you goin'?"

"This is just waaay too much. I'm drunk, and you're high and trippin'."

"Man, close the door." His tone was low but commanding.

Gray locked eyes with Gunz and wondered what it was about him that made her want to stay.

"Please."

Inhaling deeply, she took a much needed breath and placed her foot back into the car and closed the door.

"What you runnin' for?"

"I wouldn't call it runnin'. I just know what's good for me."

"Trust me, ma." He kissed her lips again. "I know what's good for the both of us."

"Well, if you know what's good, then you know you need to be taking me home."

"Is that what you really want?"

Gray thought for a minute before speaking. "No."

The scene was like something out of a film. Gunz and Gray entered his condo in complete silence. Nothing had to be said. Each of them knew what they were there to do. Gunz didn't even turn on the lights. The room was already dimly lit. That night, they would use the light from the city skyline as their guide.

Gray did a quick assessment of his place and was impressed. Gunz's crib looked like a mini mansion. Unlike your regular condo, this one came equipped with a living room, kitchen, two bedrooms, two baths, game room, sauna, and elevator. The bedroom itself was amazing. It had a sensuous, contemporary feel to it. It was beautifully decorated with the colors pale blue and grey. In the center of the room was a platform bed with a massive wooden headboard. Gunz had a flat screen television, but it was cleverly hidden in a slot at the foot of the bed. The only other things in the room were a stereo system and a life-sized telephone booth aquarium filled with African Cichlids and Puffers.

After throwing her purse on the floor, Gray sauntered backward to the bed, never breaking eye contact with Gunz. Turning around, she gazed over her shoulder, winked her eye, and slowly began to peel the upper half of her dress down. Gunz couldn't take his eyes off her ass. It sat up just right.

With a look of lust in her eyes, she turned around and unsnapped her bra. As it fell to the floor, she bit down into her lower lip and signaled for him to come to her. Gray aggressively took his face into the palms of her hands and kissed his soft lips.

Gunz was on cloud nine. He'd waited all night for this. Ready to do her thing, Gray pushed him down onto the bed. Standing before him, she continued her erotic strip tease by massaging her breasts and licking her nipples until Gunz couldn't take it anymore.

"Come here, man." He spoke barely above a whisper because he was so dazed.

Gray did as she was told and switched her way over to her prey. Tired of playing games, he grabbed her by the waist and made her straddle him. Eagerly, he took each of her breasts into his hands.

"Not yet," she moaned, pushing his hands away.

With her arms wrapped around his neck, Gray twirled her hips to an imaginary beat. Gunz's dick was rock hard, and she could feel every inch of it. Smiling at a job well done, she ran her hands through her hair and then slid them down her body slowly while rolling her torso like a belly dancer. Gray was in absolute control and loved every minute of it. She swung her hair over to the side and made sure that he had a good view of her caramel-colored breasts.

This chick love to play games, Gunz thought. His dick couldn't take it anymore, so he placed his strong hands onto her full breasts again. This time Gray didn't protest. Gently, he took one of her nipples into his mouth and sucked. It tasted just like Hershey's Kisses.

The experience of his tongue on her nipples was sensational. Every lick was sinful and soft to the touch. The two didn't even realize it, but after a minute, they had unconsciously begun to clothesburn one another. Gray was now grinding her hips even harder on his dick. Every time her pussy pressed up against his dick, she moaned.

The sound of her sweet groans sent bolts of intense electrical sparks throughout Gunz's entire body. He knew if he didn't stop her soon he would bust in his pants, so he took control of the situation by standing up and roughly laying her down on her back. Gunz quickly snatched off her dress, leaving her in nothing but a pair of four-inch stilettos. Grabbing the remote control, he turned on the stereo. "You Already Know" played in the background as he removed his thermal, boxer briefs, jeans, and Tims.

"You know I'm about to fuck the shit out you, right?" he stated, now on top. "But first you gon' let me taste the kitty?"

Gray didn't even get a chance to reply before Gunz's mouth and tongue were devouring the lips of her pussy. Normally, he wouldn't go down on someone so soon, but he was drunk, and tonight was different. Her pink clit was begging to be tortured and teased.

Pushing her knees up to her chest, Gunz smiled. She had to have the prettiest pussy he'd ever seen. Gunz buried his face between her thighs and proceeded to give her insides an oral education. He used two of his fingers to spread her lips apart so that his tongue could toy with her clit. In a matter of seconds her pussy began to make it rain. Hot, creamy juices dripped from her lips and into his mouth. Gunz was eating her pussy so well she had no choice but to holler and scream.

"Oh, God!"

"You like that, huh?" he asked.

"Yeah, don't stop!"

"I'm gon' make you cum real hard, a'ight?"

"Mm-hmm."

"You ready?"

"Yeeeeeeeeeeeeeeeeeees," Gray squealed.

Never one to renege on a promise, Gunz placed two of his fingers inside her warm tunnel and started working them all around, while zoning in on her clit with his tongue. In a matter of seconds, Gray's thighs began to shake.

"Ooh, baby . . . I'm cumming! I'm cumming!" she screamed, clawing the sheets.

Wiping his mouth, Gunz made his way back up and said, "You want this fat dick, don't you?"

"Yes." Gray panted, still reeling from her orgasmic high.

"You want me to work the middle?"

"Yes."

"Goddamn, you wet. You gon' throw that pussy back?" He toyed with her by sliding his dick up and down the opening of her wet slit.

"Yes."

"Then stop wit' the good girl act and tell a nigga how bad you want it." He licked then bit her neck.

"I want it bad. I want it real bad," Gray moaned, about to lose her mind.

"Say it again."

"I want it real bad. Fuck my pussy until I—"

Gray couldn't finish her sentence. Gunz had already rammed his thick, ten-inch dick inside her pussy, hitting bottom.

"Ahhhhhhh!" Gray's eyes rolled to the back of her head. Her pussy was being suffocated by Gunz's dick.

"This how you want it?" he groaned while pumping in and out as sweat dripped from his pores.

"Yes . . . yes!" Gray screamed, feeling possessed.

Grinding his dick in and out, Gunz made sure that Gray came at least three times before he even came once. All ten inches of his rock solid dick filled her insides. She barely had enough room to breathe.

"Yo' pussy tighter than muthafucka, ma," Gunz roared, biting down on his bottom lip so he wouldn't scream out like a bitch.

"You gon' cum for me? I wanna see you cum." Gray rubbed his back as his hips roughly rotated in a circular motion.

Obliging her request, Gunz came long and hard inside of her.

"Ay." Gunz shook Gray's leg as she lay sound asleep.

She looked so peaceful he almost didn't want to wake her. For a minute he just sat back and examined her features. There was no doubt Gray was pretty; no scratch that she was beautiful. Her skin was as smooth as water. The arch in her eyebrow was even more distinct with her eyes shut, and on her right cheek were a few small freckles. If she played her cards right, Gunz could almost think about locking her down and making her his wife.

"Yo, Gray! Wake up!" He slapped her hard on the ass this time, causing it to jiggle.

Gray's eyes instantly popped open. The first thing she spotted was Gunz standing before her with a stern look on his face. He was dressed in nothing but a white cotton towel, which hung low on his defined waist. Focusing her eyes, she made a trail from his washboard abs to the imprint of his dick. Gray couldn't have woken up to a better sight. The only problem was that she couldn't remember exactly where she was or how she'd gotten there.

This wasn't her bed or her sheets. And who was this nigga telling her to get up like he was some kind of drill sergeant? As she went to sit up, Gray was hit with the excruciating pain of a splitting headache. Holding her head, she tried to stop the pain and figure out where the hell she was.

"What time is it?" she asked, shielding her eyes from the blinding light of the sun.

"Going on eight." Gunz sat on the edge of the bed and out on his watch.

"Oh."

As if she were a patient suffering from amnesia, Gray suddenly got her memory back. Flashes of the night before filled her mind. She remembered leaving the club without telling her girls where she was headed. She could see Gunz leading her up to his crib. She could feel his big black dick thrusting inside her, making her cum over and over again.

Utterly embarrassed by her actions, she shook her head in disbelief. Gray was sure that her hair was all over her head and that she looked a hot mess, but at that moment, she couldn't care less. All she wanted was to get into her own bed, take a couple of aspirin, and get some rest.

"Yo, you good?" Gunz took a sip of orange juice. "'Cause it's about time to make that move."

"Yeah, my head just hurts; that's all."

"Well, look . . . last night was fun, but a nigga gotta jet. But don't even trip, though. I left you a li'l something on the nightstand."

In total shock, Gray turned to her right, and sure enough, on the nightstand next to his cell phone and wallet was three hundred dollars.

"You need me to drop you off somewhere, or is that gon' be enough for a cab?"

Gray was speechless. She'd never been made to feel so low and dirty before. She'd hoped that he could look past her sexual whim, but as her eyes connected with his and she saw only her reflection, she realized that all she could ever be to him was the darkness they knew.

"Are you serious?"

"What? That ain't enough? You need some more?"

"Oh, uh-uh. You have seriously lost your mind." She pulled the covers from over her naked body and got up.

Gunz was once again taken in by her curvaceous frame. If she didn't look so mad, he would've attempted to hit it again.

"Do I look like some kind of ho to you? Yeah, nigga, what we did last night was fun, but don't get it twisted. You got what you wanted, and so did I."

"Yoooooooo, ma . . ." He cocked his head to the side and waved her off. "You can stop wit' all the dramatics, 'cause I ain't even for all that."

"Excuse you? Who the fuck you think you talkin' to? Yo, I swear cats like you really fuck me up. You think 'cause you look halfway decent and got a li'l change that you God's gift to the world, but let me tell you something. You got me and life all the way fucked up, 'cause Gray don't need you!" she yelled, snatching up her clothes. "And you can keep that measly-ass three hundred dollars! That shit ain't even enough to get my hair fixed!"

She tried to shoot past him, but instead of letting her walk by, Gunz grabbed her hand and pulled her back.

"What the fuck is yo' problem?"

"Umm, you need to be letting me go." She looked him up and down.

"Nah, damn that. Sit yo' ass the fuck down." He pushed her back onto the bed and lay on top of her. "Ain't nobody tryin' to play you." His full lips were inches away from hers. "And all that slick shit you was just kickin' ain't even for you, so act right, ma. A nigga could see you as his wife, but if you keep showin' yo' ass, I'ma quit fuckin' wit' you, you dig?"

"Gunz, get off of me."

"Nah, you bad. Talk that slick shit now." He slid down her body, kissing her stomach and navel along the way. "You don't want the money, Gray?" he asked, pushing her thighs back. "You don't want me?"

"Gunz." She squirmed as he parted then licked the lips of her pussy.

Instead of responding, Gunz sucked her clit. Gray's body was paralyzed with pleasure. His tongue was on a mission to please, as his mouth rotated between stroking and sucking.

"Gunz," she moaned, rubbing the top of his head. "Baby, stop."

"Nah, you gon' let me suck this fat-ass pussy." He licked even faster.

"But if you keep it up, I'ma cum." Gray could feel sticky cream building between her legs.

"That's what we want, ain't it?"

"Yes."

"A'ight now, get used to it. A nigga finally found home, ma." He ran his tongue across her stiff clit before gently biting the lips. "This my new home."

My every thought is you . . .

Kelly Rowland, "Every Thought Is You"

Chapter Two

It was the middle of the night and Gray lay in the center of her bed dressed in only a nude panty and bra set. Thoughts of her steamy night with Gunz ran rampant through her mind. For the first time in a year, she had thrown caution to the wind and let go. Gray was tired of being cautious and always doing the right thing. That night, she had decided to live life and not worry about the repercussions of her choices. It was time to have fun and allow herself some pleasure; but now, as she lay alone, she wondered if she had made the right decision.

A week had passed, and she hadn't seen or heard from Gunz. And even though she felt some kind of way about it, no matter how hard she tried, all she could think of was him. For the past seven days she ate, slept, and drank Gunz. Every night, she lay dreaming about what they could be. Either she was envisioning his sly grin, dreaming of his sweet kisses, or dying for his touch.

Sometimes she swore she even smelled the scent

of his cologne. In her dreams, she could feel his firm hands gripping her waist and pulling her close. She just wanted to be next to him, bathe in his touch, drink in his smile. The only thing she could think was, *Why did I fuck him so soon?* Rolling her eyes, Gray tossed and turned under the white sheets, which cascaded over her body like ripples, until she felt somewhat comfortable. As she lay gazing absently at the ceiling, she wondered if it was possible that Gunz could be thinking of her too.

"He couldn't be," she spoke out loud as she sat up and ran her hands through her thick, curly hair. "He hasn't even called me yet."

Restless, Gray got up and headed downstairs. Her two-story loft was huge; two thousand–plus square feet, to be exact. She'd decorated it beautifully with a mixture of her two favorite design concepts: artistic, but edgy. In her living area, the walls were an electric shade of blue. Gigantic windows and a black and white photo of Gray dressed in nothing but a pair of jeans, cupping her breasts, consumed the walls.

Also in the living area was a zebra print chaise with yellow throw pillows. In front of it was a steel fireplace with an L-beam mantel. A two-toned black and white sofa, two sleek '60s-inspired chairs and a crystal chandelier finished off the room. With thoughts of Gunz consuming her mind, Gray looked out the window and admired the sky. It was one of those nights where the horizon was darker than usual. Not a cloud was in sight, and millions of stars twinkled, shining a stark light onto her face.

Should I call him, I wonder but quickly nixed the

idea. *This is too much. Shake this nigga off, girl. You barely know him. Get it together, bitch!*

Gray knew her conscience was right. She needed to get over the feelings that tortured her heart and plagued her mind. It was just that their one night together had made a strong impact on her life. Although she didn't know Gunz that well, he was the first person she'd slept with in over a year. Never before had she behaved that way. She'd never been that aggressive, but she liked it. She liked that Gunz brought out the bad girl in her. She was almost sure he was a no-good-ass nigga, but there was just something about the chemistry they shared. If given the opportunity, she had to give him one more chance.

Gunz stood at the window of his luxury condo, looking upon the city as the sky dripped heavy drops of rain. His perfectly sculpted physique stood tall while he puffed on a freshly lit see-through blunt. The sun was just beginning to peek above the horizon. It was 5:55 AM and he hadn't slept a wink.

Gunz rarely slept more than two hours anyway, but on nights like these, he knew he wouldn't be able to sleep at all. He hated the way darkness fell each and every night. It only served to remind him of his own mortality. Gunz didn't fear much in life, but for some reason, dying was one thing he did fear. He didn't understand why, especially since he'd ended so many lives.

Maybe it was because as a young child he realized that you didn't have to be grown to go. When he was eleven, his sister died in an accidental drowning. Gunz couldn't pinpoint when the fear had set in. All he knew was at night, while he tried to rest, he'd awaken, jumping out of his sleep at the thought of his life slipping away. So, instead of sleeping, he grinded hard in the streets or preoccupied himself with unnecessary company.

That night, Devin, the pecan beauty lying in his bed sleeping peacefully was his diversion from reality. She was a brave girl that was down to do brave things. For an hour and half, she did nasty things to Gunz that most men only dreamed of.

They met five years ago. He'd been in the club with his mans when she approached. From the look in her eyes, he could tell that she was a project nympho. His theory was proven true when after only one drink they were in the bathroom and she was giving him head. Gunz was a sex fiend. Getting pussy was like Kryptonite; it made him weak.

That morning, after winning a couple of grand at the casino, he met up with Devin back at his place. She'd cum multiple times, and he'd enjoyed turning her out, but in a couple of hours, it would be time for her to go, just like all the rest. Being with only one woman didn't excite him. If anything, it scared the shit out of him. After the death of his sister, Gunz's heart was permanently cemented under his foot, so it meant something that, while banging the pecan beauty's back out, visions of Gray's face flashed before his eyes. There was something about the half-black and Korean mami. He loved the way she snapped her fingers, rocked her hips, and bit her bottom lip.

She was the perfect size and weight. There was

no fighting it. His every thought was of her. He could see her bouncing up and down on his dick, feel her nails scratching his back, and hear her calling out his name. Her feisty ways only made him think of her more.

He wasn't trying to be rude or disrespectful by offering her money. Gunz was only trying to show her love. That's how he got down. What he couldn't say with his mouth, he showed through his pockets, and although he didn't know her that well, he was almost sure she wasn't a ho.

With thoughts of Gray drowning his mind, Gunz picked up his cell phone and called her.

"Hello?" She answered on the first ring.

"You been on my mind all week. You miss me?"

"No."

"Damn, that's fucked up." He chuckled. "Here I been missing you like crazy, and you ain't even been thinking about me."

"Gunz, please."

"Well, if you don't miss me, I know ya li'l mami do, 'cause I been missing the hell out of her."

"She miss you. Now, why you up so early?" Gray turned over to her side, happy as hell.

"I don't sleep." His mind went back to thoughts of death.

"Why not?"

"I just don't. Now, what you got on?"

"Nothing," she lied. Gray could almost bet his dick was hard.

"That's what's up?" Gunz adjusted his hard dick. "Can I come I see you tonight?"

"Yeah. What time?"

"Umm, around eight."

"That's cool."

"When you open the door, you better be naked," he joked.

"Bye, Gunz." She laughed.

"A'ight, ma. One."

Gray hung up the phone with a huge smile spread across her face. She was smiling so hard her cheeks hurt. She couldn't wait to see Gunz later on that night. Closing her eyes, she hoped and prayed that he wouldn't be like all the rest and live down to her expectations.

Jitters filled Gray's stomach, causing her lips to quiver as she made her way through the doors of *Haute Couture* magazine. It was just as she thought it would be: vibrant, full of possibilities, and fast paced. The walls were stark white, and the furniture was mod, yet very contemporary. Swallowing the huge lump in her throat, she held her head high and prepared for her first day at work.

She'd landed her dream job as the assistant to the creative director of style, but first Gray had to have a sit-down with *Haute Couture*'s editor-in-chief, Sienna Saint James. Sienna was the black Anna Wintour of the fashion industry. Black Hollywood looked up to her. Her words were like gospel written from the Bible. With one word she set trends and jumpstarted careers.

Besides her mother, Soon Yee, who now lived in Korea, Sienna was Gray's only other role model. She prided herself on the magazine. Gray had been reading it since she was ten. *Haute Couture* was the go-to classic, edgy fashion magazine that African American women from the ages of sixteen to forty-five read religiously. It covered the most coveted designers, up and coming models, runway trends, beauty concepts, and A-list celebrities.

Gray could vividly remember as a child waiting in line for the next edition to hit newsstands. Once she got her copy, she would race home, lock herself in her room, and fantasize about being one of the models in the magazine. When she was little, Gray wasn't comfortable living in her own skin. It was hard for her growing up as a mixed race child because she didn't have her father, who was African American, in the house to teach her his culture. All she knew was her Korean heritage and traditions.

And to make matters worse, there were no other Korean kids in her neighborhood. So, all she had to relate to were the African American kids, but they felt as if she weren't black enough. Gray didn't know what to say, what to do, or how to prove herself. Nothing she said or did helped. None of the girls liked her, and the boys from around the way constantly teased her; but to be poor on top of that made life even worse. Every day she was taunted by her peers for not being able to afford the latest fashions. Her mother couldn't afford to buy her expensive clothes, so instead, she sewed or shopped at thrift stores.

Gray despised going to school, until she met Kema in junior high school. They instantly became friends. Kema didn't judge her for being biracial. She respected Gray for who she was, and in turn, this made Gray feel comfortable in her skin. She realized that she didn't have to prove herself to be liked. All she had to do was be who she was. No longer being a social outcast, Gray got on the grind.

She worked her ass off through high school and college so that she could live out her dream of working with the fashion elite. She wanted nothing more than to be able to afford the one-of-a-kind pieces of clothing she saw in *Haute Couture* magazine. She didn't want to struggle anymore. Gray knew there was more to life than the confines of her neighborhood, and to be working for Sienna Saint James proved her point even more. Dreams really did come true.

With her hair filled with loose, free-flowing curls, Gray walked to the front desk, dressed in a sleeveless black scoop neck bubble dress and black patent leather open-toed heels.

"Hi. Welcome to *Haute Couture*. How may I help you?" the perky front desk clerk spoke.

"Hi, my name is Gray Rose. Today's my first day. Sienna Saint James should be expecting me."

"She is. Take the elevator up to the twenty-fifth floor and then make a right."

"Thank you."

Once upstairs, Gray checked in with Kema, Sienna's personal secretary, and then stepped into her office. To her surprise, there was a homey feel to the space. Gray was in awe. Sienna's office overlooked downtown St. Louis. Tons of black and white photos of her and her famous friends adorned the wall. An array of flowers scented the room. A crystal vase filled with fresh calla lilies sat in the corner above an antique mirrored desk. Behind it, sitting in a matching chair with her legs crossed was "the" Sienna Saint James.

She hadn't uttered a word, but she was still everything Gray thought she would be. There was an air of confidence and power that oozed from her pores. She was forty-six years old, but with the help of dieting, exercise, and Botox, Sienna didn't look a day over thirty.

"Hellooo," she spoke dryly, giving Gray a once-over look.

"Hi, I'm Gray." Gray stuck out her hand.

"Sorry, dear, I don't shake hands."

"Oh."

"You're late."

"Umm,"—Gray glanced at her watch—"I was told to be here at eight o'clock. It's eight o'clock on the dot."

"Being on time is late. I never arrive on time. I always show up at least fifteen to twenty minutes early. Remember, the early bird gets the worm. Have a seat." Sienna sat back in her chair and squinted her eyes.

Taken aback by her attitude, Gray quietly sat down.

"So tell me, what is it that brought you to *Haute Couture* magazine?"

"Since I was a child, I've loved *Haute Couture*. I grew up on the magazine, and I've followed your career since you took over in ninety-nine. *Haute Couture* was almost extinct, then you came along and singlehandedly revamped the magazine and made it the fashion leader it is today. Without your influence, *Haute Couture* would be just another magazine that folded."

"So you've done your homework? *Haute Couture* caters to women on the go, the type of woman that is glamorous, chic, sophisticated, and thin. Tell me, Gray, where do you think you fit in to that picture?"

Gray felt as though she had been sucker punched in the stomach. Unwilling to let Sienna see her crumble, she chose her words carefully before deciding to speak.

"First of all, I am glamorous, sophisticated, and chic. The only thing I am not is thin. I'm a size fourteen, and there are a lot more women in the world that look like me than the models in your magazine. Maybe that's something that *Haute Couture* should look into."

Impressed by her answer, Sienna simply pursed her lips and inhaled deeply. "You know that working for this magazine is not an easy task. In the last month alone we've fired six assistants. Are you really sure that you can handle the demands of this job?"

"If you don't have challenges in life, then how will you grow?" Gray countered back on point.

"Okay, Gray,"—Sienna arched her eyebrow—"we're going to give this a try. You'll be on probation for ninety days. Kema will fill you in on everything you need to know."

"Thank you so much, Miss Saint James." Gray happily hopped up.

"It's *Ms.*"

"Oh, I'm sorry, Ms. Saint James."

"Get it right, dear." Sienna diverted her attention as if no one else was in the room and began working.

Once again caught off guard by her rudeness, Gray stood dumbfounded.

Sensing her uneasiness, Sienna looked up from her work and said, "That will be all."

Gray left the room somewhat in a daze. She wasn't sure if she should jump for joy or run for the nearest exit. Sienna was the most unpleasant person she had ever met, but Gray would never quit. She hadn't come this far for nothing. After going over do's and don'ts and signing paperwork with Kema, the rest of the day was a blur. If she wasn't pulling clothes, she was answering phones, picking up purses from Chanel, getting coffee, confirming appointments, or dodging Sienna's smart remarks. By the time she got home, Gray was mentally and physically exhausted.

All she wanted was to take a hot bath and crawl into bed, but Gunz had called twice confirming that he was still stopping by. Beyond tired but excited by the thought of seeing his face, she quickly took a shower. After drying off, she brushed her teeth then massaged scented lotion into her skin. Since they would be in the house, she decided upon wearing a white camisole and leggings.

Once she was dressed, Gray lay across her bed sideways. It felt good to be off of her feet. Grabbing the remote control, she turned on the television. A rerun of one of her favorite television shows, *Harlem Heights*, was on.

Twenty minutes into the episode, her cell phone began to ring. It was Gunz. Happy that he was keeping true to his word, she answered the phone.

"Hello?"

"What's up, Future?"

"Future?" she repeated, confused.

"Yeah, my future wife."

"That's really how you feel?" She laughed.

Gunz couldn't help but laugh too.

"I'm just fuckin' wit' you. What you doing?"

"What you think I'm doing? I'm waiting on you."

"Well, look, I'm kinda running late, so give me about an hour and a half, a'ight?"

"Okay, but you need to hurry up, 'cause I gotta be at work in the morning."

"I'm sure one of your coworkers at McDonalds can cover your shift if you're late," he joked.

"For your information, I work for *Haute Couture* magazine, thank you very much."

"You know I'm just fuckin' wit' you, ma. But look, let me handle this business real quick and I'll be there in a minute."

"A'ight."

"One."

His family called him Gavin, but to the world he was known as Gunz Marciano, the young, heartless creator of the Marciano Crime Mob, better known as MCM. For the past seven years he'd been the boss, the leader, el capitan, Mr. 17.5 of the largest black crime family the world had ever seen. Gunz's rep in the streets was impeccable. He wasn't to be fucked with. When he talked, niggas listened, and when niggas listened, Gunz made money.

He had a crew of niggas rolling with him, and they all moved like soldiers. The MCM Empire stretched from St. Louis, over to Detroit, past Baltimore, up to Jersey, and across the country to Cali.

Everybody was out for the same goal: get money. Their code of ethics was honor, loyalty, and respect; the one rule they lived by was 'don't snitch.'

Dressed in all black with his favorite girl—a nine millimeter—by his side, Gunz sat comfortably with his hat draped low. Out of the corner of his eye he could see a rat scurry across the concrete floor and into a rotted hole in the wall. Glass crackled underneath his feet as his tongue toyed with a toothpick dangling from the side of his lips. His two best friends, Watts and Bishop, held court behind him. They were both strapped with pistols and AKs.

A small portion of his squad stood patiently waiting for him to speak as the stark white florescent lights flickered on and off around the warehouse. Gunz was used to people hanging on to his every word, so he chose them carefully. Niggas had been fucking up, so he studied his squad. Like a dog, he could smell fear.

They all had unsure looks on their faces. Gunz could tell they were wondering why he had called an impromptu meeting at eleven o' clock at night. He could tell that they were concerned.

He hated that he had to take them out of their comfort zone because when they were comfortable, they worked harder; but there were some issues at hand that needed to be discussed. The feds had been nosing around too much. Every other week someone from his crew was being knocked. Suddenly, the police knew when and where drops were being made.

Weapons and bricks of cocaine and heroin were confiscated. In Gunz's mind, this meant one thing: somebody from his crew was breaking the rules.

This put Gunz in a predicament because being the go-to nigga meant he had to be feared yet respected without being too giving, too strict, or too friendly. It was fucked up that he had to do one of his men in, but a point had to be made. Nothing got past Gunz Marciano. Nothing.

"It's a beautiful night, huh?" He gave his men a slight smile as he toyed with the lighter in his hand, flicking it on and off.

"Not a cloud in sight . . . but y'all niggas didn't know I could make it rain." Gunz's upper lip curled as his head cocked to the side. "Young Gunna, what's the one thing MCM niggas hate the most?"

"Snitches," the devoted young soldier responded with conviction.

"And what happens when niggas snitch?"

"They get wet up."

"Exactly. So, tell me . . ."—Gunz rubbed his chin—"why somebody from our crew has been working with the feds."

Surprised faces filled the room as everyone stood in shock—except for one. One member had his head down low and was shuffling his feet.

"Rich? What you got ya head down for, man?"

"Wh–wh–what you talkin' about, boss?" he asked nervously.

"You stuttering now, nigga?"

"I–I–I–I'm just saying—"

"Nah, nigga, you ain't saying shit! Yo, Bishop, shut this muthafucka up! I'm tired of listening to this bitch-ass nigga talk!"

Without hesitation and with pure joy written all over his face, Bishop walked over to Rich, reared his hand back, and slapped him in the mouth with the butt of his gun. Like Sylvester Stallone in a *Rocky* movie, blood spewed from Rich's mouth and into the dust-filled air. Pissed, Rich clutched his jaw in agony and decided it was best to keep his mouth shut and listen.

"Now, that's better." Gunz eyed Rich and his crew. "It's fucked up 'cause I thought you could go far in this game, but you ain't built for this shit. You's a weak nigga. You chose to fuck wit' my life and work wit' the feds over riding wit' your man, so you know what?" He stood up and placed the hood of his jacket over his head. "I'ma see you in hell, muthafucka. Yo, Bishop."

"What's good, fam?"

"Make it rain."

Fear rested in Rich's eyes as the realization that his life was about to end became clear. Gunz knew that look like he knew the back of his hand. He'd seen it too many times before. This was the part of the game that he hated. He was tired of going to funerals and wakes, faking condolences while mothers screamed why.

He was sick of waking up in a cold sweat from nightmares of the men he'd killed or had members of his crew kill. Gunz didn't want to hear another man beg for his life as if he were God. Something had to give, he thought, as his driver, Lorenzo, opened the back door to his Phantom. Gunz got inside and rested his head back up against the seat. He couldn't continue to live life this way, but just as he came to that conclusion, the sound of a gun pop brought an end to yet another life.

* * *

The central air in Gray's loft hummed softly as she lay stretched out, asleep underneath the covers. The atmosphere was still and serene, even though on the inside, Gray's emotions were stirring. She tried to stay up, but after watching television, gossiping on the telephone, and dozing off twice, she'd had enough of waiting on Gunz. He must have had her confused with the next chick.

Gray was heated, and she refused to be duped into playing silly cat and mouse games with Gunz or any other man. After her last serious relationship, she set a couple of rules for herself. The first was not to be so readily available for a man. She would be the one to keep them waiting and wanting more. She wouldn't answer the phone every time the guy called. She'd always say what she meant and not beat around the bush about how she felt. And most importantly, she wouldn't put all of her eggs in one basket by just dating one man.

She was done with falling so quickly only to be disappointed in the end, and the way things were going with Gunz, it looked like he was feeding her the same ol' lines she'd heard a million times before. His excuses sounded too familiar. He was just like all the other dudes she'd met, full of broken promises and excuses.

For a minute she thought about calling to see what the holdup was, but Gray wasn't the sweating type. No man was that important, or at least that's what she wanted to believe. Instead of going the desperate route, she would just play him to the left, or better yet, turn her phone off. Yeah, that's what she would do.

But Gray was too open for that, so she kept her

phone on and prayed that he called with some kind of excuse so she could cuss him out. It was 3 AM when Gray got her wish. She was just turning over when her cell phone began to ring.

"Hello?" she answered groggily.

"Yoooooo, ma, don't be mad. A nigga got caught up."

"Mm-hmm, tell me anything."

"Straight up. I wouldn't even do you like that."

"It don't even matter. I'm 'sleep."

"Well, it matter to me, 'cause I still wanna see you. Now, you gon' get up and open the door?"

"Gunz, I'm not fuckin' wit' you." she huffed, hating the fact that she still wanted to see him too.

"Yo, for real, my fault. Don't do me like that. You got me standing outside your building lookin' all good, wanting to see you and shit. Come on, yo, for real, don't do me like that. Open the door."

Gray knew that she was bending all of her rules for Gunz, but there was something about him that had her past intrigued.

"Don't think I'ma be doing this all the time." She rolled her eyes before hanging up.

A minute later, they were standing face to face, basking in the essence of one another. Gunz didn't utter a word as he wrapped his strong arms around her waist. His fingertips massaged the fabric of her shirt. She was instantly taken in. The smell of his cologne was intoxicating and spellbinding. Gray never knew an attraction to someone could be so strong.

Her tongue wanted to explore his skin; he was so sexy. Diamond studs were in each of his ears. They weren't big or gaudy; they were just the right size.

Black aviator shades shielded his eyes, while a black hoodie and jeans draped tailor made over his body. Gunz was a ghetto Adonis.

His height and masculinity overpowered her. She felt so small in his embrace. Lost in his touch, she allowed her hands to roam freely over his muscular back as he whispered in her ear how much he missed her. From that moment on, she knew he had her.

Pulling back from their embrace, Gunz noticed for the first time how rare of a beauty Gray was. He'd never seen anyone like her before. Her features were so exotic they were mesmerizing. Even with no makeup, she was still as beautiful as he remembered. He had to taste her. Hugging her just wasn't enough.

Before Gray knew it, his lips were pressed against hers. She missed his touch. She couldn't fight it. Her mouth welcomed his kisses.

"You know I missed you, right?"

"Yeah, you missed me so much it took you all night to get here." Gray stood back and rolled her eyes.

"Man, please. We already discussed that, so dead all that noise, ma."

"Whateva. Look, I'm tired, so let me go and get you a pillow and blanket."

"A pillow and blanket?" Gunz repeated, looking at her crazy.

"Yeah, a pillow and blanket." Gray retrieved the items from the linen closet and handed them to him. "I know you didn't think you were sleeping in the bed with me."

"It's cool, ma. I got you. I can ride the dog house for the night. As long as you promise to ride my dick in the morning." He cracked a smile while taking off his hoodie.

"You are so nasty."

"You like it." Gunz grabbed her waist and gave her one more kiss, this time adding a little tongue.

"Baby, I gotta go to bed," Gray pleaded, knowing if she stayed a minute longer she would be on her back instead of upstairs asleep.

"A'ight, but just give me one more kiss."

Rolling her eyes but loving every second of being in his presence, Gray stood on her tiptoes and did what she was asked.

"Thank you."

"You're welcome."

"So, what are you, one of those artsy types or something?" He looked around her place with a skeptical eye.

"Why you say that?" She followed his gaze.

"'Cause of the way you got your place decorated. It's a lot of color up in this muthafucka."

"No, it's not."

"Yeah, it is."

"What, you don't like it?"

"Nah, the shit look hot. I was just wondering."

"I wouldn't call myself artsy. I just don't like being like everybody else."

"I feel you."

"Anything else you want to make a comment on before I go upstairs?"

"Nah, I think that's about it, but if I do think of

something else, I'll let you know." He cracked her favorite crooked smile.

"Good night, Gunz."

"Good night, ma."

Gray was lying flat on her back, asleep, when she felt the familiar sensation of two hands creeping up her thighs. Gunz licked the face of her pussy as she squirmed in her sleep. Once she opened her eyes, she found him between her legs.

"Gunz," she moaned, rubbing the top of his head. "Baby . . . what are you doing?"

"Damn, I miss tastin' this shit." He ran his tongue across her stiff clit, looked at it in awe, then kissed the lips of her pussy. "Mmm."

Gunz buried his face in Gray's pussy and went to work. Gray swore with each lick that her body had been transported into space, where the stars were so close you could reach out and grab one. She didn't know whether to sing, squeal, hum, or rhyme. His grip on her thighs was so tight. She liked the constraint, but it was all too much to handle. His tongue strokes set off a spark in her pelvis that she couldn't or didn't want to control.

Gunz felt her legs shake as cum escaped from her valley and onto his tongue. The average man wouldn't be able to handle her sweetness; they'd overdose. Gunz could never have too much. Thoughts of the way her butterscotch skin melted in his hands stayed in his mind. He didn't know what this was he was feeling, but had to have his fix and quick.

Gunz swiftly made his way up her body. The desire in his eyes was as evident as the moon. Between her legs, he took a hold of her thighs and pushed them back. Gunz inserted his dick into her pussy inch by inch. Her wet walls devoured him. Together they rocked to a slow, steady beat, while Gray wondered if this was the beginning of a promising relationship.

A love to call my own . . .

Teedra Moses, "Rescue Me"

Chapter Three

Gray lay half awake. A slight smile graced the corners of her lips. Months had passed since she shared the company of a man she actually liked spending time with. She'd dated guy after guy, and nothing seemed to come of it. It was always the same routine: meet a man, put up with his bullshit, and then kiss his sorry ass good-bye. Gray was so sick and tired that *sick and tired* were not even the words to describe how she felt.

None of the men she met lived up to her expectations. First there was White Mike. They'd met a year and half ago, when she was twenty six. He was flyer than fly, with a buzz cut, boyish good looks, great job, and expensive cars. Slick lines were his entire conversation. Romance and companionship were what he offered when really all he wanted was a warm pussy to slide his two-inch pink dick into.

For weeks he'd sweet-talked the pussy, promising Gray sexual pleasure. Then when the time came, all she got was a, "Why, God?" and a slight tingle. Mike did everything from licking and sucking to biting the pussy to make up for his lack of manhood, but nothing he did could take Gray there. In the end, all she could remember was her legs wrapped around his big back as his penis played peek-a-boo with her pussy for three minutes. Needless to say, after that fiasco, it was a wrap on White Mike.

Then there was Dion, but everyone knew him as The Home Depot Guy. He was twenty-two, tall, with big feet and benefits, but the chemistry just wasn't there. He was too much of a square for Gray's taste. She wanted the full package: a man with a heart of gold who could knock the pussy out.

She longed for a man who liked taking long walks on the beach, could provide her with security, and take care of her every need. Gray yearned for someone she could call her own. He didn't have to be a gangsta or a baller. All she wanted was for him to come and rescue her from the pain that other men so selfishly left behind.

She was finished with getting her hopes up only to be disappointed. She was fed up with praying to God for a husband that seemed destined not to come. How many more nights would she have to beg for him to finally catch on? It wasn't like she didn't attend church, pay tithes, or believe in the Word. She'd done everything. Gray tried being patient. She asked God for discernment. She described the type of man she wanted down to a T, but what had that gotten her? Nothing but bitter nights alone.

All of her friends had men, so this left Gray with

wondering what it was that she was doing wrong. Was it the vibe she put out that kept attracting "ain't shit" niggas, or were the words *sucker for love* written across her forehead? Every man she met seemed to be full of shit, not on her level, or a waste of her time.

But Gunz was different. He had heartbreak written all over him, but for some reason, she just couldn't walk away. He had a certain aura about him that intrigued her. With him, she wanted to swallow her pride. She wanted her emotions to show. If he allowed her to, she would be everything he ever hoped and dreamed.

Happy that he was only a few feet away, Gray got up from her bed and headed downstairs. She was so excited to see his face, but to her dismay, he wasn't there. He had already left. The covers she'd given him the night before were neatly folded on the sofa. There wasn't a note or anything left behind to say good-bye.

Stupid was the only word that came to mind as Gray stood stunned. Once again she felt played. She thought about calling him, but changed her mind. Instead, she carried on with her day as if he didn't exist.

An hour and a half later, she was at work. Gray had just walked through the doors when Kema rushed up to her.

"Seems to me like you have an admirer, girl-friend."

"What are you talkin' about?" Gray asked, confused, as she placed down her suede Lauren Merkin clutch.

"Read this and find out." Kema handed Gray a small note dressed in a white envelope.

Eager to know who it was from, Gray sat down at her desk and opened up the note. It read: *Have breakfast on me, Gunz.*

"Have breakfast on me," Gray repeated as she looked across the room and noticed a huge buffet table filled with food.

How she hadn't noticed it as soon as she walked in was beyond her. There were muffins, croissants, fruit, eggs, and bacon. You name it, it was there. It was enough food to feed the entire floor, and it was all courtesy of Gunz. Gray was on cloud nine. Nobody had ever done anything so sweet for her before.

"So, who is Gunz?"

"The guy I met that night at Dolce." Gray blushed.

"He must be one hell of a guy."

"He is." Her cheeks were now burning bright red.

"Damn, he got you cheesing like that? Please tell me he got a brother, 'cause I wanna be cheesing too."

"Shut up, Kema."

"I'm for real, girl. So when do I get to meet this Gunz?"

"I don't know. Like I said, we just met. Things between us aren't even that serious yet."

"From the looks of this spread, it seems to me like he's serious about you."

"We'll see, but look, give me a second so I can call him and say thanks."

"A'ight. While you doing that, I'ma go and get me some French toast."

"Bring me some too."

Once Kema was out of ear distance, Gray dug into her clutch purse and fished out her iPhone. She couldn't wait to hear Gunz's voice.

Five rings and no answer later, she was left with no choice but to leave a message. "Hey, Gunz, it's me. I just wanted to say thank you for breakfast. That was so sweet. I can't believe you did that. Hope you have a good day. Call me when you get a chance later. Bye."

After making passionate love to Gray the night before, Gunz hopped on a private plane to the Sunshine State. He now sat back on his eighty-foot yacht, allowing the rays from the Miami sun to bless his skin. Gray's voicemail message sang in his ear, as visions of her face danced in his mind. Holding his head back, he let out a much needed sigh. He knew that if he stuck around Gray too long, he'd continue to make promises he'd never be able to keep.

His lifestyle was too wild, dangerous, and unpredictable. He was constantly out of town. It was nothing for him to receive a phone call at the crack of dawn about a shipment that needed to be picked up. Droves of women yearned to be in the midst of his grace.

By the looks of Gray, he could tell she couldn't keep up. He was too hood, and she was too high maintenance. Sweetness poured from her skin. She was nothing like the ghetto chicks he was used to dealing with. If he made her his girl and allowed her into his life, she'd become like all the other hustlers' wives, insecure and needy. But none of that mattered. He and Gray could never be.

Gunz was too stuck in his ways. He was the type of nigga that stayed on the go. He answered to no one. He wasn't the one to be questioned or quizzed. Nobody's feelings mattered but his. That's why he never wifed a chick; being in a relationship came with too many responsibilities. He liked Gray and wanted to keep her around, but not anyone, even Gray with her trusting eyes and winning smile, could have his heart.

"I know my nigga ain't on the phone cakin'," Bishop joked as Gunz closed his cell phone.

"What?" he asked, coming back to reality.

"You over there smiling and shit. Some broad got ya nose wide open."

"Man, please. You know me. I'll never give my heart to a woman."

"That's the same thing I said. Now look. Me and Keisha been married five years, wit' three kids and one on the way."

"Damn, nigga, do y'all ever use rubbers?"

"Hell naw. Keisha know I like to go up in mines raw. That condom bullshit be in the way."

"Yo' ass is nuts." Gunz laughed, shaking his head.

"Yo, Gunz, you got a visitor," Watts announced, peeking his head around the corner.

"Who is it?"

"Fortune."

"Let him up."

Fortune, one of Gunz's soldiers from Miami, boarded Gunz's yacht with a look of admiration written on his face. He knew Gunz was doing it, but damn! From the looks of it, he could tell the yacht had to be worth at least four million. It held four large staterooms, a galley equipped with gourmet appliances, a fully stocked kitchen, sky lounge, living area, movie theater, and pool. Gunz also had a staff of maids, bodyguards, and cooks on board. Four bad chicks dressed in bikinis lounged on the deck, sipping champagne as if it were their daily routine. This was the life, and Fortune was going to do everything in his power to have a piece of the devil's pie.

"What's up, Gunz?"

"How you doing?" Gunz reached out his hand for a shake.

"I'm straight."

"You sure? I know Rich was ya man."

"Yeah, I'm cool." Fortune tried his best to hide the hate in his eyes. Over the years, he and Rich had become close friends. When he heard about his death, Fortune was devastated, and to sit in front of the man who ordered his best friend dead was the hardest thing he had to do in his life thus far.

"Good. That's what's I like to hear. As a matter of fact, let me get you a drink. Locia," Gunz called out to one of the bathing beauties.

For a minute, Fortune lost track of why he was there as the cocoa-colored mami sauntered over. She was lethal, cute, and petite; just how he liked 'em. And her titties were more than a mouthful. Homegirl didn't have any shame in her game. He could almost swear that she placed her small round ass in his face on purpose as she bent over and poured Gunz's drink.

"Anything else, papi?" she asked after giving them both their glasses.

"Nah, you good, shorty." Gunz cocked his head to the side and looked at her ass too.

Locia's curves had Fortune in a daze. Her impeccable good looks were too much for the young solider to handle. Instead of focusing on Gunz, he was too busy watching Locia's butt cheeks bounce as she walked away.

"You a'ight? You act like you ain't never seen a woman before."

"My bad, boss." Fortune coughed, clearing his throat. "You know I been down with the crew for almost two years now, and I'm still at solider status."

"And why is that?"

"Shit, that's what I'm tryin' to figure out. I've put in the work. Ask anybody in the crew and they'll tell you how I get down."

"My man," Gunz said with a laugh. "You still ain't tellin' me what it is that you came here for."

"I wanna move up in rank. I wanna become captain."

"Is that right?"

"Yeah."

"Let me ask you something." Gunz meanmugged Fortune. "What makes you think I wanna fuck wit' you like that?"

Fortune wanted to reply, but couldn't find the words to say. The look on Gunz's face screamed that it was time for him to talk and for Fortune to listen.

"Fortune, I like you. You're a good dude. I ain't never really heard anything bad about you except for the one time you got bagged."

"That whole thing was my fault. I know I fucked up, but I ain't going back to jail. Straight up. The next time the county see me, it's gon' be in a body bag. I mean, come on, Gunz. I know you good and all, but a nigga like me tryin' get put on. I'm hungry. I'm ready to put in work."

"So if I do this, what I'ma get from you?"

"Anything you want. Whatever you need. I got you. That's my word. I got you," Fortune assured.

Gunz rubbed his chin and contemplated whether he should make that move. Fortune seemed trustworthy enough. He could see the hunger burning in his eyes. It was time to put him on.

"So you think you can handle being a captain?"

"I know I can. I know it."

"Well, look, check this out. I dig what it is that you tryin' to do, so I'ma put you up on game. I got this li'l airport scenario that I want you to be a part of. You wanna captain some shit, here's your shot.

"I got these two shorties from the Dominican Republic, right? They sistas, they kinda fly . . . but I digress. They old dude, Estebon, he got the whole game on lock. That White Girl shit everybody so hyped up about, he the one supplying it."

"Oh, word?"

"Yeah, so what we gon' do is have ol' girl and them smuggle the shit in the passengers' luggage. Then once it get here, I got two luggage boys that's gon' transport the shit to an unsecured room and unpack the shit."

"That's what's up? So what you want me to do?"

"You gon' be my luggage bitch—I mean boy," Gunz joked, laughing.

"Yeah, a'ight." Fortune nodded his head with a slight smirk of embarrassment.

"Don't take it personal. I'm just fuckin' wit' you." Gunz adjusted himself in his seat so he could feel more comfortable. "So, what's the deal? You in or you out?"

"I mean, I wanna get down, but what's in it for me?"

"If you don't fuck this up, you get twenty grand once the job is done, and maybe I'll put you on as captain."

Fortune tried to maintain a steady expression as Gunz and Bishop looked on. Twenty G's wasn't shit. Fortune knew all too well about guys putting in work for the bosses only to get hemmed up in the end. He needed more money and more assurance that he would be okay. Since Gunz wasn't willing to provide him with that, Fortune decided in that moment to take matters into his own hands.

"This my last time askin' you. Are you in or are you out?" Gunz's upper lip curled. He detested repeating himself.

"Of course I'm in. I got you," Fortune lied.

"Ay, Locia, come show my man the way out."

"All right, daddy." She got up and seductively walked toward him.

Wanting to get to know Locia better, Fortune tugged at the string of her red polka dot bikini and said, "Why don't you g'on and let me see what's under that two-piece?"

"Baby, please. You ain't got enough money. Holla at me when you get your own yacht."

"Mmm, this is sooooo good." Gray licked her chocolate brownie ice cream cone, savoring the taste. She was in the Central West End and had just left Ben & Jerry's. It was a glorious spring afternoon. Tree branches swayed in the wind. Couples dined outside at different restaurants throughout the strip. Gray wished she was sharing her down time with Gunz, but she hadn't heard from him in days.

In her mind, this meant one of two things: he was with another chick, or full of shit. Whichever one it was, Gray didn't have time. She swore not to be beat for another no-good nigga. Been there, done that. Those days were over.

Gray just hoped he wasn't married. If he was, she'd die. She just wished she could understand him. She wanted to know where they stood. Her heart was tired of playing guessing games. With each day that passed, she grew wearier of his egotistical ways.

"What you thinking about?" her best guy friend, Truth, asked.

"Nothing," she lied.

"Yeah, right. Something on your mind."

"Why you say that?"

"'Cause I know you, Gray. When you're deep in thought, you get quiet, and plus, you've been checkin' your phone every five seconds since we been together. Don't worry. That nigga gon' call," he joked.

"Shut up. You don't even know what you're talkin' about."

"Mm-hmm. Anyway, let me get some of that." He tried licking her cone.

"No. You got your own cone!" Gray blocked him by turning away.

"But yours look better than mine."

"You better take yo' ass back in the store and go get you one then, 'cause you ain't gettin' none of this."

"Well, since I can't have none of your ice cream, you gon' give me some of that?" He pointed between her thighs.

"If you don't stop." Gray twisted up her mouth, trying her best not to smile.

She'd known Truth since high school, when they were carefree, seventeen, and in the eleventh grade. He'd wanted her from the day he laid eyes on her in the school cafeteria. Gray, on the other hand, only saw him as a friend, so for the years that followed, that's all they would be. She and Truth told each other their deepest, darkest secrets. Many nights passed where they fell asleep on the phone, discussing their hopes and dreams.

Truth was Gray's shoulder to lean on. He schooled her on how niggas were, how they operated, and how they got down. In return, she helped him decipher between dimes and gold diggers. Like 50 Cent and Olivia, they were best friends; but one lonely night, all that changed.

They were twenty-one and in college. Gray was

between boyfriends, horny, and in need of some attention. Truth's feelings for her were still there, lying underneath the surface of being her best friend, so she called him up. She knew that if given the opportunity, the feelings he'd hidden would arise. A phone call later, Truth was caressing her body the way he'd envisioned for years.

Two orgasms later, they lay spent on her twin-size bed. Truth wasn't a slouch in bed by any means. His head and dick game were on point to the fullest, but Gray knew they could never be more than what they were. Truth was disappointed by the news, but dealt with her decision like a man. He didn't want to lose Gray as a friend. Without her by his side, he felt lost in the world. Hope still sprung eternal in his heart that one day Gray would change her mind and see him for the husband he could be and not the friend he was.

"So, how is everybody doing?" she asked as they window shopped.

"Good."

"Where is Rich? I haven't seen him in a minute."

"Who knows? I ain't heard from that dude in a couple days. I've called him, went by his house; I don't know what's going on."

"Rich is a mess. That boy ain't gon' never change. But that's your li'l brother. Knowing him, he probably just got up for a minute. He'll show up eventually, like he always does."

"Right. I just wish he would chill out on all these li'l dope boy fantasies."

"He still running with them dudes you was tellin' me about?"

"Yeah, and I'm tellin' you, them niggas ain't nothing nice, G. It's a whole squad of them cats all over St. Louis. I'm tellin' you if my li'l brother don't sit down soon, something gon' happen to him."

"Don't think like that, Truth. Rich gon' be okay," Gray assured, rubbing his back. "How is your mother doing?"

"She good." Truth inhaled deeply. He was happy to change the subject. "She been a little sick lately, but she'll be a'ight."

"I'm gon' have to come by and see her."

"Yeah, and she been asking about you." He looked down at her and arched his eyebrow.

"Don't be making me feel bad." Gray used her elbow to poke him in the stomach. "You know how hard I been working."

"I know. I'm just fuckin' wit' you."

"You better be." She flashed a broad grin as her cell phone began to ring.

Gray quickly checked the screen with high hopes. She wanted nothing more than for the caller to be Gunz. Unfortunately, it wasn't. It was Kema.

"Hello?" she answered dryly.

"Eww. What's wrong wit' you?" Kema popped gum in her ear.

"Nothing," Gray lied.

"Where you at? I tried callin' your house."

"Having ice cream wit' Truth."

"I told you about hanging around that psycho."

"Kema, what do you want?" Gray ignored her comment.

"Nothing. I was just callin' to see if you wanted

to go to this Freakum Dress Party they having at 1108 Friday."

"I don't care. That sound cool."

"A'ight, well, call me later."

"Will do."

"Bye, girl."

"Bye," Gray said before hanging up.

Friday couldn't come fast enough. Hitting the club with her girl was just the thing she needed to get her mind off of Gunz.

Too grown for that . . .

Tamia, "Too Grown for That"

Chapter Four

Sparkles of light from the disco ball danced across Gray's face as she did a slow whine to the beat. She was in the center of the dance floor at 1108, which was the hottest new hip-hop, R&B, and reggae club St. Louis had ever seen. There were three different levels accompanied by three different DJs. Exposed brick decorated the walls, while vintage furniture and black and white art adorned the room. The atmosphere was very spacious and rustic, but there was still a sensual appeal to it.

On the first floor, Enoch spun "I Love Them Girls" by Tank, causing every female in the spot to take to the dance floor. From left to right, everybody was droppin' it like it was hot, but none outshone Gray.

Unlike every other woman, she had something to prove. The harder the bass thumped, the more she grooved. Dressed in the skimpiest outfit she owned, Gray sauntered over to Truth and slithered her backside like a worm down his chest. She knew she was wrong for teasing him, but the intense look of

desire which lay deep in his eyes told her to continue. Every dip, twirl, and pop of the hip drove
him insane. The way she torqued it only made
Truth want her more. Besides, he deserved to be
tortured. It was supposed to be a girls' night out.
Nobody invited him to come; yet and still, he insisted on tagging along.

And Kema, Gray could kick her ass too. They
weren't even in the club five minutes before she
spotted some nigga she knew and got lost. At first
Gray didn't mind being left alone with Truth. They
always had fun when they went out; that was until
Truth got amnesia and morphed from her best
friend to an insecure boyfriend. Gray couldn't turn
left without him being up in her face. All night he'd
been following her around the club like a lost dog,
saying, "Let me get a dance" or "Can I buy you a
drink?"

Truth was straight up on some bug-a-boo shit.
When she went to powder her nose, he stood outside the ladies' bathroom door. If a dude tried to
holla, he'd flip and try to hold her hand. At one
point, Gray thought she'd lost him, but when she
turned around, lo and behold, who was standing
behind her? Truth. Gray didn't know what to do. She
wanted to pull her hair out. Truth was always very
overprotective, but damn, could a chick breathe?

Why he was all up in her personal space, suffocat-
ing her lungs, she didn't know. He knew they
weren't together, and by the way he was acting,
they would never be. If he didn't enjoy the music
and let her breathe soon, Gray was sure to grab her
shit and leave. She was too grown to be babysitting
some grown man's ego.

As they danced, Gray wished to the love gods up above that somehow Truth could magically transform into Gunz, but her wish didn't come true. Gunz was still nowhere to be found, and Truth was still wreaking havoc, making her night miserable.

"Okay, I need a drink," Gray panted as she stopped dancing and placed her hand on his chest.

"I got you. What you want?"

"A Cosmopolitan, please."

"A'ight, I'll be right back. Don't go nowhere."

"I won't." She faked a smile.

As soon as Truth was out of sight, Gray made her way to the other side of the club in hopes of finding Kema. On the second level of the club, Gunz and his crew stood posted up like kings. They'd ordered bottles of Ace of Spades, Moët, and Dom Pérignon. Don Lino cigars were being passed around, while women of all different persuasions exchanged "fuck faces."

Bobbing his head to the beat, Gunz puffed on a blunt and zoned out as "The Infamous" by Mobb Deep traveled through space and into his ears. He loved living the lifestyle of the young, black, and rich. Any and everything he ever wanted was at his disposal. Money was piling in by the boatload. Everybody in his crew was eating good and living lavishly. This was the life. Gunz couldn't imagine living any other way. No matter how many times he thought about it or how hard he tried, Gunz just couldn't leave the game alone.

It needed him as much as he needed it. One couldn't exist without the other. They were each other's addictions. His presence in the streets was a must. No other hustler was getting it like he was. In the last three years, Gunz's net worth had grown to be well over fifty million dollars, and it was all because of the devil's drug of choice, cocaine. Only in America could a young black man from the hood be so rich and never have graduated high school or did something legit.

And yes, at times, being at the top felt lonely. Most of the dudes he came up with were either dead, on some jealously shit, or sworn enemies. His mother stayed in fear for his demise and constantly prayed for his safety. Gunz hated to see his mother in such a predicament, but without sacrifice, there was no gain. All of the blood, sweat, and tears he'd shed were well worth it in his eyes. He had a mansion on the outskirts of St. Louis that he'd only slept in once. He'd drunk the finest wine, shopped in the most exclusive stores, traveled the world, and fucked the baddest bitches. Still, at the end of the day, he didn't trust or have anyone but himself.

After finishing off the last of his blunt, Gunz told his boys that he'd holla and was up. With a pair of brown Tom Ford shades shielding his eyes, Gunz glided his way down the steps, where he ran into his man King. There weren't too many people besides Watts and Bishop that Gunz knew had his back, but King was one of them.

At the ripe age of thirty-five, with skin that resembled fresh coffee and a muscular body covered with tattoos that any woman would want to caress, King Lewis was that dude. Long dreads filled his head, while a smooth but trimmed and precisely lined beard decorated his face. Just like Gunz, King stayed dipped in the latest fashions, but unlike

Gunz, King knew that there was more to life than clothes and expensive cars.

For years Gunz had tried to persuade King into his way of life, but King wasn't having it. King wanted nothing more than to build a family, own a couple of clubs, and stack his chips. As far as he was concerned, Gunz could have the dope game; he'd conquer the nightlife.

"My man." Gunz smiled brightly as the two men gave each other a pound and a hug.

"What's up? I was just about to come up and holla at you. Where you heading?"

"Shit, I was just about to burn out."

"Man please, go ahead with all that" King teased.

"C'mon now, you know I'm gettin' old."

"Old? Nigga, I'm the one gettin' old. Yo' ass only thirty."

"But it feel like I'm forty." Gunz laughed. "On the real, though, you doing your thing with this club, man. This muthafucka hot."

"That's what's up. You know, I'm tryin' to do me. Tryin' to get this muthafucka poppin', but, uh, let me walk you out. I ain't tryin' to hold you up our nothing. I know you a busy man and all," King joked, wrapping his arm around Gunz's shoulder.

"Man, please. Get the fuck outta here." Gunz chuckled, pushing him away.

"But for real, holla at me. I got a chocolate party coming up soon, and you know it's gon' be mad chicks up in here."

"Right," Gunz said, halfway listening. He had just spotted Gray out of the corner of his eye. Although her back was turned, Gunz knew that ass anywhere. He thought about just walking away as if he hadn't seen her, but the way her body looked in the dress she wore told his dick to think otherwise. Gray's physique was dangerous. It had more dips and curves than a little bit. Gunz knew that he should back away now before one of them got hurt, but since childhood, he'd loved playing with fire.

"A'ight then." He stopped King in mid-sentence. "I'ma holla at you."

Making his way through the crowded room, Gunz approached Gray's backside. Without saying a word, he wrapped his arms around her waist, leaned down, and placed a soft kiss on her exposed shoulder. A smile instantly formed on Gray's face. Gunz didn't have to say a word. She knew his scent anywhere. For days she'd dreamt of it.

"We gotta stop meeting like this, ma," he whispered, lightly biting the side of her neck.

"Who said we were meeting?" Gray pulled away from his embrace and turned around.

"Yo, what I tell you about pullin' away from me?" He took her hand. "Stop doing me like that."

"Are you serious? Gunz, please. I haven't heard from your ass in over a week."

"I know that." He pulled her back into his embrace. "Quit trippin' off old shit."

"Old shit?" Gray cocked her neck back.

"I'm just sayin' everything ain't as it seems."

"And what is that supposed to mean?"

"Don't worry about it. You coming home wit' me tonight?"

"No."

"Why not?" He gazed deep into her eyes.

"'Cause." Gray looked away, feeling overwhelmed.

"I'm right here." He turned her face back toward him. "Why you lookin' over there? Now, why you ain't coming home wit' me?"

"'Cause I'm not fuckin' wit' you like that, that's why."

"Well, guess what? I'm still fuckin' wit' you, so fuck all that bullshit you talkin'."

"Gunz, please."

"Gunz, please my ass. I'm coming over tonight."

"No, you're not!" Gray laughed, trying to convince herself.

"Yeah, a'ight. C'mon, ma, quit bullshittin'. I miss you."

Everything in Gray at that moment wanted to say kick rocks because she knew Gunz was full of shit, but the way words dripped like sweet honey from his lips had her hormones entangled. She couldn't explain it. Her mind was saying walk away, but her legs wouldn't cooperate and move. For some reason, she wanted to give him the best of her. She had to have him, no matter the cost.

"So what you gon' do if I let you come over my house?"

"I'ma put it on yo' ass if you giving it up."

"Well, I'm not, so I guess you ain't coming over," she countered.

"That's what your mouth say, but we'll see."

"I bet we will."

"Be quiet." Gunz gently kissed her lips.

His hands were roaming all over Gray's butt and thighs. She was voluptuous and thick in all the right places. All Gunz could think about was laying her down and pinning her legs back. He needed to hear her moan, so he backed her up into a dark corner, took his hand, and placed it underneath her dress. So what if someone saw? For days he'd been missing home, and as the tips of his fingers caressed the hardness of her clit, he knew that home was right where he wanted to be.

"What are you doing?" Gray asked, becoming nervous.

"Didn't I tell you to be quiet?" He rotated harder.

In a matter of seconds, the lips of Gray's pussy were covered in cream. She knew that there was a possibility that someone could be watching, but it was a risk she was willing to take. The sensation building between her legs was too strong to deny.

"And you ain't got no panties on. That's what's up."

"Yeah," she spoke between moans of pleasure. "I did that just for you."

Gray's entire body was on fire. She wanted nothing more than to ride Gunz's fingers until cum exploded onto his hand, but they were in public, so instead, she came to her senses and told him to stop.

"Nah, you don't want me to stop." His voice was low and raspy. "Do you?"

"No, but we need to, 'cause in a minute I'ma cum."

"But I thought you wanted me to taste it."

"I do," she moaned.

"So why you want me stop?" he asked with an intense look of desire in his eye. With each stroke, he could feel the folds of her pussy melting.

"I don't." Gray's voiced cracked.

"You sure?" Gunz kissed her lips intensely as he dipped his long fingers into her wet slit.

Unable to respond, Gray placed her head onto his chest so no one could see the agony written on her face. The more Gunz explored the depth of her pussy, the more she wanted to bite his skin and scream out his name.

"Don't make me ask you again." He pulled his fingers out and smeared sticky cream onto her clit. "You want me to stop?"

"Gunz . . ."

"You can call my name later. Right now I'm asking you a question." He stroked faster.

"Baby." She gripped his back.

"You cumming?"

"Yes," Gray panted as her thighs began to shake.

"So I guess you didn't want me to stop." He gave her his infamous crooked grin and removed his hand from underneath her dress.

"You know you wrong for that, right?"

"You liked it."

"I know I did."

"What's going on over here?" Kema interrupted with a drink in her hand. Gray could tell she was already tipsy.

"Where have you been? I've been looking for your ass all night," she responded.

"Girl, you know me. I can't be standing around. I gots to enjoy the party, and anyway, excuse your rudeness. Hi, how you doing? I'm Kema."

"My bad. Gunz, this is Kema. Kema, this is Gunz," Gray spoke.

"What's up? So y'all partying tonight, huh?" he asked, with Gray still wrapped up in his arms.

"And you know it." Kema danced while taking a

sip of her drink. "And who is your pot'nah over there?"

"Who?" Gunz looked over his shoulder.

"Ol' boy over there with the dreads." She pointed.

"How you know we cool?"

"'Cause I just saw y'all on the steps talkin'."

"Oh, that's my man King."

"Well, tell King Kema said what's up."

"I got you. You done partying for the night?" Gunz turned his attention back to Gray.

"Yeah."

"Good, 'cause I'm ready to go."

"Okay, well, I guess I'll catch up with you later." Gray air-kissed Kema good-bye.

"Right, and just remember, don't get nothing on you," Kema teased.

"You are a mess."

"And make sure he tell ol' boy I said what's up."

"I will."

Gray and Gunz weren't even out the door a good five minutes before Truth reemerged with his and Gray's drinks.

"Where Gray at?" he asked with a concerned look on his face.

"She just left," Kema answered, downing the drink in her hand.

"Who she leave with?"

"Some nigga name Gat. I don't know. Don't get me to lying." She took the extra drink from Truth's hand and gulped it down as well.

"You don't know? So you just let her leave the club with somebody she barely knows?"

"Shit, she looked like she knew him to me. Calm ya ol' extra nervous ass down."

"Fuck you, Kema. You be on some bullshit, man." Truth shook his head as he retrieved his cell phone. "I'm up," he declared while dialing Gray's number.

"How you just gon' leave me? I rode wit' you," Kema yelled.

"Well, bring yo' ass on then!"

Nervous jitters fought for space in the pit of Gray's stomach as she approached the door to her house. The palms of her hands felt like clay. She could feel Gunz's presence from behind, wanting and needing her. She wanted him as much as he needed her, but it was late, and they'd already played with the idea of him being there when she woke up in the morning. There was no way that she could make the same impulse decision twice, but visions of him caressing and licking her skin filled her mind.

Face to face, exchanging breaths, she studied his face. Just the sight of him caused the tingle in her clit to twitch. It took everything in her not to wrap her legs around his waist and ride his dick right there in the hallway. He could have her at any moment or any given time, and he knew it.

Gunz saw the fear in her eyes. His mouth tried to form the words and tell her not to be afraid, but that would be a lie. It was best she feared him. A nigga like him was no good. He was the worst kind of man to deal with. In the end, he would only break her heart. They both knew this; yet and still, here they were, bathing in the wonder of what should come next. *Is this like or lust?* Gunz questioned himself as his lips sought refuge in her silky skin. Gray had an undeniable effect on him.

The sexual attraction he had for her clouded his better judgment. Kissing her good night and heading to his car was what he should have been doing, but being in the midst of her company compelled him to stay. His tongue wanted to tour the hidden areas of her flesh no other man had dared to find. *This shit is crazy,* he thought as his thumb massaged her cheek.

"Gunz, what is it that you really want?" Gray inhaled deeply. "'Cause I'm not used to guys like you coming into my life and staying."

"To be honest,"—he pressed his forehead against hers—"I don't know what it is I want to do with you yet."

"Well, until you figure it out, I think it's best you go home."

Disappointed with her request, Gunz inhaled deeply and replied, "A'ight."

Before something happened that might change his mind, he quickly brushed his lips against Gray's. Then he left without saying another word, leaving her speechless.

For a minute, Gray stood with her back pressed against the door, trying to digest the night's events. Incapable of doing so, she turned around and placed her key into the lock and entered her loft. High off her encounter with Gunz, she grabbed the stereo remote and allowed Jill Scott's euphoric voice to serenade her ears. Alone with only Jill's words to keep her company, Gray envisioned Gunz's warm mouth torturing her skin with kisses as she peeled off her clothes one layer at a time.

She wanted him there. Since he wasn't, she went into the bathroom, turned on the shower, and got in. Beads of hot water slithered down her breasts and between her thighs, while thoughts of Gunz and the time they'd just shared ran across her mind. After lathering her body with Victoria's Secret Very Sexy shower gel, Gray grabbed her towel and dried off.

Once her body was coated with lotion, she placed on a black Juicy tank top trimmed in white, with a pair of matching boy shorts, then turned off the stereo.

Back in her bedroom, Gray lay sideways on her ivory chaise lounge, gazing out of the window. Silence overtook her as she sat all alone, harboring feelings for Gunz. And although he'd just left, she yearned to hear his voice.

Gray's wish came true when suddenly, her phone began to ring.

"Hello," she answered on the first ring.

"What you doing?"

A smile instantly erupted onto Gray's face.

"Just laying around. What are you still doing up?"

"You know I don't sleep." He spoke softly into the phone.

"That's right. I forgot. We're going to have to work on that."

"So what you got going on tomorrow?"

"Nothing much. I'll probably go over one of my friend's houses. What are you going to do?"

"Me and my pot'nahs going hoopin' in the morning, then after that it's back to business as usual." Gunz thought about the large shipment of cocaine he had coming in.

"If I have time, I wanna come see you, if that's a'ight."

"Sounds like a plan to me," she replied, enthused.

That night, Gray and Gunz talked for hours under the cloud-covered moon. They discussed everything that a man and woman would when trying to get to know one another, like what their favorite colors were, likes, dislikes, hopes, and dreams. Talking to one another was so easy. The conversation was never forced or dull. Words spilled from their mouths like running water.

Gray clung to Gunz's every word. His voice captivated her. It was deep and full of bass. She didn't know it, but her voice also put a spell on him. For the first time in years, Gunz felt at ease. He didn't know if it was Gray's personality or the sincerity in the way she talked; whichever one it was, he liked it. Neither of them knew it then, but that night would be the first of many late night phone calls.

The next morning, Gray awoke with the sun beaming in her face. The cordless phone was stuck to her ear. It was evident by the silence coming through the receiver that she'd fallen asleep on the phone. Lifting herself up, she checked the clock and saw that it was 9:00 in the morning.

"Wow. I wonder how long I was asleep," Gray spoke out loud as she hung up the phone.

Twisting her torso from side to side, she popped her back and stretched before pulling the covers back to get into bed. Gray had just placed her right knee onto the mattress when the phone began to ring. Who in the hell was this, calling her at nine o'clock in the morning? she thought. Gray didn't play when it came to her sleep. Her family and friends knew not to call her until at least eleven.

"Hello?" She answered with an attitude.

"Gray!" Truth stressed her name.

"What?"

"Why haven't you been answering your phone? I've been trying to call you all night." His voice quivered.

"I fell asleep on the phone. What's wrong wit' you?"

"I found Rich."

"Where was he at this time?" she asked, getting underneath the covers.

"In the trunk of his car. . . . He's dead!"

Unofficial girl . . .

Cassie, "Official Girl"

Chapter Five

Gray swallowed the huge lump in her throat and vaguely studied her surroundings. It seemed like the whole North Side was in Truth's mother's living room. The entire house from top to bottom was filled to the brim with mourners. Everybody from his family to his best friend, Fortune, and associates were there.

All Gray saw were different forms of black clothing floating by. There were elderly women in big black hats, thugs in black suits, and curvaceous women in form-fitting black dresses, all there to mourn the tragic death of a man who died way too soon.

The way Rich died and how they found him was what fucked Gray up the most. For days, residents in his apartment complex had been complaining about a foul stench coming from his car. The smell was so profound that the building's manager stepped in. Once he couldn't get a hold of Rich, he reached out and called Truth, since he was listed as the "In Case of Emergency" contact on his application.

After attending sunrise services, Truth and his mother, Ms. Moore, went by Rich's place. Using the set of spare keys he had, Truth opened the trunk only to find his twenty-three-year-old brother bloody, beaten, and dead. Tears and vomit seeped from his insides.

Seeing her eldest son in such a state prompted Ms. Moore to get out of the car and see what was going on. She had no idea what she was about to see. Truth tried to block her path and stop the heartache she was about to feel, but his attempts were of no use. Ms. Moore spotted her son, and screams of loss exploded from the pit of her gut. The vision of her son lying on his side with his mouth and eyes wide open, a bullet wound in the front of his head, would never escape her memory.

Now, here they all were, trying to be hopeful and supportive, when really deep down, no one knew the right words to convey. Deciding it was her time to step in line and console Ms. Moore, Gray left the corner she'd been hiding in and approached the elderly woman.

Donny Hathaway's soul-stirring ballad, "For All We Know," played delicately from the record player sitting beside her. Ms. Moore was one of the few people left that still used an old school record player to listen to her oldies. She sat to herself in her favorite chair, a sky blue Laz-Z-Boy with a handful of tissues in hand. Her face was stone. The only emotion that showed was one of sorrow. Streaks of tears stretched across her cheeks, under her chin, and down her neck. For the past hour, her attention had been focused on one particular spot in the middle of the floor. It was the same spot Rich used to sit in and watch television as a child. *The Cosby Show* was his favorite.

Gray felt horrible as she kneeled down, placed her purse on her lap, and gently took Ms. Moore's pudgy hand. She was so incoherent that she didn't even notice Gray was there until she called out her name.

"Oh, hi, Gray." She took her attention off the floor and looked at her face.

"How you doing, Ms. Moore?" Gray massaged the outside of her hand with her thumb.

"That's a difficult question to answer, dear. I guess I'm just here; that's all I can say right now."

"Have you eaten anything? You know you have to take your medicine."

"No, I'm not that hungry, but thank you."

"But, Ms. Moore, you have to eat something, even if it's just a little bit. I don't want you to get sick. Just let me fix you a little something, please."

"Okay, but not a lot. I won't be able to stomach much."

"Okay." Gray patted her hand and picked up her purse. "I'll be right back."

As she went to turn around, Gray collided head first into Gunz's chest. She hadn't talked to him since the night they fell asleep on the phone. Shocked to see his face at Rich's funeral, she quickly stepped back and looked him up and down. As usual, his attire was immaculate. Gunz was dressed in a gray Dolce & Gabbana suit and black Prada loafers. His hair was freshly cut, and the goatee surrounding his mouth was lined to perfection. For the first time, he looked like a businessman and not a thug.

"What are you doing here?" she finally asked.

"Get outta my house!" Ms. Moore began to scream as she got up. "You killed him! You did this to my boy." She pounded her fists into his chest. "How could you?"

"Ms. Moore, I'm sorry." Gunz tried his best to apologize.

"No, you're not! You and those sorry sacks of shit you run with killed my son! You killed him!" She doubled over, sobbing. "Oh Lord! I can't take it! Just give 'im back to me, Lord! Give 'im back!"

Gray stood alongside Gunz and Ms. Moore, speechless. For the life of her, she couldn't figure out how Gunz and Ms. Moore knew each other. *Were Gunz and Rich friends*? she thought.

"I just want my boy back! Lord, why? Why?" Ms. Moore continued to shout as onlookers began to whisper.

"Mama?" Truth appeared suddenly. "Mama, sit down. You're going to make yourself sick again."

Truth sat his mother down and kissed her forehead before getting into Gunz's face. "You got a lot of nerve showing up here like this."

"You two know each other?" Gray questioned Truth, perturbed.

"Yeah, I know this sorry-ass muthafucka," he responded, unafraid.

"Gunz, what's going on?" Gray nervously searched his eyes for answers.

Ignoring her, Gunz directed his attention to Truth. "Let me hit you with something real quick," he spoke low enough so only Truth could hear. "Don't you ever in your life come at me like that again. I will kill you; then your mother will be mourning two sons instead of one. Ya dig? Now, get the fuck out my face. Gray,"—Gunz turned his attention to her—"I'll be in the car."

And with that being said, Gunz left the house as quickly as he came.

"You fuckin' with that nigga?" Truth yelled as spit spewed from his lips.

"Umm, you can quit yelling at me," Gray said sternly as she looked around at the people watching them.

"I'm sorry. I just can't believe that nigga." Truth paced back and forth. "How the fuck y'all know each other?"

"Gunz is the guy I've been tellin' you about."

"That's the nigga!"

"Yeah, now, how do you know him?"

"Gunz is the dude Rich was working for." Truth pulled Gray far enough so his mother couldn't hear. "And I bet you anything he had something to do with him being killed."

"Don't say nothing like that." She absently shook her head.

"So what, you siding wit' that nigga? My word ain't good enough no more?"

"I'm not siding with anybody. I'm just saying you can't be going around accusing people of stuff like that. What you're saying is serious. It could ruin someone's life."

"What, like he ruined mine? My fuckin' brother is dead and it's because of that nigga, I'm tellin' you."

"Look, calm down. Let me just go and tell him good-bye and I'll be right back." Gray said before she walked away, not giving Truth enough time to respond.

A cool April wind kissed the side of Gray's face as she descended the steps and got into Gunz's car. Once inside, she sat quiet. So much was going through her head.

Gunz didn't bother to speak either. He never expected in a million years to run into Gray at Rich's funeral. He hadn't even planned on attending. The only reason he came was because he felt in some strange way he owed Ms. Moore that much.

"I was surprised to see you in there." She finally spoke up.

"Yeah, them my peoples."

"Really? Well, how come I've never seen you around before? I've been cool with Truth for years."

"I haven't talked to you in a couple of days. Is this really what you wanna talk about?" Gunz shot, not in the mood.

"I mean, damn, excuse me. I was just asking you a question," Gray shot back.

"Look, ma, I ain't tryin' to argue wit' you. I'm tryin' to kick it wit' you. As a matter of fact, I'm tryin' to get something to eat, so are you riding, or what?"

"I'll go with you, but I just need to know some things."

"Some things like what?"

"What is it exactly that you do for a living?"

"I shovel snow," Gunz answered without hesitation.

Gray inhaled deeply. She had pretty much already figured out that Gunz earned his money the illegal way.

"And did you kill Rich?"

Gunz looked at Gray and swallowed hard. Everything in him wanted to tell her the truth, but if he did, what little relationship they'd built thus far would be over. He couldn't risk losing her, so he took her by the hand, gazed sincerely into her eyes, opened his mouth, and said, "Baby, I swear to God I ain't have shit to do with that. Rich was like a li'l brother to me."

Gray wished that she could completely trust in his answer, but something inside her soul told her that Gunz was lying. She wanted to push the conversation further, but the look in his eyes screamed that now was not the time, so Gray tucked her suspicions away, vowing to press the issue later.

The buzzing sound of printers and fax machines rang in Gray's ear as she sat alone at her desk. Taking a moment, she looked at the ceiling and thanked God that it was Friday. She couldn't wait for the day to be over. From the time she got into work, she'd been busy with one task after another.

Sienna was driving Gray crazy with her insane demands. She'd been given the opportunity to write an article on "Fabulous Women over 40," but it had to be finished and turned in by seven o' clock the next morning. Gray didn't know how she would finish on time. Not only did she have to complete her article, but that weekend she was hosting the girls' monthly Saturday night get together.

Every month, they'd go all out with decorations, food, wine, and music. Gray's theme for this month's get together would be Parisian chic. To add to her stress, she also had an eleven o'clock hair appointment, and if she had enough time, she'd try to squeeze in getting her nails and feet done. Gray was tired already, and the weekend was just starting.

Checking the clock on her desk, she saw that it was only 12:30. Gray collapsed onto her desk and sighed. She still had four and a half hours to go. She needed a cup of coffee or a shot of espresso to perk her up. The cafeteria was only two floors down. Gray grabbed her clutch purse and got up. After pressing the down button and waiting a couple of minutes, she boarded the elevator. Halfway down, her cell phone began to vibrate. Gray tried not to smile once she saw that it was Gunz.

For a second she wondered if she should even answer. The last time she'd heard from him was two days after the funeral, and that was a week and a half ago. They were supposed to go out and kick it, but after waiting three hours, Gray realized that she'd been stood up. That time, she wasn't having it. Gray called Gunz's cell phone and left him a message, letting him have it. Later on that night, he called and apologized, but Gray wasn't trying to hear him. His apology went in one ear and out the other.

"What?" She finally decided to answer on the fourth ring.

"Who you *what* in'?"

"You. Who else on this phone?" she snapped back.

"Be easy." Gunz ignored her sarcasm as he purchased a brand new pair of sneakers at R Sole. "What you doing?"

"About to have lunch."

"Why you ain't call me? We could've had lunch together."

"Gunz, please. The last time we had plans together you stood me up."

"Gray, I don't have the kind of schedule where I can be on you the way I want to, so chill out and quit bringing up ol' shit. I told you I got caught up on business, but that's irrelevant. That happened like two weeks ago and I apologized. Besides, I ain't even call you for all that."

"Then what you call me for?" she asked, picking up a tray.

"I called to see if you wanted to come to this chocolate party wit' me tonight."

"Where?"

"At 1108."

"Nah, I'm good. I got a lot on my plate."

"So, that's how it is? You act like you don't miss me." Gunz got into his car and started up the engine.

"It ain't got nothing to do with me not missing you." Gray's heart dropped as she picked up a chicken Caesar salad. "I got a lot of stuff I got to do in the next twenty-four hours, and going out isn't one of them. Besides, I ain't fuckin' wit' you like that."

"Why not?" He pulled off.

"'Cause I'm not. You be on some bullshit. Every

time we make plans, you always breakin'em, so I'll see you another time."

"That's what's up. Well, I'm sorry you feel that way," he spoke, stunned.

"Yeah, me too."

For a minute, the two held the phone in silence, unsure of what to say next.

"Well, I'll holla at you then." Gunz hung up reluctantly.

Gray stood in line with her cell phone in hand, shocked. Had the almighty Gunz showed some type of emotion? From the sound of his voice, she could tell he was hurt. She didn't want to do him that way, but it had to be done. He had to see that she wasn't that easy.

Now that she'd proven her point, Gray contemplated what she would wear to 1108.

Throughout the years, one special woman held the key to Gunz's heart. It was his mother, Vivian. Gunz was her oldest of two, and the only one who gave her no pain during birth. In the years to follow, though, even though it wasn't intentional, he would cause her unnecessary grief. Gunz was a wild child with a "fuck the world" attitude. After his father Joseph became addicted to heroin and left for the streets and his sister Adriana passed, there was nothing else for him to live for.

Everything he loved had been snatched away in the blink of an eye. And yes, his mother constantly reminded him that if he didn't live his life according to God's Word that he would be punished, but what was the point of caring and doing right? Nothing in his life was as it should be. His father was God knows where, and his sister was dead. All he had left was a traumatized heart and a resentful memory.

Gunz stepped out of his car and walked up the sidewalk leading to his mother's row house. He hated the fact that she still lived there. Too much bad stuff had happened in that house, but his mother was determined to stay. Refusing to accept any of her son's drug money, she worked hard as a school teacher to pay off the mortgage. The house was hers, the only piece of property she owned outright.

Vivian was proud of her investment. Back in the late seventies when she and Joseph purchased it, the house was only $90,000. Now, because of the recent interest in the area and proper upkeep, it was worth $250,000.

Gunz knocked on the door.

"Who is it?" his mother asked.

"Me! Who else it's gon' be?" he responded as she opened the door.

"You coulda been my man." Vivian hugged her son.

"Ma, don't play wit' me."

"Who said I was playin'?"

Gunz shook his mother's comment off. In his mind, his mother had no business dating. Besides, he couldn't fathom the thought of some man being around "his" mama. He couldn't front, though. Vivian still had it going on for her age. A head full of smooth black hair hung past her shoulders. Her skin was an immaculate shade of copper, while her eyes were almond-shaped and brown. Her smile was the most exquisite thing about her. Vivian had the type of smile that with one glimpse, captured your heart.

"Anyway, what you doing, and better yet, why don't I smell nothing good to eat?"

"'Cause I didn't cook anything good to eat. You better call one of them li'l hot-tail girls you fool wit' and tell them to cook you something 'cause my days of slaving in the kitchen for you are over."

"You see how you do me? Ya only son."

"Boy, hush and hand me my gloves." She pointed toward the kitchen counter.

"What you about to do?"

"Go work in my garden. You wanna help?"

"I'm good."

Gunz went into the refrigerator and grabbed a soda.

"I ain't never seen a lazier man in my life." Vivian shook her head as she placed on her gloves.

"Mama, please. You must ain't seen me without my shirt on."

"And I don't want to either. I have seen enough of ya li'l scrawny body to last me a lifetime," she joked, opening the back door. Gunz followed.

"Damn, Mama, you got it lookin' like the Botanical Gardens back here."

"Quit all that damn cursing."

"My bad." He looked around in awe.

The entire backyard had been transformed into something even Martha Stewart would have been proud of. A huge white picket fence closed off the area. Surrounding it were pink, yellow, and red roses. A table for two with an umbrella sat near the back on top of a red brick pathway.

Gunz's mother got down on her hands and knees and began pulling up weeds. "You know I talked to your grandmother the other day."

"Word? How Granny doing?" Gunz took a seat. "I've been meaning to go by there and go see her."

"She's doing okay. She says her chest been hurting."

"I'ma go by there tomorrow."

"Your daddy's been staying over there too lately."

Gunz's jaw tightened at the mention of his father. At the age of ten, he wrote him off as a deadbeat junkie. He hadn't seen nor talked to him in years, and Gunz liked it that way. Fuck him. He didn't have a father. The streets raised him.

"Your granny says he's been clean now for almost a year."

"Good for him."

"I talked to him for a while. He said that he would like to see you."

"Next time you talk to him, tell that nigga he twenty years too late."

"Gavin, that's not right. He's tryin'."

"Tryin'?" Gunz scrunched up his face. "Don't tell me you gettin' high too. That nigga ain't did shit for me or you. When Adriana died, that muthafucka couldn't even come to the funeral."

"Now wait just a goddamn minute!" Vivian rose up and looked at him. "I am not one of them sorry-ass negros you got hustlin' that poison for you! I am your mother! You will respect me, and if you can't, then you know what you can do." She pointed to the door.

Gunz sat quietly and collected himself.

"Yo, I ain't tryin' to disrespect you, Ma . . . but if you wanna forgive and forget, then that's on you. Me,"—he placed his hand on his chest—"I ain't got nothing for him. That nigga been dead to me."

"Gavin, I know you're hurt, but you gotta let all that stuff go. Life is too short to be holding on to a whole bunch of negative stuff. You can't live like that. It will tear you apart."

Gunz knew what his mother was saying was right, but wasn't it plain to see that he had a mountain load of pain that would always remain in him? No one could save him from his own misery. He was stuck there like time in space. Since as far back as he could remember, he'd been alone, and Gunz liked it that way. He wasn't willing to allow anyone, especially his father, into his life knowing there was a possibility he could be hurt again.

The green lights on the dashboard of the cab flashed 12 AM as Gray pulled up to the club. The environment was live, as party hopefuls stood awaiting their turn to get inside. Eager to see Gunz, she checked her hair and makeup, which was flawless, then hit the driver with a twenty dollar bill and stepped out. From the looks she was getting as she approached the door, Gray knew she was the shit.

That night she wore her hair pulled back in a sleek ponytail. The makeup on her face consisted of bronzer and nude lip gloss. On her body she rocked a copper Donna Karan jersey wrap dress. The plunging neckline accentuated her full, shimmering breasts, while a pair of Gucci corset-style 5-inch heels highlighted her firm calves.

Unlike the last time she was at 1108, the décor was completely different. The entire club was filled with bouquets of red roses, streaming twinkling lights, chocolate fountains, fondue sets, and fruit. Up in the booth, DJ Needles made sure to remind everyone that the drink special for the night was chocolate martinis. The music, as always, was on point. Atlanta native Keri Hilson's smash hit "Turnin' Me On" was playing, hyping up the crowd.

Gray thought she would have to call Gunz and let him know she was there, but to her surprise, he was standing right up front. A slight smile crept onto the corners of her lips as she stood and watched him from afar. He looked simply divine in a brown vest. A cream-colored handkerchief peeked from the breast pocket. Underneath he wore a cream-colored V-neck T-shirt. On his lower half he rocked a pair of distressed Diesel jeans and Cre8tive Recreation high top sneakers. As always, his signature aviator shades covered his eyes, while small diamond studs gleamed from his ears.

Gray was just about to approach him when she noticed a petite woman dressed in a purple spandex dress walk over and get his attention. Gunz seemed to be excited by seeing her because the infamous crooked grin he normally gave to Gray exploded onto his face. Disturbed by this, she stood and watched. The entire time he talked to the woman,

Gunz never removed his hand from around her waist. *What the fuck is that shit about?* she thought.

Feeling someone staring, Gunz looked over his shoulder and spotted Gray looking sexier than ever. Happy that she came, he left the woman's side and stepped to her.

"I thought you said you wasn't coming." He kissed her cheek.

"I wasn't," she replied sarcastically, unsure of how she should feel after what she saw.

"A'ight, Gray, whateva. Anyway, you want something to drink?"

"Nah, I'm good." She turned her face and looked away, mad. "It seems like you've drank enough for the both of us." She could smell liquor on his breath.

"Why you lookin' over?" Gunz followed her gaze and saw her staring at another guy. Heated, he cupped her chin and turned her face back toward him. "You see something you like?"

"Don't play wit' me."

"Then what's your problem?" Gunz could tell she had an attitude. "'Cause I'ma be honest wit' you. I ain't for that sarcastic shit tonight."

"I said I'm good."

"You sure? 'Cause I don't wanna have to fuck you up," he joked.

"Yeah, a'ight. Picture that."

Changing the subject, Gunz took her by the hand and said, "C'mon. Let me introduce you to my peoples."

By that time, the woman had already walked away.

"These are my homeboys, Watts, Bishop, and King."

"Hi," Gray spoke to everyone.

"What's up?" The three men responded.

"So, you're King?"

"Yeah."

"Did Gunz ever tell you that my homegirl wanted to holla at you?"

"Nah. Nigga, you cock-blockin'?"

"Man, don't even play me like that. You know how fucked up my mind is." Gunz finished off his third drink.

"How she look?" King asked, intrigued.

"Don't worry. She's a winner."

"That's all I needed to hear."

"Oh, so that's how you gon' do me, Gray?" Watts joked.

"What?" She giggled.

"I mean, I know you wit' my man and all, but c'mon, yo. Don't front. I peeped you checking me out."

Gray could only laugh. Watts wasn't a bad-looking guy, but he wasn't the most attractive man she'd ever seen either. His height and weight were the equivalent to Snoop Dogg's, but his looks resembled J.J. from *Good Times.*

"Yo, Gunz, you better watch her. Your girl got her eye on me," Watts teased, posing in a B-boy stance.

"Wow!" Gray cracked up.

"Man, fuck what he talkin' about. Take down my number so your girl can call me," King interjected.

"Hold up. Let me get my phone out my purse."

"Yo, go ahead and handle that. I'll be right back." Gunz kissed her cheek before disappearing in the crowd.

Gray didn't realize until King and Bishop walked

away and her feet began to hurt that Gunz hadn't come back. She didn't know what time he'd left, but she was pretty sure that twenty minutes came and went since she last saw him. It was bad enough that they barely talked and that when she walked in she spotted him with another girl. To leave her unattended at a party that he invited her to was downright rude.

"I don't know where my homey went." Watts pretended to scan the club.

"Me either. He said he'd be right back." Gray sighed.

"That's how my nigga is, though. You can never keep track of him."

"Right," she agreed.

"But yo, you cool? You need anything?" he questioned, concerned.

"Yeah, I'm fine. Look, let me go find this boy."

"You sure? 'Cause I can go look for him for you."

"Nah, I got it. Thanks," Gray yelled over her shoulder.

Halfway through the club, she caught up to Gunz. He and his crew were chilling in the V.I.P. section, sipping on bottles of Nuvo. Gunz acted as if he didn't have a care in the world. He had a new drink in his hand and a freshly lit see-through blunt, but to Gray's surprise, he wasn't alone. The same woman he was talking to earlier was not only in his face, but was sitting comfortably on his lap with her arm wrapped around his shoulders.

Gray couldn't tell for sure, but it looked like the woman was either whispering in his ear or licking it.

Gray was so outdone she was dumbfounded. To add to her embarrassment, when Gunz noticed her watching, he simply gave her a look that said *deal with it*. Her heart was shattered. This wasn't how their story was supposed to go. Gray wanted to be the classy woman she was and walk away, but fuck that. He owed her an explanation. And no, he wasn't technically her man, but hadn't the time they'd spent together stood for something?

"Hi, how are you? I'm Gray." She placed out her hand for a shake.

"Hi," the woman spoke back dryly.

Gunz, being the man he was, continued to sip on his drink as if nothing was wrong.

"Y'all having a good time?"

"Yeah." The woman looked at her funny, and then looked at Gunz. "You two know each other or something?"

"That's my homegirl. Ain't that right, Gray?"

"So it's like that?" she asked, shooting him a look that could kill.

"Like what? What you talkin' about, shorty?"

"Now you gon' try and play me crazy. Okay, that's what's up?" She sucked in her bottom lip and smiled. "It was nice meeting you, sweetheart. Y'all have a good night." And with that being said, Gray walked away.

"Yo, what the fuck is yo' problem?" Gunz caught up with her and grabbed her arm.

"I don't have time for this shit. I'm going home." She snatched her arm away.

"Time for what? You the one that told me you wasn't coming."

"Oh, so since you thought I wasn't coming you decide to invite one of your other hoes?"

"Man, I didn't even invite her." Gunz shook his head, annoyed. "That's some ol' shit. I ain't worried about it, and you for damn sure shouldn't be."

"You didn't invite her, but she still in your muthafuckin' face. As a matter of fact, the whole time I been here, she been in yo' face. What, you fuckin' her or something?"

"So that's how it gon' be? Every time I go out you gon' think I'm out here fuckin' every chick you see me talkin' to?"

"What you expect for me to think? The bitch was sitting on your lap!"

"Hold up. I'm not doing this with you. Whether I'm fuckin' her or not ain't none of your business. You not my girl. I told you I ain't want to be in no relationship, and shit like this ain't gon' make me change my mind no sooner. So I'ma tell you like this, Gray, 'cause I'm not gon' let you fuck up my night. You either gon' stay here and chill wit' me, or you gon' take yo' ass home and I'll be over there when I leave up outta here. Either way it go, I'm good, so do what you got to do," he shot before heading back to where he was at.

Left with whether she should leave or stay, Gray made her way over to the bar and ordered herself a drink. Gunz, on the other hand, took his seat and puffed on the blunt. He had too much on his mind to deal with Gray and her insecure ways. Gunz dug her a lot, but the nonstop complaining had to stop. He was a man with needs that needed to be fulfilled, and when Gray didn't step up to the plate,

Devin did. In Gunz's mind, Gray got what her hand called for. Nobody told her to show up unannounced. She brought the pain she was feeling on herself.

Wondering if she had left, Gunz scanned the club in search of her and saw her at the bar. *She better not had left*, he thought, slumping back with a mean expression on his face.

That quickly changed when his anthem by Jamie Foxx, "Blame It," began to play. The song was Gunz's shit. As he vibed to the hook, he checked for Gray again, but she had left. *Okay*. Gunz chuckled underneath his breath. He hadn't expected her to grow balls and leave. It was a good thing she had left, though, 'cause if she would have stayed, he would've lost all respect for her.

An hour and a half later, the club was letting out and Gunz was getting into his car. He was pissy drunk, but so what. Thoughts of Gray devoured his mind, so he called her; only she didn't answer. Amused by her behavior, Gunz called back, but this time, her phone was turned off. Now he was pissed. He didn't like not being able to contact her.

She had him fucked up if she thought shit was gonna go down like it was.

Back at home, Gray sat on the couch with her arms folded underneath her breasts and her legs crossed. A million thoughts ran through her head. Gray thought Gunz respected her more. The way he chased her, you would've thought she was the number one woman on his list. Evidently she was wrong. How could she be so stupid to think that he wouldn't be like all the rest? Just because he took her out and fucked her better than any other man she'd ever dated didn't mean a thing. Gunz wasn't her man when it all boiled down. She was just a person he kicked it with from time to time.

But didn't the way he gazed into her eyes mean anything? His touch was filled with too much tender loving care, and when they kissed, nothing else in the world mattered. No one could tell her that he didn't feel something in his heart for her. Yes, he was unemotional and arrogant as hell, but Gray saw past all of that. She and Gunz had a connection.

Or was Gunz just running game? Gray didn't know what to think. All she knew was that she'd been played and humiliated. She felt stupid. Gray should have never put her life, meaning her job, on hold to be with a man. "What was I thinking?" she said out loud to herself.

In the midst of her frustration, Gray heard someone buzzing her door. She didn't even have to ask who it was; she already knew. Outraged, she got up and pressed the button to allow Gunz into the building.

To his surprise, once he got to her door, Gray was there waiting for him with an angry expression on her face.

"What's yo' problem?" he asked with a glossed-over look in his eyes.

"What the fuck are you doing here?"

"Man, g'on with that bullshit, Gray. I'm tired. A nigga just wanna go to sleep."

"What the fuck does that have to do with me?"

"C'mon, Gray. Stop fuckin' around and let me in."

Gray looked at him with pure disgust and stepped to the side. She couldn't stand the look of his face, yet a part of her was happy that he'd come.

"I hope you don't think you're staying. You better take yo' ass over that bitch house."

"What I tell you? That's old shit."

"And so are we, 'cause I ain't got nothing for you."

"So what? You don't like me no more? You don't want to fuck wit' me no more, Gray?"

Gray wanted nothing more than to say no, but the fact that he was there putting up a fight did something for her self-esteem.

"If you were me, would you want to fuck wit' you?"

"That's a good question. Let me sleep on it and get back to you in the morning." He got up in her face and shined his crooked grin.

"I don't see nothing funny."

"C'mon, just let me go to sleep. I promise we can talk about whateva you want to talk about in the morning."

Gray looked at him sideways and wondered if she should take him up on his offer or make his ass leave as planned.

"We can talk in the morning," she huffed, going against her better judgment. Gray just prayed that in the morning she wouldn't hate herself for the decision.

* * *

The smell of Colombian coffee roamed through the air as Gray sat at her kitchen island watching reruns of *Project Runway*. Gray loved her kitchen. It was like a breath of fresh air. Unlike other areas of the house, her kitchen was more on the traditional side. Everything except the countertops was white. Storage cabinets lined the walls. Her refrigerator, microwave, and oven were all built into the wall unit as well. Miniature plants and greenery gave the area a sprinkle of color.

With her right hand cupped under her chin, she lazily watched television. Gray hadn't slept a wink. From the time Gunz drifted off to sleep, she'd been up working on her article. Finishing it was a harder task than she thought it would be, due to the fact that the situation between her and Gunz stayed on her mind. Thankfully, she finished with only minutes to spare.

With a little time on her hands to think, Gray realized that she was at a pivotal point, where she had to figure out if she should pass Go and head to Boardwalk, or throw in all of her chips and give up. Being disrespected by him with other chicks and competing for his attention was not something she was up to doing. It was time to put everything on the line.

Gray was tired of being his unofficial girl. She wanted to be spoken for. They'd been messing around for several months. Gunz needed to make his feelings clear. Whatever he threw at her, she could handle. What she couldn't handle was the mind-numbing feeling of being stuck in limbo.

Cool air from the ceiling fan swept over Gunz's

bare chest. As soon as he opened his eyes, the first thing he saw was Gray's lavender satin accent chairs. He hadn't felt so well rested in years. He almost hated to get up, but Gray's missing body compelled him to get out of bed. He wondered where she could be. Slowly he made his way down the steps.

Gray almost choked from the sight of him half naked. The only thing he wore was a pair of blue boxer briefs. With each step he took, his dick shifted from side to side; it was so big. Gray wanted to taste it. *Get it together, bitch,* she told herself, but it was too late. She'd already become caught up in his toned and rippled physique. His body was mouthwatering, sinfully delicious. Gunz wasn't fighting fair, and Gray didn't like it one bit.

"What you doing up?" he yawned, adjusting his dick.

"I haven't been to sleep," Gray answered, sipping on her fourth cup of coffee.

"Why not?"

"I had an article due for the magazine that I had to finish and turn in by seven this morning."

"Damn, I ain't know you had all of that going on." Gunz opened the refrigerator to see what she had to eat.

"You never bothered to ask."

"Did you finish?"

"Yeah," she replied dryly.

"What's wit' the attitude?" He shut the door and looked at her. "What I do to you now?"

"Are you serious? You don't remember what happened last night?"

"If I remembered I wouldn't be askin' you now, would I?" He looked at her, confused.

"You can save the attitude 'cause frankly, I don't have time for it. Last night was enough."

"Are you gon' tell me what happened, or do I have to figure it out myself?"

"First of all, you were drunk as hell to the point you couldn't even stand up. Then on top of that, you had some bitch sitting on your fuckin' lap like I wasn't even there."

"Damn, I did." He chuckled.

"I'm glad you find the shit funny." Gray shot past him, heated.

"Where you think you going?" He grabbed her hand and pulled her back.

"Can you please not touch me?"

"Quit actin' like a fuckin' brat," Gunz shot sternly.

Gray stood and stared into his eyes as her heart raced a mile a minute. A part of her wanted to buck and scream, "Fuck you," but the fear of how he would react prompted her not to. Instead, she released her hand from his and proceeded up the steps to her bedroom. Gunz knew her feelings were hurt, but there was only so much slick shit he was gonna let her get away with.

Was I really trippin' that bad? he thought. Gunz did a mental rewind of the night and tried to piece together the events that he could remember. He could see himself at the bar buying drink after drink. He remembered Devin pushing up on him hard. He could see Gray entering the club and shutting the whole scene down with her presence. The only thing he could remember after that was Devin coming over and sitting on his lap.

"I knew I wasn't trippin'," he spoke out loud as he walked up the steps and into Gray's bedroom.

"Yo, I just remembered she came and sat down on my lap. I ain't even tell her to come sit down."

"You really think that makes a difference?" She stopped making up the bed and looked at him like he was dumb. "It doesn't matter if you asked her or if she did it on her own. The fact is she was still there, and most importantly, you invited her."

Gunz had completely forgotten that piece of vital information.

"You right. I did after you said you wasn't coming."

"What is that supposed to mean?"

"It means you brought all of this on you."

"I brought all of this on me?" she repeated in disbelief.

"You damn right you did. I asked you to come, you said no, so what in the fuck else was I supposed to do?"

Gray didn't know what to say. She knew he had a valid point.

"The shit was still embarrassing as hell. I felt stupid. Here I was setting aside my responsibilities just to kick it wit' you, and what do I get in return? Another bitch all up in yo' face, a headache, a fucked-up night and no sleep."

"Look, that shit wit' Devin—"

"So that's her name?" Gray cut him off.

"Fuck all of that." Gunz swung his arm, frustrated. "I told you I don't fuck wit' that bitch. I apologize, but you gotta remember, Gray, me and you not together. I told you I ain't wanna be in a relationship."

"Who said anything about a relationship?"

"To me that's what it seem like you want us to be."

"Well, I don't." She turned her back to him and resumed making up her bed. Hearing those words come out of his mouth were like stab wounds to the heart. Gray never felt so insignificant and small. Here she was trying to be all she could be for him and for what? He was absolutely right. She wasn't his girl, nor did he want her to be, so why did it hurt so bad when this was something she already knew? The air in her lungs felt short, like she was having an asthma attack. There was no way she could be back in this moment of rejection again. It was time to reevaluate some things.

"Look." Gunz gently turned her around to face him. Holding her hands, he said, "I ain't tryin' to hurt you. I'm just tryin' to be honest. I like you . . . a lot. I enjoy spending time wit' you, but I'm the type of nigga that just can't be in a relationship. My life is too dangerous, and I'm not gon' take the risk of you being hurt."

"So what do you suggest I do?" Gray shot back.

"I don't know. That's up for you to decide. I mean, hopefully you still wanna fuck wit' me, but if not, I'll understand."

"I'ma tell you right now, I'm not into fucking you when there is a possibility that you could be fuckin' somebody else."

"Say what you mean, Gray."

"Are you seeing anybody else?"

"No."

"Do you want to see other people?"

"I mean, at this moment, no." He got in her face and placed his arms around her waist. "I don't anticipate me wanting to see anybody else but you."

Gray hated that when she was in his arms, everything felt right. If she could stay there forever, she would.

"Then just promise me this: if things change and you do want to see other people, let me know."

"Why you worrying about other people?" he asked, kissing on her neck. "All that matters is us."

"Gunz . . . stop." Gray tried her best to protest, but the flicker of his tongue on her skin had her feeling as if she were going in circles.

"Come on, baby. Daddy missing home. Let me taste you."

That was all Gray needed to hear. Before she knew it, her back had met with the sheets and her legs were bent and spread open. Gunz looked at her. Confusion and agony were written all over her face. He wanted to promise her the world and everything it had to offer, but lying to Gray was something he just wasn't willing to do. He cared for her too much, but just didn't know how to show it. Gunz would never admit it, but he was falling hard for Gray. He loved each and every part of her, from the gentle spirit of her soul to the way she laughed at his corny jokes.

Gunz placed a trail of loving kisses from the back of her left knee all the way to the heartbeat of her clit. An impatient desire for his mouth to devour the lips of her pussy consumed Gray.

Gunz had waited all night for this moment. He wondered if she had noticed. The second the tip of his tongue met with her hard clit, she lost it. Gray could hardly breathe. She felt out of place, but in a good way. Getting her pussy eaten shouldn't feel so good. If he kept on licking and biting her clit the way he was, she was sure to cum in a matter of minutes.

Sounds of ecstasy filled the air. What Gunz was doing to her pussy was crazy voodoo black magic. Screams of pleasure arose in her throat and spilled out into the atmosphere. Gray tried to back away, but Gunz simply stopped, looked her in the eye and said, "Be still," then pulled her right back into his embrace. Gunz held her thighs in his hands so tight she swore his fingerprints would leave a mark. He wanted her to feel every stroke. With each lick he lusted for more. Gray was beyond wet. The sweet taste of her wetness lathered his tongue.

"Gunz," she moaned as her body ached for more. In the pit of her stomach she knew he was giving her just enough string to hold on, but the cream lava that was building in her pussy was too hard to ignore.

With fire in his eyes, Gunz made his way up top. His dick was rock solid and throbbing to be licked. Gray, without hesitation, took a hold of him and led him up to her mouth. This shit was crazy.

Gray knew deep down inside that she should give up and let go. Destruction was ahead. She could see it a mile away. If she held on, he was sure to make her cry. Lonely nights, forgotten promises, and lies would all be thrown her way, and in some way it would all be her fault because she should've walked away. Gray wished she was strong enough to tell him to bounce, but the enthralling kisses he placed on the base of her neck dulled any common sense she thought she had. Pain shouldn't feel so good. She felt weak and cared for at the same time. Something had to give.

Transformer . . .

Gnarls Barkly, "Transformer"

Chapter Six

Estelle's hit song "American Boy" bumped throughout Gray's house as she finished putting the final touches on the décor in her dining room. The space looked beautiful and chic, just like she'd hoped. A stark grey silk organza with pearl-studded patches covered her wooden table. In the middle was a beaded mesh runner. On top of the runner were four silver vases filled with Sarah Bernhardt peonies and sweet peas, which gave the décor an almost angelic look. Glass candle holders and candlesticks of various sizes lined the runner as well. Streamlined stemware and flatware finished off the table.

The girls would be arriving at any second. Gray couldn't wait to see her friends. It had been a minute since they were all together. Gray stood in front of the full length mirror and did a quick assessment of her outfit. Girlfriend Saturdays meant you had to go all out. A pair of jeans and a T-shirt just wouldn't do. Gray looked stunning in a pale pink halter dress with a satin tie around the waist and a feathered bottom, designed by Vivian Westwood. The dress was on loan to her from the magazine. Two huge square bracelets graced her right wrist, while a pair of lavender sequin Miu Miu closed-toe heels completed the ensemble.

Her hair was pulled to the side in a bun. Just as Gray gave herself a wink and a smile, there was a buzz at the door. Only one person would show up thirty minutes early, and that was Heidi. Gray happily went over and buzzed her up.

"Heeeeeey." Heidi air-kissed each of her cheeks. "You look cute. I brought some wine."

"I see somebody's excited."

"I am. Shit, I've been waiting all month to get away from Jerrod's ass."

"You stupid." Gray laughed.

"I'm for real. That muthafucka been gettin' on my last nerve."

"What he do now?"

"I'll tell you as soon as everybody get here, 'cause this some shit that all the girls gon' need to hear."

"Damn, is it that serious?" Gray walked toward the dining room.

"Yes." Heidi entered in behind her. "Gray."

"What?"

"You have outdone yourself. This room looks gorgeous."

"Thanks. Here you go." She handed Heidi a frozen cranberry martini.

"This shit is hot, but I'm afraid to drink it. What in the hell is this smoke shit rising from the glass?"

"Dry ice, fool."

"Oh, I was about to say . . ." Heidi took a sip.

"Now that's what I'm talkin' about! I'm 'bout to get fucked uuuuup!"

"You are an idiot." Gray laughed as someone else buzzed her loft. "Who is it?"

"Me, girl. Open up the goddamn door," Kema joked through the intercom.

"I knew it was somebody that I forgot to leave off the guest list," Gray replied, letting her up.

"Bitch, please. You know I'm the life of the party," Kema announced once she got upstairs.

"I can't stand ya ol' tall, pretty ass." Gray gave her a hug.

"Don't hate me because I'm beautiful. Hate me because I'm rich."

"Here, girl, you got to try one of these." Heidi handed Kema a drink.

"Damn, can I at least sit my purse down?"

"Ain't shit in there but a tube of lip gloss, some condoms, and KY Jelly."

"You know me so well." Kema smirked, winking her eye.

"Y'all are ignorant," Gray chimed in.

"Who else is coming?"

"Tee-Tee."

"I talked to that bitch early this morning and he said he wasn't coming."

"Y'all know how he is," Heidi reasoned. "His ass gon' come in here and make a big ol' dramatic grand entrance."

"If he do, I'ma punch him in his damn face." Kema devoured the last of her martini. "Give me another one of these."

Just as Gray was about to fix Kema another

drink, there was another buzz at the door. Without asking who it was, Gray buzzed the caller up. Once she opened the door, she found Tee-Tee posing like a Madam Tussaud wax figure.

"Tyra Mail!" He waved his hand in the air, coming through the door dressed head to toe in drag.

Gray was outdone. Teyana, aka Tee-Tee, aka Miss Tee If You Nasty, was a bona fide diva. He was six foot one and had a body any woman would die for. His skin was a flawless shade of sweet honey molasses. That day, he was dressed very old Hollywood. He rocked a golden blonde Beyoncé-inspired wig. Black eyeliner, which was wing-tipped on the end, gave his eyes a catlike effect. Bright ruby red lipstick finished off his face. His dress was the showstopper. It was a cream-colored halter dress that plunged to the middle of his stomach. A row of ruffles trimmed the neckline. The bottom of the dress fanned out like a fishtail.

"I know, darling." He smiled. "I'm fierce." He snapped his finger.

Everybody wanted to hate, but they couldn't. Tee-Tee had put every last one of them to sleep.

"Yo' ass always tryin' to outdo somebody." Kema twisted up her lip.

"Bitter, bitch?" Tee-Tee questioned.

"You wish, and anyway, I thought you said yo' ass wasn't coming."

"I know what I said. Why you all up in my business?" He flicked his hair to the back and sat down at the dining room table.

"Whateva." Kema rolled her eyes toward the ceiling.

"Gray, have you talked to Truth since the funeral?" Heidi questioned.

"No, I've been meaning to call him."

"Oh."

"Listen up, ladies." Gray clapped her hands together. "To start, we will be having crepes for appetizers. The main course will be mussels served over a bed of pasta that has been steamed in white wine with shallots and garlic, and for dessert, crème brûlée."

"Sounds finger-lickin' good." Tee-Tee licked his fingers with each word.

"You are so gross." Heidi giggled.

"Like T.I. said, you can hate if you want to, but you'll just be wastin' ya time."

"Since when you become a homo thug?" she teased.

"Since ya man stopped taking baths."

"Oh, no you didn't," Heidi shot up.

"What?" Gray asked, surprised, bringing in the crepes.

"I can't stand yo' big-mouth ass," Heidi said.

"Hmm." Tee-Tee crossed his legs then pointed his index finger toward Heidi. "Man down!"

"Heidi, what the fuck is he talkin' about? Jerrod over there not washin' his ass?" Gray continued.

"Girl, I don't know what the fuck is wrong wit' that nigga." Heidi placed her face in her hands. "Like, I'm straight-up fuckin' wit' a D.B."

"As big as you say Jerrod dick is, I know y'all still been fuckin', so he ain't too much of a Dirty Boy," Tee-Tee instigated.

"For your information, trick, we haven't been

having sex. I just started back giving his ass some last week 'cause I felt sorry for him. But what make it so bad, y'all, is that I have to run him a bath and sit on the side of the tub just to make sure he wash his ass."

"Oh, hell no. That's too much muthafuckin' playin'." Kema looked at Heidi as if she'd lost her mind.

"And he let you do that?" Gray asked, stunned.

"He so dumb. He didn't know what was going on. He thought I was tryin' to be romantic."

"Wow."

"Shit, if you did all of that, you might as well have washed in between his legs." Kema chuckled.

"That's not a bad idea. My man like to get his asshole wet from time to time," Tee-Tee confirmed.

"You just don't care what come out your mouth, do you?" Heidi snapped.

"No, boo, it's more about what I put in."

"All right." Gray's upper lip curled. "That's enough. Heidi, finish."

"Okay, one time we had sex in the morning, right? After we finished, I took a bath. When I got out of the tub, this nigga had on his gym clothes and I'm lookin' at him like, you ain't gon' hit nothing? So I got past that. We went to the gym and worked out for an hour. He drove us home, and I swear to God, I almost fainted twice. I mean, it smelled like badussy, y'all. I had to make him wash my car as soon as we got home. Then I had to go in after him and wipe my seats down 'cause I could still smell his ripe-ass balls on the inside."

"That's some funky shit." Kema shook her head.

"Ummmmmmmm, ah." Tee-Tee pursed his lips like an old lady in church and rocked back and forth.

"Hold up, but I ain't finished. After he washed my car, he cleaned up the house, went to bed, then got up, and went to the shop."

"So he ain't take no bath?"

"No, that nigga didn't even wash up. Not a half bath, a bird bath, a ho bath, nooooooooooo bath."

Gray had to hold her stomach because she was laughing so hard.

"Then his ripe ass be having the nerve to come to me talkin' about he want some head. I be lookin' at him like, nigga, are you tryin' to kill me? You ain't even put a rag on that dick. No air freshner, no Febreze, no Air Wick, no Glade, no hand sanitizer, no nothing."

"You better tell him to g'on somewhere with them organic, all nat-ur-al, no preservatives, low sodium, sugar-free-ass balls," Tee-Tee joned.

"I swear y'all are a bunch of coons." Gray continued to laugh. "So are you going to say something to him?"

"How do I go to a thirty-year-old man and tell him to wash his ass?"

"Nigga, get yo' nasty, musty, sweaty-balls-having ass in the goddamn tub!" Kema snapped, almost done with her second drink. "That's how you say it."

"You stupid. I can't do that," Heidi remarked.

"Well, then you like smelling his funky ass. Quit complaining."

"Whateva."

"Anyway, how are the crepes?" Gray said, changing the topic.

"They're good, girl," Heidi said, taking another.

"Yeah, girl, these things so good I wanna lather them all over my body," Tee-Tee agreed.

"I am officially not talkin' to you anymore today." Gray laughed on her way back into the kitchen.

"Uh-uh, Stormy Weather, I know you don't think you off the hook. What's been going on between you and Tommy Gunn?" Tee-Tee said.

"His name is Gunz, ignorant ass." Gray smiled, pushing him in the back.

"Shit, I thought his name was BB Gun." Kema laughed.

"Fuck the both of you." Gray gave them both the middle finger.

"Whateva. Spill the beans, bitch," Kema ordered.

"I don't know. It's hard to explain. It's like sometimes I know where he's coming from, then sometimes I don't. Like . . . I know he likes me, but this whole thing with him not wanting to be in a relationship is not gonna work for me too much longer."

"Is it workin' for you now? From what you told me, you only see him every couple of weeks," Kema countered.

"I mean, that has to be understood, though. You have to consider what he does for a living. He's the fuckin' leader of a major drug cartel."

"Let me tell you something. When a man wanna spend time with you, he'll find a way, so all of that is a bunch of bullshit," Kema advised.

"You're right." Gray nodded her head.

"So his career choice doesn't bother you?" Heidi asked.

"I mean, of course it does, but it's not like I can just go to him and say 'you need to stop sellin' drugs.' It's like we both know what's going on, but we don't discuss it."

"I mean, c'mon, let's be real. What is it about Gunz that's keeping you around besides the fact that he's fine and got dough?" Heide inquired.

"What other reason she need? Hell, that's reason enough for me," Tee-Tee remarked.

"Tee, you know how I am. I'm not the relationship type, but Gray is. That's all she's wanted for the past year, and you know how she fall into shit quick. I'm just tryin' to make sure her feelings don't get hurt, and dealing wit' a nigga like Gunz, her feelings are sure to get hurt. And guess what? We gon' be the ones left to pick up the pieces."

"Well, damn, I'm glad to see y'all think I'm such a fuckin' weakling," Gray spoke up for herself.

"It's not that, boo-boo. We just know how you are." Heidi rubbed the back of her hand. "You're too fuckin' nice and people take that for granted."

"Look, I know that Gunz is a handful, but at the end of the day, despite the bullshit, I know he cares for me."

"Nobody said he didn't care for you. What we're sayin' is be careful. Don't put all of your eggs in one basket. If the man is tellin' you he doesn't want to be in a relationship, then it's for a reason, so listen to him. And I know sometimes we as women get caught up in the sweet words that they tell us, but like the old sayin' says, actions speak louder than words," Kema stated, hoping Gray would take her advice.

"I feel you. Now, if you ladies will excuse me, I'm about to go get dinner."

Gray stood at the kitchen counter and glared out the window. She could hear her friends in the other room, laughing and talking as if what they'd just said hadn't hurt her. It didn't matter, though. Kema, Heidi, and even Tee-Tee had somebody. Gray wasn't willing to be the single friend with no man anymore. She was at the point were she would rather have a piece of a man than no man at all. Gray had become accustomed to having someone to talk to and hold at night, and so what if Gunz didn't want a girlfriend?

He liked her, probably even loved her. If she stuck around and showed him how great a woman she was, he'd change his mind. There was no point in stopping now. Half the battle had already been won. With a little bit more persistence and finesse, Gray was sure to win the fight.

Gray and Gunz sat quietly outside of Bar Louie in the Central West End. It was a scorching hot July afternoon. Gray's meal wasn't even appetizing to her anymore. The lemon chicken pasta she'd ordered looked like mush. The sight of it turned her stomach every time she took a look at it. Gray fanned herself with a black napkin. The sun beamed against her right thigh, making her feel hot and uncomfortable.

Gunz, on the other hand, was in heaven. Shade covered him while he sipped on a fresh scotch and soda from the bar. A huge smile covered his face as he texted nonstop on his cell phone. He'd been texting for the last fifteen minutes. Gray was beyond annoyed. He was being rude and didn't even seem to care. It was as if she wasn't even sitting there.

If he hadn't looked so good, she would have left a long time ago. Gunz sat across from her dressed casually in a black T-shirt, jeans, and Nike Blazers, but his face and physique were what did it for her. Gunz was sporting a new look. As always, his hair was freshly cut, but now he rocked a punked-out curly Mohawk. The black beard with sprinkles of grey hair that formed into a goatee had Gray's adrenaline running overtime. His barber must have used a razor on his lining; it was so precise.

Gray cleared her throat in hopes that would get his attention, but it didn't. Rolling her eyes, she situated herself in her seat and called out his name. "Gunz."

"What's up, babe?" He finally looked up from his phone.

"What are you doing?"

"Taking care of something."

"Taking care of what? I'm sittin' here trying to have lunch wit' you and you're ignoring me."

"My bad. I ain't tryin' to ignore you. This just had my attention."

"What has your attention?" she snarled, leaning forward.

"Why you so nosey?" He couldn't help but laugh. Gray trying to be tough was the funniest thing he'd ever seen. She didn't have it in her to be mean.

"That's what's up. Don't answer my question." She sat back in her seat and crossed her arms, heated.

"Look, man, don't start that shit today. We having a good time. Chill . . . out."

"Who said I was having a good time? Last time I checked, I wasn't. You've been ignoring me the whole time."

"Hold up. Let me get this." He placed up his up index finger and answered his phone. "Hello? What up, Shanice?"

Gray's forehead immediately wrinkled at the mention of another woman's name.

"'Bout time you finally picked up the phone and called. This text messaging thing is not that deal. Yo, but hold on. Gray,"—Gunz took his mouth away from the phone—"give me a second. Let me take care of this. I'll be right back."

"Oh my God." She threw up her hands in defeat as he left her alone. "I can't believe this muthafucka is on the phone with another chick. Like, is this shit really happening?" she questioned herself.

At that point, Gray didn't know if she had it in her to keep on trying. Why she continued to let him treat her like shit she didn't know. Maybe it was his looks or the way his strokes felt like thunderbolts when he hit it from the back. Whatever it was, she had to get it out of her system. Gunz had her fucked up. Her pride couldn't take much more disrespect. She felt stupid. He'd played her one too many times and gotten away with it. Things had to change immediately.

"Please don't be mad." Gunz sat back down. "That was my homegirl. I had to holla to her."

Gray shook her head and looked off to the side.

"What's wrong wit' you?" he asked once he noticed she wasn't responding.

"Nothing."

"You gotta get up outta here in a second, don't you?"

"Yep."

"I wanna see you this weekend. You gon' make time for me?"

"No." She shook her head.

"No? What the fuck you mean, no?" Gunz repeated, appalled.

Gray didn't even answer. She simply hit him with a roll of the eye and looked the other way, which she knew he hated.

"A'ight . . . so that's how you wanna be?" He nodded in disbelief. "I tell you about muthafuckas who try to be hard. Yo' ass gon' learn to quit fuckin' wit' me. So I guess I should call Shanice back and tell her to cancel our flight to Chicago this weekend for your birthday."

"What?" She perked up.

"Now yo' ass wanna talk."

"How you know my birthday was coming up?"

"Don't worry about it. I know. That's all that matters."

"So that was really just a friend?"

"That's what the hell you been over there trippin' off of? You really ain't the sharpest tool in the shed, are you? You really think I would holla at another chick while I'm sittin' here wit' you? You must think I'm as dumb as you look."

"Okay, all of that ain't even necessary. I apologize. I assumed—"

"Don't start assuming shit," Gunz said, cutting her off, " 'cause that'll get you fucked up every time. I don't like that shit. Don't do me like that."

"Like I said, I'm sorry." Gray sincerely apologized, feeling bad. Getting up from her seat, she walked over to him and wrapped her arms around his neck.

"You forgive me?" She kissed the side of his neck.

"Yeah, I forgive you, but cut that shit out." He dug into his pocket and pulled out enough money to cover the check. "You ready to head out? I don't want you to get back to work late."

"Yeah." Gray placed on her shades and grabbed her purse. "Let's go."

It was the phone call Gray had been dreading for months. Dressed comfortably in a long fitted V-neck tee and polka dot leggings, she sat Indian-style on the floor, polishing her toes black. For the past hour, she'd gazed at the phone, wondering was now the time to call. She'd done a very shady thing by leaving Rich's funeral the way she did. Night after night she tried figuring out a way to explain herself, but there was no excuse for her behavior.

Her best friend needed her, and instead of being there, she bailed. If she were Truth, she'd cuss her out, which she was almost sure he would. Unwilling to allow her fear to take over once again, she picked up the cordless phone and dialed his number. To her surprise, he answered on the first ring. It was almost as if he'd been waiting on her call.

"Hello?"

"Hi," she spoke almost in a whisper.

"Who is this?"

Gray knew he was trying to play her, but instead of reacting with an attitude, she answered, "Gray."

"Oh . . . what's up?" Truth leaned back in his chair.

"I was just callin' to see how you were doing."

"I'm good," he responded dryly.

Gray swallowed the huge lump in her throat. She was so nervous, if there was a glass of water nearby, she would've finished it off in a matter of seconds.

"Is that what you called me for? To see how I was doing?"

"Well, yeah. I did wanna see how you were doing, and I also wanted to say I'm sorry for leaving the funeral the way I did. It was just so much stuff going on and I didn't know what to do. I hope you can forgive me 'cause I really miss talkin' to my friend."

"To make things clear, we haven't been talkin' not because of the way you left the funeral. It's been because of you. I guess you been too busy hangin' wit' ol' boy to be concerned with me."

"It's not even like that. I just know y'all don't like each other, and that puts me in an awkward position. Plus, I didn't know how you would feel about me continuing to date him."

"Gray, me and you been friends for how long? Over ten years. It's not no secret that I don't like that nigga. He killed my brother—"

"You don't know that." Gray cut him off.

"You're right; I don't know, but something in me is tellin' me he did."

At that point, Gray figured that Truth was allowing his hatred for Gunz to cloud his better judgment.

"Beside," he continued, "you and I both know you can do better, but that's for you to see. Regardless, I'ma still be there for you. You my homegirl. Just don't ever play me like that again."

"I won't. I promise." She sighed with a sense of relief.

"Now that all of that female shit is out the way, turn on the Travel channel. *No Reservations* with Anthony Bourdain is on."

The next day, Gunz went by his mother's house. She'd left him an urgent message saying he needed to come by. He'd asked over and over again what the problem was, but she wouldn't say. The only thing she would admit was that he needed to be at her house by 1:00 PM so they could talk.

Normally Gunz would knock, but in a situation like this, he opted to use his key. To his surprise, when he opened the door, he found his mother and father sitting side by side on the couch, having tea.

Silence filled the room as the two men stared each other down. Gunz was the spitting image of his father. It was like he was looking at himself in the mirror. This man who he was supposed to call Dad stood two inches taller than him, but their skin was the same exact shade. Years of drug abuse had caused him to look years beyond his age, but a youthful sparkle still glimmered in his eyes.

"Hey, son." Joseph stood up.

"This what you called me over here for?" Gunz glared at his mother with daggers in his eyes.

"I knew that it was the only way you would come," she replied anxiously.

"Don't be mad at ya mama. I just wanted to talk to you, son."

"Either call me Gunz or Gavin, but never . . . ever in your life call me son, ya dig?"

"I apologize . . . Gavin. Will you please sit down?"

"Like, y'all gotta be kidding me right now." He shook his head, heated.

"I know that you're upset. You have every right to be, but there are some things that I need to say to you before it's too late." Joseph sat back down.

"You can save the sob story for somebody who cares, 'cause frankly, I don't give a fuck. When I wanted you to be there, you wasn't, so I'm . . . good."

"Just hear him out," Vivian pleaded.

"Is it some cameras up in this muthafucka? Am I being punked? I gotta be, 'cause this is some straight Oxygen, Lifetime channel bullshit." Gunz sat down on the love seat. "Say what you gotta say, man." He deliberately looked the other way instead of in his eyes.

"First I wanna start by saying I'm sorry. I was wrong for doing you and your mama the way I did."

"You fuckin' right." Gunz cut him off.

"I take full responsibility for what I did," Joseph continued on. "I should've been there, and I regret every day that I wasn't. Understand, though, there was never a day where I did not miss or think about you. I hate that I let drugs take over my life, but it got to a point where . . . drugs became bigger than me, you, and everybody else. I just hope you can forgive me, Gavin. If there is a way you and I could start anew . . . you just don't know what that would mean to me."

"You done?" Gunz finally gave him eye contact.

"Yeah." Joseph nodded his head.

"You ain't had a muthafuckin' thing to say to me all these years, but now you got so much to say. Nigga, fuck you! Don't . . . say . . . shit . . . to . . . me. I'm a grown-ass man. Don't try to tell me shit now. You ain't never been no father to me, so as far as I'm concerned, Mama, you even callin' ya baby daddy over here was pointless. This was some bull-shit." He stood up and walked toward the door. "I'm outta here."

"Gavin, just stay for a little while longer," his mother begged, taking his hand.

"Nah, let him go, Vivian. I spoke my peace and he spoke his," Joseph interceded.

"But there is so much more that you need to say." She looked at him with distress in her eyes. "Gavin,"—she turned and faced her son—"please stay. . . . He's still your father."

"Why are you going so hard for this man?" Gunz snapped, snatching his hand away. "Have you for-gotten how he used to go upside yo' muthafuckin' head and beat yo' ass? How he stole from us? This sorry-ass-nigga couldn't even come to Adriana's fu-neral! But I guess that don't matter, 'cause he ain't no crackhead no more. I mean, what's really good?"

"Watch ya mouth, Gavin."

"Nah, fuck that." He waved her off.

Vivian stepped up to Gunz and slapped him with so much force her hand burned. The minute she did it, she regretted it, but she wasn't going to let her son talk to her any kind of way just because he was grown.

"Now, I have told you about your goddamn mouth!"

"That's what's up." He chuckled, rubbing his jaw. "So let me get this straight, just so we can all be clear. You'll ride for this reformed crackhead that left you wit' two kids and a mortgage for heroin, but you'll slap me, your son who has done nothing but stand by your side? That's how the shit is now?"

"Gavin, there is just so much that you don't understand."

"I know everything I need to know. I see now that all I got is my damn self. I can't even depend on you anymore, but it's good. I'ma get up outta here. Y'all two go 'head and finish drinkin' tea and gettin' acquainted."

With that being said, Gunz left angrier and more confused than ever. He realized that his words would hurt his mother to the core, but who gave a fuck? He couldn't care less about the agony in her beautiful brown eyes. All that mattered were his feelings. She'd made it perfectly clear that all of the struggles they'd gone through together were no longer of importance. She'd done the godly thing and forgiven Joseph for all of his sins, but Gunz could never forgive and forget. Fuck that. His life had always been a lonely one, and he wasn't willing to transform it for anybody.

Yellow 2 my blue . . .

Coultrain, "Blue"

Chapter Seven

Bursts of color and beautiful one of a kind chic vintage pieces filled Paperdolls boutique located on Washington Avenue. The boutique had a loft-like appeal to it. At the back of the store was a seven-step staircase which led to a showcase of clothes. There was even a seating area outside. Some of the clothing was actual pieces of art designed by the artist Macu. The owner also sold jewelry and designer handbags.

Gray was ecstatic. Her surroundings only intensified her feelings more. She couldn't wait to go out of town with Gunz. This was the opportunity she'd been waiting for. Finally he'd be able to see all of the wonderful things about her that a couple of hours together couldn't provide.

"This is ca-uuute." Tee-Tee picked up a nude-and-black Alexander Wang dress.

"Oooooooh, I do like that," Gray agreed, coming over.

They were trying to find outfits for her and Gunz's weekend trip.

"I can most definitely rock the hell out of this, so I will be gettin' it." She took the dress over to the counter and placed it down.

"So what time y'all leaving tomorrow?"

"I lied and told my boss that I had a family emergency, so she let me have the day off tomorrow, so we'll be leaving in the morning."

"Yo' ass gon' get fired."

"No, I'm not. Don't be burning bread on me like that." Gray knocked on wood. "Besides, I've been working my ass off. I arrive earlier than anybody else, and I'm the last one to leave at night. And plus, when I get back, I'll be coordinating all of the looks for the September cover, which will feature Halle Berry."

"That's what's up. I mean, I'm excited that you done found you a li'l boo and e'rthang, but don't start takin' unnecessary time off just to be with him, 'cause please believe he would not do it for you."

"Trust me, I'm not. This is just a one time thing. Speaking of my boo, this him callin' me right now." She cheerfully grinned as her cell phone vibrated vigorously in her hand. "Hello?"

"What the fuck you doing?"

"Nothing." She giggled at his silliness. "Just out . . . picking up a few things."

"A few things," Tee-Tee repeated. "Has this bitch forgotten that she has her whole entire paycheck sittin' over there on the counter?"

Giving him the evil eye, Gray placed her index finger up to her mouth and warned him to shush.

"Who was that in the background? I know you

ain't wit' some nigga," Gunz questioned, about to flip.

"Calm down. That's my friend Tee-Tee."

"Tee-Tee? What kind of bullshit is that? You know what? I don't even wanna know. Just call me when you get home, a'ight."

"Okay."

"Ay," Gunz called out before she hung up.

"What?"

"Before you do that, I want you to do one thing for me."

"What, babe?"

"Turn around."

Gray quickly spun around on her heels. To her surprise, Gunz was right outside the boutique, leaning against an SLR McLaren Roadster. The car cost almost half a million dollars. Gray damn near shitted on herself he looked so good. Gunz posted like the king. He stood dipped in a fitted white tee, dark blue dirty wash jeans, and all-white shell toe Adidas. A gold rosary hung delicately from his neck, while a gold Audemar Piguet watch gleamed brightly from his wrist.

"Close your mouth, quit lookin' at me, and come here," he said before hanging up.

Gray happily left Tee-Tee behind and greeted him outside. Gunz couldn't help but appreciate Gray's thick thighs and firm legs as she sauntered out the boutique's door, and although other people swarmed past, no one but her mattered. The crisp white Marc Jacobs tank top and indigo blue True Religion cuffed denim shorts accentuated her curves to the fullest. A long beaded necklace that reached her waist enhanced the casually chic outfit.

"What you doing wit' these little bitty-ass shorts on?" Gunz asked, pulling her into him by the belt loop of her shorts. "You want niggas to be lookin' at yo' ass and shit?"

"Nope, only you."

"You miss me?" He placed his hands inside her back pockets and situated his dick so she could feel his hard-on.

"The question is, do you miss me?" Gray challenged, biting down onto her bottom lip as she ran her hands up and down the center of his crotch.

"You feel how hard my dick is; that's obvious."

"Why you so nasty?"

"'Cause I know you like it."

"How you know I was here?" she wondered.

"I was riding through and seen you."

"But how did you know it was me?"

"Gray, I know that ass from a mile away."

"Ha ha, funny." She playfully hit his chest.

For a minute they stood in silence. Gunz stared off into space as if something was on his mind. The whole family intervention with his parents had him off balance.

"Hey," Gray got his attention. "What's wrong?"

"Nothing. It's just been a long-ass day."

"You wanna talk about it?"

"Nah, not right now."

"You sure? 'Cause we can go somewhere and talk. I don't mind."

"That's sweet, ma." He lovingly placed a kiss on her forehead. "But nah, I'm good. You finish doing your thing. I just wanted to see you for a minute."

"Okay," she replied, not really wanting to leave the conversation alone.

"Here,"—he dug into his right pocket—"Go buy me a box of Lemonheads." Gunz handed her a stack of hundred-dollar bills totaling up to ten grand.

"I am not taking that." She handed him the money back knowing full well she needed it.

"I ain't ask you to take it. I asked you to go get me some Lemonheads."

"You think you slick. No, go buy your own candy; I'm good."

"A'ight, you gon' quit tellin' me no. But look, I'm about to head on out." He cupped her chin and made her look directly at him. "You be good, a'ight."

"I will."

A delightful melody by Emily King called "U & I" came to Gray's mind: *Finally, finally my love has arrived. Once there was me . . . now there's you and I,* Gray thought as she became trapped in his gaze. *Handsome* was not the word to describe him. Gunz was beautiful. The hold that he had on her was beyond her control. Since forever she'd prayed for a man like him. Gray's lips desperately wanted to form the words *I love you*, but the timing just wasn't right.

"I'ma call you later." He softly kissed her lips. "Answer the phone."

"Okay," she replied, on cloud nine.

After Gunz pulled off, she reentered the store.

"It's just fuck me, right?" Tee-Tee cocked his head back with his hand on his chest. "I swear a bitch that's gettin' some dick ain't shit."

"Shut up. You just mad."

"I mean, look at you."

"Look at me." Gray rolled her neck then turned

around slowly in a circle so that he could get a good view of her.

"That killa really got you sprung. If the dick that good, let a nigga like me get a taste." Tee-Tee flicked his tongue like a snake.

"Trick, please. You better fall back. I will cut a bitch over that big, black ten-inch dick."

"Oooooh, why you have to go into details? Now my panties all wet."

"Okay, that was just too much." Gray shook her head, repulsed.

"It's never enough. You can never have too much dick in your life." Tee-Tee did his best Eartha Kitt impression.

"Yo' ass is certifiably crazy."

"And so are you. I can't believe you are about to spend all this money just to impress some man. I hope he's worth it."

"He is."

"You love him, don't you?" Tee-Tee said more as a statement than a question.

"How you figure that?" Gray challenged.

" 'Cause he's everything you never said you wanted but apparently need."

No one on the corner has swagger like us, was the melody that ran through Truth's head as he walked through the mall. You couldn't tell him he wasn't the shit. Truth was tall with pecan-colored skin, and although his pockets weren't deep, his dick was long. Every time he stepped outside chicks were on him, but he couldn't sweat that none. Only one woman had his attention and that was Gray.

Just because she and Gunz were doing their thing didn't mean that he was gonna give up on them one day being together. In time, she was sure to see what he'd known from the start—that they were meant to be. He was willing to do anything to make her his. It didn't matter. If he had to lie, cheat, or kill, she was gonna be his.

Plus, Gunz needed to pay. There was no way he was going to get away with killing his brother and not deal with the repercussions of his actions. Truth was gonna make him suffer in the worst way imaginable. Gunz didn't know what was in store for him.

Truth made his way out of the mall and into the parking lot. As he approached his car, his cell phone began to ring.

" 'Bout time you called nigga. I was starting to get worried," he said, opening his car door.

"My bad. I got caught up. What's poppin'?" Fortune asked.

"I'm just callin' to make sure everything is good."

"Yeah, the shit about to go down tomorrow."

"That's what I'm talkin' about." Truth smiled.

"You got everything covered on yo' end?"

"I'm good."

"Now, you sure that I'ma be straight?" Fortune questioned, unsure.

"As long as you follow the plan. Get that shit and get ghost. Lay low for a minute then set up shop. Just don't be spending mad money and drawing attention to yourself."

"A'ight. Well, look, I'll holla at you in a minute then," Fortune confirmed.

"One."

With a devious smile plastered on his face, Truth got inside his car. Operation Ruin Gunz's Life was in full effect. Now it was time for Truth to sit back and watch as Gunz's life crumbled into pieces around him.

After a quick flight, Gray and Gunz arrived in Chicago. Everything was perfect. Gray couldn't ask for more. The flight was smooth, and there was hardly any turbulence. There was no problem with finding their luggage, and the weather was sunny with not a cloud in sight. A driver picked them up from the airport and swept them away to their destination at The James Hotel.

Everything from the exterior of the building to the lobby was well thought out. The James was modern, but still had a sense of classic hospitality. They offered everything from a spa to an exercise room to a lounge called the Jbar.

Gray couldn't wait to get up to their room. Gunz had gotten them the penthouse loft. As soon as the door opened, she was in love.

A contrasting palette of earth tone colors filled the space. The minimalist layout and custom designed furniture included a streamlined dark wood platform bed, private dining, plasma screen TVs, and a slate-tiled and marbled bathroom. Other amenities included Kiehl's bath products, commissioned art, 100% Turkish cotton towels, and daily newspaper delivery.

Once they were showered and dressed, Gray and Gunz left the hotel and did a little sightseeing on

Michigan Avenue. Due to the fact that Gray had never been to the Chi, Gunz took on the position of being their tour guide. The Chanel store, Max-Mara, and Louis Vuitton were just some of the spots they hit before heading back to the hotel for lunch. Gunz was pleasantly surprised that in each store they went to, Gray never once asked for a thing. He even went so far as to offer to buy her something, but she flat out refused.

Now they lay resting comfortably, chest to back, in a tub filled with pink rose petals. Coultrain's laid back melody "Blue" set the mood. Flickers of light from the twelve tea candles strategically placed around the room danced across the walls. Gunz laid in between Gray's legs as she used a sponge to wash his broad chest. Hidden thoughts crammed the room. There were so many things Gray wanted to unveil, but the words were stuck on pause in her throat.

Tee-Tee was right. Gray held a love so strong for Gunz in her heart that it scared her. Before him, she never knew the true definition of the word, but with him, she wanted to explore each way it could be displayed. Gray didn't have to look for love anymore because she'd found it in him. And even though the feeling might not stay, she cherished the change in her life. Captivated by his presence, she dipped the sponge in water then washed his right pec.

Gray watched intently as the hot water slid down his chiseled chest and back into the tub. Her tongue wanted nothing more than to lavish his body with sweet kisses. Flashbacks of him pounding her pussy while playing with her clit sent chills up her spine. Gunz could do what he wanted with her, and she'd gladly succumb to his will.

"What you back there thinking about?" he asked, interrupting her thoughts.

"Making love to you." She tenderly bent her head and kissed the left side of his neck.

"Cut that out." He rubbed her thigh.

"What? You asked."

"You ain't talkin' about nothing."

"Try me and find out," she challenged.

"Later."

"You so wack." She playfully mushed him in the head.

"Whateva. You ever heard this song before?"

"No, but I love it."

"Yeah, I like this cat. He's from St. Louis."

"Really?"

"Yeah, this is like my favorite song off the whole CD. Every time I play it I think of you."

"That's so sweet." Gray lovingly kissed the side of his face. "So since I love this song and so do you, I declare that this should be our song."

"You so corny." Gunz laughed.

"Whateva. You like the idea." Gray giggled.

"Ay?"

"What's up?"

"Why wouldn't you let me get you anything while we were out?" He wanted to know.

"I didn't need anything. Besides, spending time with you is enough for me."

"Remember you said that." He laughed.

"Don't get it twisted. I won't say no next time."

She laughed too. "Why have you been so quiet? You haven't said a word since we got back."

"I just got a lot of shit on my mind, man."

"Talk to me."

Gunz wondered if he should open up about his father's unexpected appearance back in his life or deal with it on his own. Opening up about his feelings was something he didn't do often, especially with a woman, but with Gray, he felt a sense of comfort.

"When I was ten, my old dude burnt out on me, my mom, and my sister. He was on drugs and shit. You know, when I was younger, it really fucked me up that he would do that. And for a long time, I wished he'd come back and we'd be like we was, but . . . my li'l sister ended up passing—"

"I'm sorry to hear that," Gray cut him off.

"It's cool." He looked down at the water.

"How'd she die?"

"She drowned in a pool."

"Oh my God. How old was she?"

"Six."

"Gunz, I am so sorry." She wrapped her arms around him tight.

"Yeah . . ." He stared off into space. "Shit was crazy, but the most fucked-up part about it was . . . you know . . . my peoples got word to my old dude that Adriana had died, and you know this muthafucka didn't even give a fuck. He ain't even come to the funeral to see his own baby girl off."

"Wow." Gray shook her head.

"After that I wrote that nigga off. I ain't want to have shit to do wit' him. Now twenty years later this muthafucka wanna come play daddy."

"You've seen him? You talked to him?"

"Yeah. Remember that day I came by the store and hollered at you?"

"Yeah."

"That day him and my old bird ambushed me on some forgive and forget, let's be a family bullshit. Supposedly he's clean."

"How did you feel?"

"I was pissed off. I couldn't believe my mama would do some shit like that. She knows all the heartache we went through behind that man."

"The question is, do you want to have a relationship with him?"

"No. I'm grown. There ain't shit that nigga can do for me now."

"The only thing I can say, Gunz, is that . . . everybody goes through stuff in life, and along the way, their choices may hurt people. But it's up to that person to decide whether or not they want to right their wrongs. And that's what it sounds like your father is trying to do."

"I don't know." He situated himself, slightly agitated.

"I mean, it's up to you. You have to search through all the pain and abandonment issues and see if you can open your heart and accept him in your life again. I know that it's a huge decision . . . so I suggest you take your time while making it. 'Cause I know how you feel."

"I don't even know who my father is, but I do know that if he were to come in my life today or tomorrow, I would want to talk to him, so I could get to see who he is as a person and whether or not we have the same characteristics, or better yet, a chance at even building some kind of relationship."

"I hear what you sayin', man, and that sounds good on paper, but after all the bullshit my old man has put me through, I don't know if I can do it."

"Well, like I said, just think about it." Gray stared at the side of his face then kissed his cheek. She prayed that one day soon Gunz would be able to let down his guard and let people into his life. If he didn't, she knew they didn't have a chance in hell for any kind of future together.

After talking some more, the two washed each other's bodies then got out of the tub and began to get dressed. Since they were going to a Latin restaurant, Gray decided to wear an ultra sexy asymmetrical red mini dress by Rachel Pally. One side of the dress had a long, flowing sleeve, while the other side was completely sleeveless. Gray didn't even rock a lot of jewelry. A pair of oversized rusted bronze earrings and two matching bracelets was all she needed. To finish off the look, she rocked a pair of edgy, zebra print, four and a half-inch Manolo Blahnik peep-toe heels.

Gunz didn't look too shabby himself. He sported a gray T-shirt with gold writing, a gray pinstriped vest, jeans, and gold Lanvin high top sneakers. A thin gold rosary and Patek Philippe watch was all the jewelry he donned.

Rumba was one of Gunz's favorite restaurants. Every time he stopped in Chicago, he made it his business to visit. He was almost sure Gray would grow to love it as much he did.

As soon as she entered, she felt as if she'd been swept off to a 1940s super club. The sounds coming from the live entertainment instantly made her want to dance. The opulent entranceway provided an unobstructed view to the bar, main dining room, as well as the entertainment focal point, the stage. Over to the side was the dance floor.

Oversized tufted red conga booths, floor to ceiling curtains, authentic Moroccan antique lamps, Spanish wall sconces, and white linen tablecloths with candles gave the place a sensual vibe. The smell of authentic Latin cuisine intoxicated her nose.

Gray and Gunz took a seat right next to the dance floor.

"So what you think?" he asked.

"I love it. Like, I wish there were more places like this back in St. Louis."

"Me too," Gunz replied, opening up his menu. "So you really have never had Latin food before?"

"No, growing up all I ate was Korean food. I didn't get my first taste of soul food until I met my friend Kema."

"You gon' have to hip me to some Korean food. All I know is a whole order of special fried rice with no onions, and crab Rangoon."

"You silly." Gray laughed. "That is not Korean food. That's some shit Chinese people made up for y'all to eat."

"Are you serious?"

"Yeah, we don't eat that shit. We eat plain fuckin' rice."

"Fuck naw."

"So what do you suggest I order? I don't really like spicy food, so anything besides that is good."

"Well, jerk chicken is out of the question then. Do you like seafood?"

"I love seafood."

"Well, I suggest you get the coconut plantain-encrusted sea bass."

"That sounds wonderful. What are you gonna get?"

"I'm gettin' the muthafuckin' Caribbean seafood parrillada."

"What's that?"

"It's a lobster tail with shrimp, scallops, tilapia, and calamari grilled in a garlic lemon butter sauce. A jalapeño corn cake and *tostones al mojo* come with it."

"Your food sounds good."

"You just don't know. I love this place, man."

Once their orders were placed, Gray and Gunz sipped on Merlot and bobbed their head to the band's rendition of Hector Lavoe's "El Cantante."

"You lookin' kinda good in that dress, ma." He leaned forward and admired her breasts with lust in his eyes.

"Thanks." Gray blushed, sipping on her drink.

"You know I'm pretty happy you decided to come wit' me."

"I'm pretty happy I decided to come too."

"You really like me, don't you?"

"What?" She giggled, almost choking.

"Admit it. You do."

"You cool."

"I know I'm cool. Shit, I'm the coolest nigga you know. I asked if you liked me."

"Why? Is me liking you gon' change anything?"

"Who knows . . . it might." He chuckled.

"Whateva." Gray threw her napkin in his face, laughing.

"For real, you do?"

"It's obvious that I like you. If I didn't, I wouldn't be here. The question is, how much do you like me?"

"Here are your meals," the waitress announced.

"Saved by the bell," Gunz replied as she placed his plate in front of him.

"That's some bullshit." Gray pursed her lips together and shook her head. She hated that he'd gotten off easy.

"Will there be anything else?"

"No, thanks," they both spoke in unison.

"This looks delicious." Gray placed her napkin on her lap, starving.

"Close your eyes and open your mouth."

"What?"

"Just trust me. Close your eyes and open your mouth."

Gray looked at Gunz suspiciously then did what she was told and closed her eyes. Reluctantly, she opened her mouth. Gunz, using his fingers, picked up a plantain and placed it into her mouth. A cornucopia of delectable sweetness exploded into her mouth. The taste of the sugary plantain and the saltiness from Gunz's fingers took her to forbidden heights of pleasure. She relished the taste of him in her mouth. As his index finger slipped from her lips, Gray made it her business to flick her tongue against the tip. Gunz's penis sprang to attention at the thought of his finger being his dick.

"That was nice. Thank you," she spoke in a low, raspy tone.

"You welcome."

"So tell me, where do you see yourself in five years?"

"Hopefully out of the game. I never really planned on doing this the rest of my life. My plans are to open up a couple of restaurants and art galleries."

"You like art?"

"Yeah, I mean, that's something a lot of people don't know about me, but over the past couple of years, I've bought a couple of nice pieces."

"Wow." Gray gave him a warm smile. "I would've never guessed that about you."

"It's a lot about me you don't know, Gray."

"But that's the point. If given the chance, I wanna know everything there is to know about you."

"Who knows? You keep it up, you just might."

A half an hour later, Gunz and Gray were full. Gray enjoyed every bite. Normally she would've been afraid to eat in front of a man, but Gunz made her feel comfortable. For the first time, she could be herself with a man.

Gunz, too, was enjoying himself. If he did want a woman, Gray would be the perfect candidate. He was digging everything about her, from her style to the way she smiled. More than anything, he loved the way she moved. He could see her grooving in her seat.

"Get up and do your thing, ma," he suggested.

"You sure?"

"Yeah, go 'head."

The smell of mouthwatering food, smoke, and sweat filled the air as Gray made her way to the dance floor. Shakira's megahit "La Tortura" had everyone up on their feet. Bodies were plastered together, but none of that mattered. The only thing that mattered was the music.

Gray loved to dance, so she quickly got into the groove. She could see Gunz out of the corner of her eye, staring her down. The whole scenario reminded her of when they first met.

Turned on, she connected eyes with him and began doing her thing. She knew he enjoyed watching her put on a show. Bending over, Gray bit her lower lip and wound her hips slowly clockwise to the beat. The entire time, she envisioned his firm hands caressing her thighs.

Gunz's dick was brick hard. The way Gray shook her ass mesmerized him and threw him off track. Here he was, trying to be hard and keep his composure, but a bead of sweat had begun to form on his forehead. Gray wasn't fighting fair and she knew it. The look in her alluring blue eyes said it all. She wanted to make love until she begged God for mercy. Wanting a better view, Gunz lit up a Djarum clove cigarette and leaned forward.

The band must have read Gray's mind because her jam by Shakira, "Hips Don't Lie," started to thump. A wicked grin traced the corners of her mouth. The dim lighting melted all of her inhibitions away. The heat coming from the beat caused her to grind even harder. Gray was tired of playing games. She was starting to wonder if she was too much for Gunz. Kissing and hugging was cool, but there was so much more a man and a woman could do. Gray wanted Gunz to put it on her in the worst way. Every part of her could be his, but it was up to him to take it.

Running her hands across her breasts, Gray stared Gunz dead in the eye and sang, "And I'm staritng to feel it's right . . . All the attraction, the tension . . . don't you see baby, this is perfection."

Far from being a punk, Gunz took one more puff from his cigarette then mashed the rest in the ashtray. It was time for him to step to Gray like the man he was. Face to face, he took her by the hand and kissed her passionately. Neither one of them had ever enjoyed someone's company so much. They laughed, they drank, they ate, and before they knew it, the lights were coming on and the restaurant was closing.

The ride back to the hotel seemed to take forever. Gunz couldn't keep his hands off Gray. Once they reached the hotel, he pulled her inside and locked the door behind them. Things were moving so fast that she didn't have enough time to catch her breath. Gunz's milk chocolaty colored physique towered over her. She felt so small in his presence. An undeniable need for him to put his mouth on her skin consumed Gray. With her back pressed up against the door, Gunz took a handful of her hair into his hand and tilted her head back.

An obsessive look of desire shone from his eyes. Using his thumb, he ran it across her lips like he was applying lipstick. She couldn't help but to take him in her mouth. Gray loved the taste of him. Eagerly, she ran her hands up his shirt. Muscles that she hadn't expected swelled underneath her fingertips.

Gray's neck was pleading to be licked. Gunz satisfied her craving by saturating her skin with soft, wet kisses. Making his way down, he stopped at the center of her chest. Gray's hardened nipples poked through the fabric of her dress like missiles. Enthralled by his touch, she bit her lip and watched as he took a hold of both her thighs and placed them on his shoulders.

Gunz suffocated the lips of Gray's pussy with succulent licks and kisses. It was unavoidable; in a matter of seconds, she was sure to cum. Gunz flicked his tongue across her clit even faster. Cumming, she let out a whimpering moan.

Nowhere near done with her, he carried her over to the bed and placed her down on her stomach. Gray eagerly lifted her butt in the air so he could enter from behind.

Seeing her face down with her ass up only heightened Gunz's hunger for her. The lips of her pussy were covered in hot, sticky cum. He quickly stepped out of his clothes. Once they were off, he placed himself in behind Gray and slid his rock hard penis inside her wet slit. With his hands on her waist, he grinded in and out of her at brisk pace. Gray was driving him crazy.

The folds of her pussy suffocated his dick. Tenderly, he kneaded her butt cheeks. Her pussy was first class. Gray was overwhelmed with desire. Her insatiable appetite for dick escalated with each stroke. She wanted to explode.

"Oooooh, Gunz, just like that."

"You like that?"

"Yeah, baby, go deeper," she moaned.

Each stroke felt like New Year's. The anticipation

of an orgasm nearing was spellbinding. Gray's lips trembled. Nothing could prepare her for the size of his mammoth dick. She could feel it all the way in her rib cage. The side of Gray's face rubbed up against the sheets as she screamed out in agony.

She wanted to kiss him, ride him, and suck him all at once. This was bliss. Gunz's groans were intensifying her pleasure. At any second, he was due to burst. Gray shamelessly thrust her ass into his shaft. She wanted him to cum on her butt. The mere thought of his hot lava on her skin caused her stomach muscles to contract.

"Ooooooooooooooooooooh, baby! Awwwwwwwwww, yeah! This dick feel so good!"

"Ahhhhhhhhhhhhhhh," Gunz roared as he pulled out and came on her butt just as she'd desired.

Gray came harder with each drop. Seconds later, they were on to round two.

What's in a name if we got what we need?

Mario, "No Definition"

Chapter Eight

Gray lay in Gunz's arms, sound asleep. They'd made love until neither could physically go any further. Gunz lay on his back, staring absently at the wall. A million thoughts ran through his mind. He'd never been so put at ease by a woman. Gray was the type of chick who naturally went with the flow. Yeah, sometimes she nagged and complained, but to see her blue eyes twinkle made him want to lock her down and make her his wife. But Gunz wasn't ready for that yet.

What he and Gray shared was rare and complicated. He wasn't her man, but they were more than friends. They made love, but he didn't call her his lover. She was his heart, his ace, but a part of him still wanted to stay open to other situations. And although he tried to play it off like he didn't, Gunz thought about Gray all the time. Every time his phone rang, he hoped it was her. With any other, he would've been done, but Gunz just couldn't shake Gray off.

Tired of thinking, he grabbed the remote control

off the nightstand. The clock read 3:33 AM. It was officially Gray's birthday. Using the remote, he turned on the television. CNN popped onto the screen. A news bulletin about ten Miami Airport workers charged in a major drug ring ran across the screen.

"It can't be," he said out loud as he sat up and turned up the volume.

"A drug ring comprised of airport and airline workers who were smuggling large quantities of narcotics into passengers' luggage bound for Miami International Airport has been broken up by federal authorities. Federal agents seized more than forty-two kilograms of heroin and fifteen kilograms of Ecstasy in the bust, and arrested seven Southwest employees, one American Airlines employee, two airport workers, and eight others in connection to the ring," headline news reporter Brooke Anderson reported.

"This is some bullshit," Gunz said as his cell phone began to ring. "What?"

"Yo, you watching the news?" Watts asked, shocked too.

"Yeah. Call Shanice and tell her to book me a flight. I'm coming home." He hung up in Watts' ear before he could reply.

Gunz ran his hands down his face and inhaled deeply. He hated to cut the trip short, but business came before everything—even Gray. Shit had to be taken care of and quick. He'd paid close to a half million dollars for drugs the feds had confiscated, and what made matters worse was that he was almost out of product, so unfortunately, for a while there would be a drought. Plus, it hadn't slipped his mind that there were twenty-eight kilos of cocaine unaccounted for, and Gunz needed to find out who had them.

First he had to tell Gray the trip was over. He felt horrible, but it had to be done. Gunz looked over his shoulder at her. An expression of tranquility covered her sleeping face. The way her lips formed the perfect pout brought a slight smile to Gunz's face and calmed him down a bit. He could watch her sleep forever and never get tired.

"Ma." He slid back in bed and tenderly kissed her forehead.

"Huh?" She groggily opened her eyes.

"Happy birthday." He kissed her lips.

"Thank you." She kissed him back. "What time is it?"

"Almost four."

"Why are you still up? Oops, I forgot you don't sleep." She chuckled.

"Okay, smart ass. I see you just a regular ol' Bill Cosby." Gunz joined in and laughed.

"Shut up." She playfully hit his chest.

"But nah, for real. I got bad news."

"What? Everything is okay, isn't it?" Gray shot up, worried.

"Everything's straight. We just gotta head back early. I gotta handle some things."

Gray knew that there was more to the story, but she dared not ask. She was fully aware of what Gunz did for a living, so situations like this were expected. That still didn't stop the fact that she was disappointed; but Gray being Gray sucked it up and pretended to be okay with the circumstances.

"You had me scared for a second. I thought somebody had died or something. You want me to start getting my things together now?"

"So you not mad?" Gunz asked, surprised.

"No. Why would I be? I've had a great time. Besides, I told you, spending time with you is the best birthday present I've gotten so far."

Once again Gunz was shocked by Gray's willingness to cooperate with his lifestyle and more importantly, the gentle, sweet words that poured from her heart for him. She was showing traits of a woman that when shit was fucked up, she would rub his back and tell him everything would be okay. If she kept this attitude up, maybe she would find a permanent place in his heart.

"Yo, I'm outside," Gunz said as he parked his brand new silver Aston Martin V8 Vantage in front of PCS barbershop.

The shop was located in the heart of south St. Louis. Gunz loved his old neighborhood. Ten years ago, the area was filled with rundown houses, vacant school buildings, and crackheads. Back in the day, niggas would start clappin' at any given second of the day. Kids didn't know the meaning of going in the house when the street light came on. Old ladies stayed bitchin' about niggas sellin' product in front of their homes. Chicks fought over the neighborhood Nino Brown. Heavy bass bumped from the trunk of old school cars. The smell of fresh piss and dog shit continuously filled the air. Single mothers bore the look of shame each time they boarded the bus with their babies in pumpkin seats or strollers. The corner store and Chinese restaurants were the residents' only source of food and nutrition.

Now, condominiums, lofts, boutiques, and a renovated project livened up the once destitute section. White families occupied the once empty brick row houses, while black families were being forced into the county. The children of white families attended the best private schools money could buy. Expensive cars that most middle class people couldn't afford lined their driveways. A look of pride filled their faces every day they took their morning jog.

For the most part, Gunz was happy about some of the changes, but to no longer see people who looked like him when he walked down the street saddened him to the core.

Gunz leaned against his ride, dressed fresh to death in a black short-sleeve button-up white V-neck, distressed denim jeans, and all black Chuck Taylors. Two dog tags and a watch completed his cycle. Philadelphia Freeway's soulful hit "Baby Don't Do It" served as his soundtrack.

A second later, Watts and Bishop came through the shop's door and out into the street. The two men gave Gunz a much needed pound and a hug.

"What's the deal?"

"Man, shit is all bad," Watts confirmed. "The feds got everything."

"How in the fuck did everything go wrong? I had this shit planned to a T," Gunz asked, heated.

"That's what the fuck we tryin' to figure out. All we know is everybody got knocked except for Fortune."

"Don't nobody know where that nigga at," Bishop added.

"What I wanna know is who got my other twenty-eight ki's of coke." Gunz looked at them both. "Either the feds got it or Fortune do. Either way, I'm fucked."

"Man, I knew we shouldn't have never let that nigga get involved." Bishop shook his head.

"The shit done happened now. Now it's time to fix it."

"And how do you propose we do that?"

"We gon' have to put our funds together and re-up. But what I want y'all to do right now is tell the li'l homies that it's hundred stacks for the man who can bring Fortune to me. Niggas need to understand that anybody who lies or steals from me got a death wish, flat out, and I'm gon' fulfill it."

Later on that night, Gunz arrived at Gray's building with a dozen purple tulips in his hand. Guilt still plagued his soul. More than anything, he wanted to give her a birthday she would never forget. Unfortunately, circumstances beyond his control got in the way. Gunz was determined to make it up to her, though.

After buzzing her loft, Gray let him up. The sight of fresh flowers and the man she adored holding them brought a huge smile to her face.

"Thank you," she gushed, running into his awaiting arms.

The feel of Gray's warm body wrapped up in his embrace pleased Gunz.

"Give me a kiss."

Gray quickly obliged his request. Standing on her tiptoes, she closed her eyes and placed her lips on his. For Gunz, kissing Gray was like the Fourth of July, Christmas, and New Year's Eve wrapped all in one with a ribbon on it.

"So what you been doing all day?" he asked, coming inside.

"Nothing. Thinkin' about you."

"Yeah, a'ight, tell me anything."

"For real."

"What is that you cookin'? It smells good like a muthafucka."

"Since I knew you were coming over, I decided to make us an authentic Korean meal."

"Word?" Gunz responded, excited.

"Yeah. Why you seem so surprised?" Gray asked as she placed the flowers in a vase.

"You don't understand; I ain't never met nobody like you. I mean, here it is your birthday and you cookin' dinner for me."

"It's for the both of us."

"You know what I'm sayin'. Right now we supposed to be in the Chi, chillin'."

"I told you I'm good. We had fun, and most importantly, we're here now sharing another moment together."

"I feel you." Gunz nodded his head, taking a seat on the couch.

Gray was nothing short of the truth. In his heart, he knew that what they shared was the start of something real. There was no use in faking. Gray held his heart in the palm of her hands and she didn't even know it.

"You know my mama always said don't let 'em

get to cookin' 'cause in a minute, they gon' want keys to your house."

"I don't want no key." Gray set down a dish. "And I don't want no house either."

"Well, at least we got an understanding," he replied, trying his hardest not to laugh.

"Don't play wit' me."

"I'm just fuckin' wit' you, ma."

"You better be." She sat down on the floor across from him. "Now, let me explain to you what we're eating. This right here is *nabak kimchi*. Kimchi is something that we eat along with everything. Right here we have *galbi-gui*. Galbi-gui is basically grilled short ribs. In this we have *udong*. Udong is a noodle dish. Last but not least we have *mandu*, which is a typical street food. Mandu is dumplings that are filled with beef, pork, and mixed vegetables."

"I don't know where to start first." Gunz looked over everything, amazed.

"Here, try the mandu. It's my favorite."

Once both their plates were full, Gray decided to spark up a conversation.

"So, Gunz, be honest with me. Why is it that you don't want to be in a relationship?"

" 'Cause, man . . . it's just a lot of shit that go into being in a relationship, stuff that I don't know if I necessarily wanna deal wit' right now. Plus, I just got out of something a minute ago."

"Really?" Gray said, surprised. "With who?"

"That's not important."

"It must have been Devin." She shook her head, feeling stupid.

"Okay, it was. And? Like I told you, that shit wit' her is in the past."

"So why you just now tellin' me this?"

"You never asked, and plus, it wasn't important."

"So why y'all break up?" Gray took a bite of mandu.

"Devin young-actin', man, and I got back wit' her for all the wrong reasons."

"Back with her," Gray repeated, confused. "So y'all messed with each other before?"

"Yeah, I used to fuck wit' her back in the day, but we broke up. Then last year we started back kickin' it again, but the shit just didn't work. But that's my fault 'cause like I said, I got back with her for all the wrong reasons."

"What reason?"

"Why are we even discussing this? This conversation is for the birds." Gunz proceeded to eat his meal in hopes that Gray would let it go.

"No, tell me," she insisted.

" 'Cause I liked fuckin' her and I wanted to fuck her again, that's why."

Gray sat silent. For some reason, Gunz's blunt confession hurt her feelings.

"Please don't tell me you mad." He placed down his chopsticks. "See, that's why I don't like talkin' about shit like that. Somebody feelings always get hurt. Look, Gray,"—Gunz scooted closer and caressed her face—"that shit in the past. Fuck what happened before you. I'm here wit' you. I ain't thinkin' about Devin. The only woman that got my attention is you."

For a while, silence consumed them.

"You believe me, don't you?"

Gray wanted to trust and believe in his words, but Kema's words kept on ringing in her head. *Actions speak louder than words,* is what kept on replaying over and over again. The last thing she wanted was to end up looking like a fool, but Gunz had her open.

"Say you believe me." He cupped the back of her head and massaged her scalp.

"I believe you."

Gunz sat back and resumed eating his food. He didn't want Gray to start losing faith in him. She could've bowed out gracefully a long time ago, but she didn't. Gunz thanked God every day for her. He drove himself crazy trying to stay out of his own way, but the secrets he kept were so sacred. Sometimes the places he went in his mind were so deep, dark, and desperate that it scared him.

"You know, sometimes I think I'm being unfair," he spoke sincerely.

"Why you say that?"

"I'm just sayin' I still can't talk about what I do. My job is dangerous. The life I lead wears people down. Sometimes it breaks them in the end, and I don't want that to happen to you. I still have commitments to other people, and I know that you say it doesn't bother you, but maybe it should."

"I can't lie. It does bother me. I mean, you say that you don't want to do this forever, but is that really the truth? Can you see yourself leaving the game?"

"Hopefully, but who knows?"

"Well, I'ma put it to you like this: I can't see myself spending the rest of my life with someone who does what you do, so eventually something gon' need to change. Either I'ma keep on fuckin' wit' you or leave you alone. But right now in this moment, I don't care about what's dangerous or illegal. All I care about is being with you."

"You love me, don't you?"

"What?" She was caught off guard.

"You heard me. Say it." He kissed her lips, rotating between the top and the bottom. "Say you love me."

"I love you," she moaned, enveloped by his touch.

Before Gray noticed, Gunz had unzipped her jeans.

"Baby, what you doing?" She rubbed his head as he made a trail of kisses down her stomach.

"What you think I'm doing?"

"But, baby, I want some dick."

"Let me just taste you. We can fuck later."

After that, Gray wasn't able to release another sound. It didn't even matter that he hadn't said "I love you" back. The passionate road of pleasure they were about to embark on was far more appealing to her. Gunz's tongue roamed her body in a fierce manic fervor.

All day he'd been itching to hear her scream for it, fiend for it, be in need of it. Unclothed, Gray lay fully naked. Gunz watched intently as she bit into her bottom lip. He could read her every thought. Gray swallowed hard. She could almost feel the kisses he was about to place onto her wanting skin.

Suddenly, without warning, his lips plunged into hers, claiming her as his own. While Gunz assaulted her lips with sinful kisses, his fingertips toyed with her chestnut nipples. Gray tried to still her raging heart, but the freaky things they were about to do and thoughts of the erotic sounds she was about to make were driving her insane. With precision, her thighs adjusted to his jaw.

Her legs poured over his shoulders as her hands roamed the top of his head. An immeasurable amount of pleasure swept through her lower stomach. Gunz placed a continuing kiss onto the lips of her pussy. Seconds later, an orgasm began to flow onto the tip of his tongue. Slowly he made his way up and aligned his dick with the slit of her wet pussy.

Gray's breasts were heavy with anticipation. This was it, the moment she'd been waiting for. Gunz's deep strokes sent shockwaves through her veins, paralyzing her lungs. And though she felt dissatisfied by his refusal of admitting love, Gray was intoxicated in the moment and the promise that maybe one day he would love her too.

The next morning, Gray was awakened by Gunz lovingly placing kisses on her nose, cheeks, and lips. Opening her eyes, she saw that he was fully dressed. Gray looked over at the clock. It wasn't even seven o'clock yet. After making love, she'd stayed up half the night talking to him because he couldn't sleep.

"Where you going?"

"I gotta burn out right quick. I'll be back later, though," he assured, running his fingers through her hair.

"Promise."

"I promise. As a matter of fact, be dressed. My family having a barbecue this afternoon." Gunz reached under the covers and put his hand between her legs.

"Okay, but I thought you said you were leaving." Gray squealed as he played with her clit.

"I am." He took her hand and placed it on the face of her pussy.

While they both massaged the lips of her pussy, Gunz took one of her breasts and lightly flicked his tongue across her nipple.

"Baby," she whined.

"That's all you get." He released his hand and stood up straight.

"Why you do that? Now I wanna fuck."

"Chill out. Later. Now give me a kiss."

Gray obliged his request and planted a deep, sensual kiss on his lips.

"I'm out." He turned and left the room.

"Bye! Lock the door on your way out!"

"A'ight!"

Gray sat up and placed her knees up to her chest with a smile on her face. Flashbacks of the love they'd made the night before crossed her mind. The tricks Gunz pulled out of his sleeve had her climbing up the wall. Gray didn't know a happiness existed like the one she felt. She wondered if the whole world could hear her heartbeat. Every day with Gunz felt like spring.

He made her feel safe and wanted. With him she could be herself without having to fake or front. She loved how at night, when they slept, he wrapped her up in his arms tight and wouldn't let go until it was time to get up. She was especially happy that he had begun to open up to her about his life and family. Everything from his smile, hands, and feet excited her.

Beaming, she got out of bed and walked toward the bathroom. On the way, she heard the doorbell ring. Curious as to whom it could be, she made her way downstairs and over to the door. To Gray's surprise, some woman she'd never met before was standing there.

"May I help you?"

"Hi, are you . . ."—the woman looked down at her clipboard—"Gray Rose?"

"Who wants to know?" Gray asked, prepared to go off.

She just knew the woman on her doorstop had something to do with Gunz.

"Hi." The lady stuck out her hand for a shake. "I'm Jada. Mr. Marciano hired me as your personal shopper. So if you don't mind, some deliverymen are going to start bringing some things in. It's a lot, so don't be overwhelmed. Oh, and before I forget, this is for you as well." She handed Gray an envelope.

Overwhelmed, Gray opened the envelope and found two stacks of money totaling up to twenty grand. Gray didn't know what to say or do. One minute she was about to brush her teeth, and the next, racks of clothes and money were being brought into her house. She was astonished by the amount of items Gunz had purchased for her. What made the moment even more extraordinary was that half of the stuff was things she'd said she liked in Chicago but refused to let him buy.

"Oh my God," she screamed when she noticed one of the boxes of shoes.

She didn't even have to open the box to know what it was. Inside was a pair of $500 Givenchy open-toe booties she'd been dying for. Gray never felt more special in her life. And yes, some of the things he bought were things she could have purchased on her own. Gray could pay her own rent, get her hair fried, dyed, and laid to the side, but it still felt good to know that someone cared enough for her to do something so sweet. Gunz was most definitely a winner.

Gunz could see smoke from the barbecue pit rise and evaporate into thin air as he made his way through Forest Park. It was almost near impossible for him to find a parking space with so many cars lined on the street. Gray sat beside him, anxious. She hadn't gone through the whole "meet the family" experience in years. She hoped they would accept her.

Once they were parked, Gunz helped her out of the car. The Gap Band's "You Dropped a Bomb on Me" serenaded them as they walked hand in hand to where his family congregated.

The scenery was inviting and cheerful. Over to the side of them was a pond with ducks. Hundreds of trees and shrubbery filled the park. The park also provided an art museum, boathouse, zoo, and science center. Over where Gunz's family was, there were five long picnic tables with red-and-white checkerboard tablecloths placed all around for people to sit. There were also lawn chairs and blankets. To eat, they had potato salad, cole slaw, corn on the cob, spaghetti, chips, and more. To quench their thirst, there were a variety of coolers filled to the brim with soda and beer.

"Yabba dabba doo, nephew," Gunz's Uncle Clyde yelled, raising his hands and drink in the air.

Gunz stood frozen stiff. It took everything in him not to burst out laughing. Uncle Clyde was a hot country mess. He didn't know whether he wanted to be a thug or a gentleman. He wore a Dallas Cowboy's baseball cap with a black wave cap underneath, football jersey, white leather pants, and blue Stacy Adams shoes. Around his neck was the biggest cross Gunz had ever seen. Uncle Clyde's ghetto fabulousness didn't stop there. He wore not one but two Cartier watches. You couldn't tell him he wasn't the shit.

"What's up, Unc?" Gunz smiled, greeting him with a hug.

"Not a muthafuckin' thang but a chicken wang. Look at ya." He stepped back and looked Gunz up and down. "Lookin' like a muthafuckin' star. I see you twinklin', nephew."

"You wild."

"Now I know you gon' introduce me to Miss P.Y.T." He leaned to the side and sucked his teeth. "How you doing, precious? You sweet, sexy thannnng, you." He stuck out his hand for a shake.

"I'm okay. How are you?" Gray giggled.

"Oh, you know my pimp hand way strong. Ain't that right, Francine?"

"Ya got that right." His wife snapped her fingers and shimmied.

"Okaaaaay." Gray looked at Gunz. "What was your name again?"

"Baby girl, just call me milk, 'cause I'll do your body good!"

"All right, that's enough, Unc." Gunz pushed him back. "Gray, this is my Uncle Clyde. Unc, this is Gray."

"Gray?" He scrunched up his face. "What in the hell kind of name is that? I see you got a little bit of that Indonasia in ya. What, ya mama didn't know Ingles? Or better yet, was she on that narcotic? You know them Chinks good for that. They the ones bought that uh, that uh, opium and uh, hair-ron over here. I seen a whole special on it the other night on the Discovery Channel."

Normally, Gray would've been offended, but deep down she knew Uncle Clyde didn't mean any harm. He was famous for using the wrong words when he spoke and half the time he didn't even know what he was saying.

"No, she just loved the word," she explained.

"I ain't tryin' to be rude, Unc, but we gon' go say hi to everybody," Gunz jumped in.

"G'on do ya thang, nephew. Don't let me slow down ya progress, ya dig. I'ma be right here by my muthafuckin' barbecue pit. 'Cause not n'all one of these niggas bet not touch it. Family or no family, I will let it loose." Uncle Clyde lifted up his shirt and revealed a nineteenth-century Beretta.

"And on that note, I'ma be over there by Granny." Gunz pointed as he escorted Gray away. "My bad. My uncle be trippin' sometimes."

"It's cool. He was kinda funny to me," she replied.

Gunz's grandmother, Emilia, sat in the shade with her legs crossed under an enormous willow tree. Sitting next to her was Gunz's mother. Even though they were no longer family by law, Emilia still treated Vivian as if she were her daughter. Gray was instantly taken in by both of the women's beauty, but Emilia's distinguished demeanor drew her in. Confidence exuded from her skin. It was easy to see she was of mixed descent. Emilia's Italian heritage showed through her piercing blue eyes. Her hair was a perfect mixture of grey and black, giving it a salt-and-pepper effect, while the complexion of her skin was a fiery shade of russet. A pair of delicate gold earrings hung from her ears. She was dressed casually in a red short-sleeve shirt, tan capris, and sandals.

"How you doing, Granny?" Gunz hugged her.

"Fine now that my no-good grandson has come to see me. It takes for me to cook for you to come by?"

"It's not like that. I just be busy."

"Yeah, yeah, yeah. Save it, Gavin." She waved him off.

"That's the same thing he tells me," Vivian added.

Gunz was still a little upset with his mother, but out of respect, he spoke anyway. Gray could feel the tension.

"Hi, Mama."

"How are you, Gavin?" she responded, unfazed by his attitude.

"I'm straight, but ah, I want to introduce y'all to somebody. Gray, this is my grandmother, Emilia, and my mother, Vivian."

"Hi. It's a pleasure to meet you." She leaned forward and shook his grandmother's hand.

"It's nice meeting you, too, sweetheart," Emilia replied with a warm smile.

"Uh-uh, I don't want no handshake. Give me a hug." Vivian stood up.

Gunz watched as Gray happily obliged his mother's request.

"Let me tell you, Gray, you must be very special to my son because he has never introduced us to any of his female friends."

"That's good to know." Gray looked at Gunz and smiled.

"Have you said hi to your father, Gavin? He's over there by your Uncle Ronnie," Emilia asked.

"Nah, I didn't know he was here."

"It would be nice if you went to go speak to him. Gray will be fine here with us."

"I'll be right back," Gunz said reluctantly as he kissed Gray on the cheek. "If you need anything, let me know."

Under any other circumstances, he would have pretended as if his father didn't exist. He would've eaten dirt rather than to speak to him, but for his grandmother's sake, he swallowed his pride.

"What's up, Uncle Ronnie?" Gunz gave him a pound and a hug.

"Look what the wind done blown through. What it do, nephew?" He happily hugged him back.

"Ain't nothing up, Unc."

"You lookin' good, boy. Not better than me, but good."

"Yeah, a'ight." Gunz grinned. Halfheartedly, he turned and looked at his father and said, "Hey."

"How you doing, Gavin?"

Before Gunz could reply, his Uncle Clyde yelled, "Y'all muthafuckas ready?"

"Ready for what, Clyde?" Uncle Ronnie asked, visibly annoyed.

"This a reunion, ain't it? Well, we about to re-unite! Clydeascope and the Ill Street Band is back together again! I done already booked us some studio time. Our first song gon' be called 'Smokin' Weed Wit' the Windows Up.' I wrote it last week. After that we gon' hit 'em wit' 'Yup, Light Dat Bitch on Fire.' You can't tell me that shit ain't hot! Fuck Jodeci and BoyzIIMen. We 'bout to take this shit over! Worldwide denomination my niggas! World denomination!"

"Uh-uh, fuck that, Clyde. I ain't wit' it. Yo' jive ass still ain't paid me for that gig we did back in eighty-seven."

"Nigga, I told you we wasn't gettin' cash for that gig. That bucket of fried chicken yo' fat-ass wife ate up was the payment, so tech-nic-ly, you . . . owe . . . me!"

"Oh, no you didn't!" Uncle Ronnie threw down his drink. "Ain't nobody said nuttin' about that big bitch you got over there! Lookin' like a big-ass porch monkey."

"Now you done did it! You ain't have to go there! You know Francine got a low metabolism!"

"Fuck you and Francine!"

"You out the group! Goddamn!" Clyde pointed his finger in Ronnie's face. "It's just me and you now, Joe! But don't get yo' ass on this stage and start embarrassing me like that crackhead Amy Winehouse."

"My singin' days is over, Clyde," Joseph replied.
"And yours are too."

"I shoulda known yo' hatin' ass was gon' say
that. You been jealous of me ever since Mama let
me get a perm."

"Sure, Clyde."

"You know what? Fuck it! I don't need n'all one
of ya! Like Swizz Beatz said, I'm a one man band
man. When my record go platinum, I don't wanna
hear from neither one of you bitches!" With that
being said, Clyde stormed off.

"Y'all wild than a muthafucka." Gunz cracked up
laughing.

"That's ya Uncle Clyde actin' a fool. As a matter
of fact, I'm about to go tell Mama," Uncle Ronnie
exclaimed. "Mama!"

"Those are my brothers." Joseph hung his head
and smiled.

A warm breeze swayed through the air. An uncomfortable silence filled the space between Gunz
and his father. Neither knew quite what to say to
the other.

"So why you don't sing no more?" Gunz finally
spoke up.

"I do sometimes. My throat kinda messed up,
though, from smokin' so many cigarettes throughout the years."

"Umm."

"I see you brought you a li'l lady friend." Joseph
looked over in Gray's direction.

She was laughing and having a good time. Her
smile brightened up Gunz's whole mood.

"Yeah."

"She's nice-lookin'."

"I know."

"Can I give you some advice?"

"Knock ya'self out," Gunz replied in a sarcastic tone.

"Treat her right. You don't want to end up like me—old, alone, and full of regret."

"I ain't even worried about all of that. Gray ain't going nowhere. I got that in the bag."

"If you say so." Joseph shrugged his shoulders.

"Look, I appreciate your concern, but you the last person to be giving me advice," Gunz said sternly.

"Your grandmother is so cute," Gray said, coming over. "We're all going shopping this weekend."

"That's what's up. Gray, this is my old dude, Joseph." Gunz wrapped his arm around her waist.

"Hi. Nice to meet you." She waved.

"Nice to meet you too, sweetheart."

"If I could have everyone's attention." Uncle Clyde tapped and blew into a customized white microphone decorated with rhinestones.

Nobody was quite ready for what he had to say or his choice of wardrobe. Uncle Clyde had changed into a form-fitting, shiny metallic jumpsuit. The front zipper was zipped down to the middle of his stomach, revealing a chest full of nappy hair lathered in baby oil. Around his neck was a white scarf tied to the side. On his feet he wore a pair of silver men's ankle boots.

"I got a little song I want er'body to hear," he said with his head down, obviously upset. "Ronnie and Joseph, I dedicate this to you."

Uncle Clyde pressed PLAY on the CD player and a funky drum beat began. Then the sound of a keyboard came through. Suddenly, before anybody knew it, Uncle Clyde had twirled around in a circle then dropped to his knees and sang, "The shooooooow must go ooooooonnn! One monkey . . . don't stop no show! If you don't want my love, you're free to go."

Everyone in attendance was flabbergasted.

"If this is how all your family get-togethers are, then when are we gettin' married?" Gray laughed uncontrollably.

"When 'Smoking Weed Wit' the Windows Up' goes number one," Gunz replied.

Two months had passed since the picnic, and the weather outside Gunz's window was bleak. Wet and dull were better words to describe it. A thick fog cascaded over the decades-old buildings. Slick rain covered the streets, while leaves fell leisurely from trees. Businessmen and women hustled for yellow cabs, but nothing else seemed to move. Everything was still, like the end of the earth was approaching. Gunz detested being alone.

The four walls that surrounded him appeared as if they were closing in. Something evil was lurking in the shadows. He could feel it in the air. Bishop and Watts said it was just paranoia, but Gunz knew better. He'd felt the same way when his sister died. There was no way he was gonna ignore the painful feeling that alarmed his stomach.

Something bad was about to happen. The only thing that kept him sane was Gray. Nine months had passed, and they'd been hanging tough like Ernie and Bert. Gunz never thought it would be, but he'd completely switched the way he lived. Rough sex with random women was a thing of the past. He didn't even stay out all night anymore. With Gray, his all wasn't enough. For her, he wanted to give everything he was and more.

Anything she requested, he intended to provide. Gray was heaven sent. The type of love she gave was the kind only God could provide. On a scale of one to ten, he couldn't rank her. She was his drug of choice.

He needed to see her. She promised that she'd be over after work. Gunz checked his watch. It was six o'clock. She'd been off for over an hour.

Tired of playing NBA Live '09, he placed the game on pause and made his way into the kitchen. He was in desperate need of a drink. After fixing himself a glass of Chivas scotch mixed with lemon-lime soda, Gunz reentered the living area. His place was too big. There was no life to it. Maybe Gray living there on a permanent basis would liven up the place.

"Nah." Gunz shook his head.

He couldn't go out like that. It was simply too soon. Anxious, he checked his watch again. Fifteen more minutes had passed. Where was she? He hadn't seen her face in over twenty-four hours. Gunz missed the way her blue eyes slanted like diamonds. If she didn't come soon, there was no telling what he might do. He needed her there to calm all of his worries.

As if on cue, a minute later she knocked on the door. Gunz made his way over and opened it.

Gray sauntered into the room like America's Next Top Model. Gunz never could get a grip on just how beautiful she was. Her long black hair was flat-ironed straight to the back. A simple but expensive pair of three-carat diamond stud earrings, which were a gift from Gunz, twinkled from her ears. Gray was elegantly dressed in a pink-and-white striped, three-quarter sleeve button-up shirt, white fitted vest, white wide-leg cropped pants, and black tie. A vintage brooch in the center of the tie added a bit of spice to the overall look of the ensemble. Smiling from ear to ear, she took off her coat.

" 'Bout time yo' ass got here," Gunz spoke while eying her.

"I'm sorry." She rushed over and kissed his cheek. "Hailing a cab was hell."

"What I tell you about that shit? I could've had Lorenzo come get you."

"I know. I'm just used to doing stuff on my own. But that's not important. Guess what?" she gushed.

"What?"

"I got a promotion!" Gray jumped up and down.

"That's what's up, babe." Gunz scooped her up in his arms.

"Thank you. You're lookin' at the new creative director of style."

"I'm proud of you."

"And guess what else."

"What else?"

"Next Saturday the company is throwing me a private party at Niche."

"Word? That's what's up, ma. You in there. I'm really happy for you, straight up."

"Thanks, babe, I'm happy too. I can't wait to pick me out something to wear. Niche is really posh, so I have to look fabulous. I'm thinking I might wear that one dress you had Jada pick out for me. What are you going to wear?"

"I . . . don't . . . know." He eyed her, confused. "I wasn't planning on going."

"Why not? It's my party."

"I understand that. I just figured we'd get up afterwards."

"Noooo. I want you there. I've already told everybody that you were coming. They can't wait to meet you, especially Sienna."

"See, I wish you wouldn't have did that." Gunz walked away, upset. Gray stood thunderstruck.

"What's the problem?"

"I'm happy for you, G, I am, but that's yo' thing. I ain't into all that."

"Okay," Gray stated, confused. "Soooo, you can't just come for me for a little while?"

"You making this hard, man." Gunz exhaled.

"Please. I never ask you to do anything for me. Just this once, please."

Gunz took one look into Gray's puppy dog eyes and melted. There was no way he could tell her no.

"A'ight, I'll go."

The next day after getting off of work, Gray called Truth.

"What's up, big head?" she joked as he answered the phone.

"Shit, on Washington having lunch at Mosaic."

"With who?" she quipped, slightly perturbed.

"By myself. Why?"

"I'm just fuckin' wit' you." She laughed. "You could've called me, though."

"I thought you and ya man might be together," he shot.

"Noooo, not today. Anyway, I was callin' to invite you to my party."

"What party?"

"I got a promotion. You are speaking to the new creative director of style."

"That's what's up, ma," Truth said, genuinely happy. "Where the party gon' be at?" He took a bite of his sandwich.

"At Niche. It starts at seven p.m., so don't be late."

"Is ol' boy gon' be there?"

"Yeah . . . but I really want you to be there. I mean, I know it's a lot to be asking, but you're one of my best friends."

"I hear what you're sayin', but I don't know if I can be around that nigga like that. I mean, have you forgotten that he killed my brother?"

"Truth, we already discussed that. You don't have any proof."

"So you still taking up for that man?"

"I'm not taking up for anybody. I just want you to be there to support me on one of my biggest nights."

"Nah, you know I ain't gon' never not support you, but I don't know. Let me think about it."

"I understand," Gray replied, disappointed. "So how have you been?"

"Good. You?"

"I've been great."

While Gray talked, Truth held the phone and wished that she would see that with him was where she was destined to be. He didn't wanna hear about her and another man, especially when that man was Gunz, who didn't deserve to wake up to her smile.

He didn't see how special she really was. Gray was the type of woman who, when she found love, she would give you her world. Gunz would never appreciate that.

Truth was the one who recognized the wonderful qualities she possessed. He wanted to be the one who kissed her lips at night and made love to her under the moonlight. He wanted to love her openly and freely. She held the key to his heart. No other woman was of interest to him, but it was up to her to give him a chance. If she didn't, he would simply have to force his way into her life.

It's like 'I checked into rehab and baby,
you're my disease . . .

Rihanna, "Rehab"

Chapter Nine

The vibe at Niche was mellow and elegant. The who's who of the industry were all in attendance for Gray's big party. Never before had she felt more special. All of her friends, including Truth, were there. Waiters dressed in black tie roamed the room, offering guests appetizers and glasses of Cristal. A smooth mix of R&B and Neo-Soul music played softly in the background.

Gray was dressed to the nines in a black tank top and super sexy charcoal grey Herve Leger miniskirt. Her hair was parted down the middle with loose curls. She wore two small necklaces and a bracelet. The shoes she rocked were what set the entire outfit off; they were a pair of $945 tribal-inspired Yves Saint Laurent heels that Gunz had bought.

Surrounded by her colleagues, Gray smiled graciously and checked her watch. The party had been in full effect for over an hour and Gunz still hadn't opted to show up. With each second that passed, her patience began to grown thin.

"Giiiiiirl, this party is nice." Tee-Tee clicked his tongue.

"Yeah, it is," she answered, barely paying attention.

"It's a whole lot of eligible men up in here, and one of them is coming home wit' me tonight."

"Tee-Tee, please." Kema rolled her eyes. "Don't none of these men up in here want yo' ass."

"Satan, please. That stallionaire over there been giving me the eye since I stepped up in this muthafucka. If he keep it up, I'ma have to let 'im get a taste."

"You are one sick individual."

"How many licks does it take till you get to the center of the—" he sang while grinding his booty on Kema.

"If you don't get yo' ass off of me" she hissed, pushing him away. "Can't take black folks nowhere."

"Umm, Gray, it is going on nine o'clock. Where is yo' man at?" Heidi asked.

"That's a good question." Gray looked down at her watch, wondering where Gunz could be.

Gunz checked his watch. He was over two hours late to Gray's party. He was sure steam was rising from her skin, but pressing business always came before pleasure. Gunz looked into the face of the person who was before him. Tears seeped from his eyes, but Gunz couldn't allow himself to feel anything for him. This was a part of the business, and showing sympathy was a sign of weakness, so Gunz bottled his feelings deep within his heart and prayed that one day God would forgive him.

No matter how much the man screamed and squirmed, no one was going to come to his rescue. There was a rope tied around his neck and hands to secure his death. The only thing keeping him alive was a rickety wooden table that teeter-tottered under his feet. Gunz wanted to feel sorry for him, but this was a part of the business. Fortune knew the consequences of his actions when he betrayed Gunz's trust. He'd allowed greed to overshadow common sense. He should have known when he stared into Gunz's eyes that he was not the man to be crossed.

Gray crossed the room with anger in her eyes. All night she'd been bombarded with questions of, "Where is Gunz?" Her friends tried being supportive, but she could tell by the look in their eyes that they'd had it with Gunz letting her down. Gray felt like an absolute idiot. As she made her way over to the door, she was stopped by Truth.

"Yo, you all right?" he asked.

"Mm-hmm," she lied.

"You don't have to lie to me, Gray. I know you're pissed off. I would be too if the person I was with stood me up on one of the most important nights of my life."

"Thanks for making me feel better, Truth." Gray rolled her eyes.

"No, I ain't sayin' it like that. All I'm tryin' to say is I'm here. Despite everything that's going on, I put my feelings aside to be here for you. I just wish ol' boy could've shown you the same respect."

"I'll be right back." Gray walked away before he could say another word.

She understood that Truth was only trying to be nice, but at that moment, she didn't want to hear anything he or anybody else had to say. The only person she wanted to hear from was Gunz.

Outside the restaurant, she dialed his cell phone number. A brisk October wind caused goose bumps to rise on her arms, but the weather was the least of Gray's worries.

If Gunz didn't answer the phone soon, she was sure to lose her mind. He knew how much she needed him by her side. All she'd thought about was sharing her big night with him. This was not how things were supposed to be. He was supposed to be there with her. Shivering and unable to breathe, she held the phone up to her ear and prayed with each ring that he'd pick up.

Gunz picked up a RIDGID ten-inch angle grinder. It was covered in Fortune's blood. Gunz had taken a sick and sadistic pleasure in pressing the metal grinder up against the skin of Fortune's face as a bloodcurdling scream roared from his throat.

Gunz's cell phone vibrated against his thigh. He took a glance at the screen and saw Gray's name. Instead of answering, he sent her call to voicemail.

Gunz stepped toward Fortune and looked him square in the eye. Sweat mixed with blood dripped down his face. He was barely even twenty-four years old. The baby boy who lay in his crib at home would never see his father again. It was a sad situation, but it had to be done.

"You should have never stole from me," Gunz whispered to him before taking the grinder to his nose and cutting it off.

Fortune's body shook violently from the pain. Once he calmed down some, Gunz could tell that he had something to say. Gunz roughly ripped the duct tape from his mouth.

"Gunz, please. I'm sorry! Don't do this! Please," Fortune sobbed.

"I can't not do it. You stole twenty-eight ki's of coke from me. Now I gotta do you in like I did your man Rich."

Tired of talking, Gunz kicked over the table. Fortune twisted and squirmed around to no avail. It was inevitable; death was approaching. The air in his lungs tightened while the veins in his neck expanded and bulged like straws. If only his hands could break loose, but they couldn't. The light in the room began to fade. Fortune unwillingly closed his eyes. This was it, the moment in life every person dreads. He should've listened to Truth and laid low, but the money was too good not to splurge a bit. Splurging got him caught. Now he was about to meet his maker. As he took his last breath, he prayed that he'd repented for all his sins.

It was 12:30 A.M. and Gray lay in wait again. Gray prayed to God that Gunz had a valid reason for standing her up. Ever since her coworker Ra'Shawn dropped her off at home, she'd done nothing but sit by the phone. Each time she tried calling Gunz, his voicemail clicked on. Stupidity munched away at her pride. Here she was thinking they'd gotten past all the games and lies, but once more Gunz was proving her wrong.

The shrill sound of the phone ringing caused Gray to jump. It just had to be Gunz. With her arms crossed over her chest, she studied the caller I.D. It was Heidi. Instead of answering, Gray let the phone ring. She couldn't risk the chance of her friend hearing the disappointment in her voice. This was not how her night was supposed to go.

She shouldn't be sitting by the phone in misery. Her lungs should be able to release a breath of air without constant struggle. Salty tears shouldn't sting the brims of her eyes. Gunz was supposed to be there whispering sweet nothings into the lips of her pussy, while moans of gratification fled from her throat.

"I can't believe this nigga. He don't give a fuck about me," she whispered out loud as the heel of her stiletto tapped against the wooden floor.

Why couldn't he just call? Didn't he know that the longer he went without communication, the more crazed Gray felt? Once again he'd made her look like a fool. Didn't Gunz know that she could have any man she wanted? She didn't have to put up with his shit.

Gray attempted not to believe that he was with another woman, but that's all her gut could go back to. The mere thought made her sick. This wasn't the first time he'd stood her up. Another woman had to be the cause. Yep, that's what it was. Gray could see him running his fingers through her hair. At that very moment, while she sat in anguish, he was probably entering the wet slit of the other woman's pussy. The pit of her stomach couldn't take it anymore.

Gray was just about to try to call him again when there was a buzz at her door. She knew it was Gunz. Heated, she hopped up from the couch and buzzed him up.

"Before you start, my bad," Gunz declared, walking past her visibly aggravated.

This pissed Gray off even more. How dare he come to her house with an attitude like she'd done something wrong? Gray's mouth hung wide open in shock as she closed the door behind him.

"I know we had plans and all, but I had some shit that I needed to take care of, and it couldn't wait."

"So you couldn't pick up the phone and call? You had me lookin' like a fuckin' fool in front of my friends, my coworkers, and my boss."

"I was in the middle of some stuff and I got here as soon as I could. I didn't have time to be on the phone arguing wit' you about why I wasn't gonna be there."

"What the fuck were you doing that was so important that you couldn't call me? I'm not stupid, Gunz. I know you was with another chick."

"Why is that always your first line of defense? I tell you I was busy and you start stressin' about some other chick that don't even fuckin' exist. What the fuck is that shit about?"

"What you mean, what is that about? You stood me up! What the fuck about that don't you get?"

"And I'm standing here." Gunz rushed toward her face. "I'm tryin' to apologize, but you just don't get it. It's like you think I like to see you hurt."

"Evidently you do, 'cause you keep on doing shit to hurt me."

"You know what? I'm out." He stepped past her and reached for the doorknob.

"So you mean to tell me you about to leave?" Gray stared at him with a look of shock on her face.

"What am I supposed to do? I'm not gettin' ready to stand here and listen to a whole bunch of nonsense. I told you what the deal was, but you don't believe me, so I'm done tryin' to explain myself. You can go through this drama all by yourself, 'cause I ain't got time for it. I got enough shit on my plate."

"Well, fuck it then. If that's how you feel, bye," Gray shot, opening the door for him.

"That's what's up." Gunz chuckled, pissed.

Gray simply rolled her eyes and shot him a look that said she could give a fuck. Gunz got the hint and walked out. She slammed the door behind him.

The Delmar Lounge was crazy packed with people. A cloud of cigarette smoke hovered over the crowd. Charlie Chan spun N.E.R.D's "Everyone Nose." Every chick in the spot took to the floor. Gunz leaned up against the wooden bar with his fourth cup of Grand Marnier and pineapple juice in hand. Being in a fun environment was a welcome invitation after the day he'd had. Nobody, including Gray, understood his life and all of the demands that came along with being him.

He'd warned her from the beginning that fuckin' with him wasn't a good idea. Hell, Gunz even tried warning himself that committing to one woman wasn't the way to go. But neither he nor Gray listened to their consciences. Now the both of them were suffering because of poor decision making. But Gunz couldn't sweat that. It was how it was. If Gray forgave him, she forgave him. If she didn't, oh well. The way Gunz was feeling, he couldn't care less.

Gunz turned around and signaled the bartender. "Ay, let me get another one." He held up his glass.

While Gunz waited, he felt someone embracing him from behind.

"I miss you, daddy." the woman purred as she licked and bit his earlobe.

Gunz didn't even have to turn around. He knew the sound of that seductive voice from anywhere.

"Is that right?" He turned around so that he and Devin were face to face.

Nothing had changed about her since the last time he saw her, except now she rocked a short hairdo. All the things he liked about her were still there. Devin's honeycomb skin felt like the finest silk underneath his fingertips. Her auburn eyes still drew him in as if she'd cast a spell. They were never good for one another, but visions of the way her ass would jiggle as he hit it from the back clouded his drunken mind. One more time wouldn't hurt. And yes, how Gray would feel if she found out entered his head, but she'd already accused him of cheating. Why not do it?

"Why haven't I heard from you?" Devin held him tight.

"You tell me."

"If I knew, I wouldn't be askin'," she countered back.

A slight grin crossed Gunz's face. He always did like that she was quick on her feet.

"Normally you call me at least once a week. Shit, I haven't talk to you since I don't know when. I hope it's not because of that one chick."

The mention of Gray brought Gunz back to reality, but resentment loaded his pride.

"What you doing after you leave here?" He changed the subject.

Devin licked her lips in a suggestive manner and said, "I'm coming home wit' you."

The sound of rain tapped against Gray's window pane as she lay on her side, curled up underneath the sheets. Blankly she stared out the window. It was ironic how the weather seemed to match her mood. Everything was dreary. Clouds filled the sunless sky. Even the trees appeared to be lifeless and unhappy. All night Gray had tossed and turned.

Sleep was impossible. Any position she lay in was uncomfortable without Gunz there by her side. Each second that passed and he didn't reach out, Gray second-guessed herself. Had she overreacted? Maybe she should have heard him out. What if he was telling the truth? Was the picture she'd painted in her mind wrong? To fade away would be great.

The insufferable pain that took up space in her gut was too much for her to handle. Checking the time on her cell phone, she saw that it was 9:00 A.M. It was early, but Gray had to speak to Gunz. Another second couldn't go by. She needed to know how he felt and where things between them stood.

Gunz lay flat on his stomach, snoring loudly as his cell phone rang. He'd only been asleep a couple of hours, but it felt like an eternity. Gunz could hardly lift up his arm to answer the phone. By the time he did, the caller had hung up. Yawning, he checked the screen. Gray's name screamed out to him. Instead of calling her back, he placed the phone on the nightstand and closed his eyes.

"I'm gettin' ready to leave, so you can call her back," Devin announced, placing on her bra.

Gunz's head promptly spun around in her direction. He'd completely forgotten she was there.

"What you talkin' about?" He rolled over onto his back.

"You ain't gotta front, Gunz. I know that was what's-her-face."

"Don't start." He yawned, rubbing his eyes.

"Trust me, I'm not." She smirked. "I enjoyed myself last night." Devin leaned across the bed and got in his face.

For a second, she and Gunz stared at one another. The look in his eyes spoke volumes. He didn't want her anymore; even after she'd been everything he wanted her to be while it was dark. Devin was his freak—pretty, yet docile. She was the picture perfect image of a wet dream. He could have her any way he desired. In the bathroom, carwash, three at a time, or over the kitchen sink. She didn't care as long as for that moment she had his attention.

And yes, she was selling her soul for emotional gain, but in life, you had to pay to play. Loneliness was not an option. So what that every time they finished having sex he discarded her like the empty condom wrapper left on the floor? During those instances of satisfaction, he was hers, and that old feeling of what they used to share was brought back to life.

"You gon' call me later?" she questioned, even though she knew he wasn't.

"Yeah."

"A'ight."

Devin grabbed her purse, blew him a kiss, and left him lying behind.

"Lock the door on your way out!"

Ready to start his day, Gunz snatched the covers from over his body, sat up, and placed his feet on the wooden floor. The remnants of his sexapade were sprawled all over the place. His John Varvatos T-shirt lay crumpled by the bedroom door, while his Dolce & Gabbana jeans and underwear rested before his feet. One unopened Trojan magnum condom was tossed at the foot of the bed.

Gunz wondered if he should call Gray back. The answer came back right away as no. She should've trusted his words and believed that he was trying to do better by her. She had to realize that in order to deal with him, trusting his word was a must. In certain situations, there could be no arguing or questioning his motives. For her to understand that, he would have to put her on the back burner. The true challenge for Gunz would be making his mind coincide with his conscience.

* * *

A little over two weeks had passed since Gray last heard from Gunz. After calling him a couple of times, she finally gave up. Gray missed him terribly, but she wasn't going to risk the chance of coming off desperate. Her friends kept on telling her to wait until he called back, but with each day that passed, the hope in her heart dwindled. She just couldn't believe that it was over. How could he just give up on them so easily? Was the way she reacted that horrible? Maybe he never cared for her as much as he said he did.

The million what-ifs, whys, and maybes that boggled her mind were driving her insane. Gray was a mess. Everything including her train of thought was off track. And yes, she should fall back, but Gray wasn't willing to let another woman swoop in and take what was rightfully hers. On top of that, she couldn't stand the idea of being alone yet again.

Gray had also received devastating news from Truth that Rich's best friend Fortune had been found murdered. Truth was overwhelmed with grief. Fortune was like a little brother to him too. Gray didn't convey her thoughts to him, but she wondered if Gunz had something to do with his murder. The autopsy report came back that Fortune had been dead since the night of Gray's party.

The mere thought sent chills throughout her body. She knew she was dealing with a thug, but the realization that he could so easily take a life alarmed Gray. Maybe the way things ended was for the best.

Gray stood in front of the copy machine and closed her eyes. The loud buzzing noise calmed her down. She didn't even realize that someone else had entered the copy room.

"Gray," Ra'Shawn called out.

"Huh?" She jumped.

"My bad. I ain't mean to scare you. You a'ight?"

"Yeah, I was just resting my eyes."

"Oh, did you and your man straighten everything out?"

"I guess you could say that." She grabbed the papers that she'd copied and placed them in a stack. "We don't talk anymore."

"Damn, that's fucked up. I'm sorry to hear that." He faked concern.

"I'll be okay."

"I know you will, 'cause this weekend I'ma take you out."

"Really?" Gray laughed.

"I mean, that's if you're not doing anything."

"I'm not."

"So it's a date," Ra'Shawn shined his megawatt smile.

"It's a date."

"So how you want your makeup done?" Heidi asked, stepping back with a foundation sponge in her hand. She and Gray were in her bedroom.

"I think I want a brown smoky eye and a nude lip."

"Now, who is this guy you're going out on a date with again?" Heidi searched through her makeup case for her M.A.C. foundation spray.

"His name is Ra'Shawn. He's the senior editor at the magazine."

"Okay, a brother with brains and bank. Now, that's what I'm talkin' about."

"Right. Ra'Shawn's a huge step up from what I've been dealing wit'," Gray said, holding her head still.

"Don't front. Gunz got hella bank too."

"I know he does. I'm talkin' about sophistication-wise."

"Mama." Heidi's eight-year-old son Harlem peeked his head into the room.

Gray loved her godson. He was the cutest, chubbiest thing she'd ever seen. His skin was the shade of Colombian cocoa. He was four feet tall and weighed a hundred and three pounds. Heidi had done an outstanding job at raising him so far. Harlem was one of the most smart, respectful kids Gray knew.

"What?"

"Can I have a snack?"

"No!" Heidi turned around, pissed.

"Pleaaaaaaaase." He placed his hands in the praying position and batted his eyes.

"Harlem, you just had two pieces of pizza, a sandwich, and chips. Hell no!"

"Well, can I least I have some water?"

"I don't care."

"I mean some chocolate milk." He changed his mind.

"No!"

"Maaaaaaan." He closed the door hard, disappointed.

"And stop slamming my goddamn door!" Heidi yelled behind him. "That's all his li'l butt want to do is eat. And I swear him and Jerrod don't bother me until I'm on the phone or got company."

"You better leave my baby alone." Gray laughed.

"Let yo' baby come live wit' you and eat up all yo' food then."

Gray sat silent.

"That's what I thought. Now, back to what I was saying. How does Ra'Shawn look? Is he cute?"

"He's cool. He kind of reminds me of a dorky version of Wood Harris."

"All right!"

"Babe." Jerrod interrupted her.

"Yes." Heidi squinted her eyes.

"What time *G's to Gents* come on again?"

"I don't know. Why don't you use the TV guide on the television?"

"I ain't even think of that. What's poppin', Gray?"

"Hi, Jerrod." Gray couldn't help but giggle.

"I know y'all in here on some sneaky shit, but that's cool."

"Boy, please. Ain't nobody on nothing." Heidi dismissed him.

"Uh-huh, tell me anything." Jerrod twisted his mouth to say he didn't believe her as he closed the door.

"Anyway," she resumed her conversation with Gray, "even though you haven't said anything, I know you're hurting over what happened between you and Gunz."

"I am, but on the bright side, at least I know where we stand now."

"So now that you've had time to think, do you think that what he was sayin' was the truth?" Heidi placed brown eyeliner onto Gray's eyes.

"I honestly don't know what to believe." Gray sat still. "From the jump Gunz didn't want to go. It just fucked me up that the one time I asked him to do something for me, he couldn't do it. Anything he ever asked of me, I did."

"Well, everybody's not going to do the same things you do, Gray. Just 'cause you chose to behave one way didn't necessarily mean that he was too. And besides, you should never allow yourself to be so readily available for a man. Let the muthafucka wonder where you at and what you're doing sometime."

"You're right. Sometimes I don't even know why I care so much. It wasn't like he was my man or nothing."

"You love him, so naturally you're gonna care. I think you should try and call him one more time and tell him how you feel."

"Nah, I'm good."

"Why?"

"Gunz has made it perfectly clear how he feels about me. Fuck him."

"Do it your way then. That's on you."

"Says the woman who's too afraid to tell her man to take a bath," Gray countered.

"Shhhhh, you tryin' to get me fucked up." Heidi looked over her shoulder to make sure the coast was clear.

"All right then." Gray arched her eyebrow.

"Fuck you. You know I'm right. Yo' ass should've told him the truth. I'm on team Gunz. Fuck whoever this other nigga is."

"Maybe you are right, but me and Gunz have already talked, and he told me flat out that he wasn't ready for a relationship. So what am I supposed to do? Sit around and wait for him to decide when and if he wants to be with me? Hell no. Fuck that. Gunz can kick rocks down the street until his feet get tired as far as I'm concerned." Gray tried her best to convince Heidi and herself.

Tiger Woods fought for the Grand Slam of Golf championship, while Black Star's underground hit "Brown Skin Lady" played softly throughout the room. Sol Lounge was a quiet afternoon hangout spot where young black professionals frequented on Sundays and sipped wine. The atmosphere was mellow yet hip and contemporary. The bar was uniquely designed with a bookshelf behind it, which took up most of the wall. Full liquor bottles took the place of fine literature, while lamps of all different shapes and colors added a funky flava to the space.

Gray sat with her thick caramel thighs crossed. A glass filled midway with Moscato wine rested in her hand as she surveyed the room. She had to admit Ra'Shawn's choice for their date was a pretty good one.

The scenery was magnificent, and the people were gorgeous, but the company Gray kept was B–O–R–I–N–G with a capital B. The entire evening, Ra'Shawn did nothing but go on and on about his Porsche 911 GT2 and million-dollar house on the beach in L.A. Gray thought he would've caught the hint when she tried to switch the subject, but that made him discuss materialistic bullshit even more.

"So are you enjoying yourself?"

"Yeah, this is nice." Gray half told the truth.

"Yeah, it's pretty nice, but there is a club in L.A. that's killin' this place. Me and the owner are really cool. I never have to pay to get in, and he gives me a complimentary bottle of Chandon every time I come in."

"Really?" Gray gave him a look that said she couldn't care less.

"If things continue to go well between you and me, I'ma have to take you there sometime."

"I'm scared to fly."

"I'll hold your hand the whole way there, baby." Ra'Shawn reached out and took her hand.

Gray wanted to throw up. She could literally feel chunks rise in her throat.

"No need." She released her hand from his and curled her upper lip.

After that, things only got worse for Gray. Coultrain's soul-touching melody "Blue" began to play, melting her heart. Thoughts of Gunz instantly popped into her mind. She didn't want to miss him, but the universe wouldn't allow it. At night, in her sleep, in her dreams, and during the day she yearned for him. Gray longed for the sound of his voice, and would give anything to be in his presence.

Suddenly, the room became quiet. Every woman in the room had her eyes diverted toward the door. Gray's eyes followed theirs. To her surprise, she found Gunz, Watts, and Bishop. Instantly, they connected eyes. Gray felt naked under his gaze. She wanted to run over and leap into his arms, but Gunz didn't have anything for her. After initially catching eyes with her, he quickly diverted his attention elsewhere. Gray felt suffocated. She quickly gulped down the rest of her drink and excused herself so that she could go to the restroom. She needed room to breathe and gather her thoughts.

Gunz shook hands with a couple of big wigs he knew then made his way over to the bar. His jaw was clenched so tight there was a struggle for him to breathe. He needed a stiff drink and quick.

"Ain't that your girl over there?" Watts pointed.

"Yeah, look like it." Gunz tried his best to seem nonchalant.

Watts could sense that Gunz didn't want to talk about it, so he left the conversation alone.

On the outside, Gunz seemed cool, calm, and collected, but on the inside, he felt awkward and out of place. He wanted to go over and grab Gray by her neck for disrespecting him. Yeah, it was his fault things were the way they were. Yes, he was being selfish, but so what? Gray was his, flat out. His biggest fear was that if they stepped from across the room and took a chance at love, they'd lose the unexpected feeling that brought them together. And yes, the way he felt for her grew more and more each day, but that didn't mean they should rush into things. Gunz didn't want to be tied down. He simply wasn't ready.

Sol's restroom area was unparalleled by any other restroom Gray had ever been in. There was no door, and it was connected to the lounge area by steps. It was unisex and had private stalls for men and women.

Gray stood in front of the sink area with her back facing the mirror and dialed Heidi's number.

"Will you give me the goddamn phone?" Heidi snatched the phone from Jerrod. "I swear you's a noscy ass. Hello?" she answered with an attitude.

"Girl, guess what?"

"What? Your date is over already?" She turned down the volume on her television so that she could hear better.

"I wish." Gray rolled her eyes. "I'm in the bathroom. His boring ass is out in the lounge area watching the golf game on the widescreen, but that's not why I called. Guess who just walked through the door."

"Who?"

"Gunz."

"Uh oh, you in troubllllllllllle.."

"Girl, I'm over here fuckin' shittin' bricks. What am I supposed to do? Should I speak, or act like I don't see him?"

"I would speak."

"You sure?" Gray was unsure.

"Yeah."

Gray leaned back and folded her free arm under her breasts. Her heart was racing a mile a minute. The way she handled things was crucial. She couldn't afford to make the wrong move. As she continued to ponder things, Gray noticed Gunz coming up the steps.

"Let me call you back." She hurried and got off the phone.

At that point, it couldn't be clearer that with Gunz was where Gray wanted to be. She was addicted to him, and if he let her, she'd overdose on him every chance she got. She needed what he gave her. With him, she felt high. What he exuded, no form of money could buy. And yes, everything about him said *proceed with caution*, but Gray was willing to take the risk.

If the circumstances were different, she would've walked over to him, wrapped one arm around his waist, and then run her other hand across his head and down his neck. They'd look into each other's eyes, then her lips would gently kiss his. But that wasn't the case. Things were all fucked up, and their pride was in the way.

Gunz saw her looking like a Maybelline queen, but none of that mattered. His pride was hurt, and more than anything, he was jealous.

"So you gon' walk past me and not speak?" she said.

"It ain't that." He stopped midway and looked at her. "I see you doing ya thing. I ain't wanna get you in trouble."

Gray knew he was being sarcastic, but that didn't stop her from reacting. She tried to rationalize the situation. "Why would I be in trouble? I told you—"

"It's cool." Gunz stopped her. "You ain't gotta explain, ma."

For almost an eternity, quietness filled the air. Both parties were on pins and needles. Gunz could sense Gray's eagerness through her body language. Her pouty lips quivered every time she spoke. Usually he would calm her tension with a kiss, but not today. The selfish part of him wanted to see her squirm.

Gray stared into Gunz's cold eyes with pain in

her own. She needed him to see the pain that lay in the space of her heart reserved for him. The distance between them was unbearable. There still had to be something for her in his heart. Fuck what her friends had to say. What they shared was real. If Gunz wanted to take things slow, she'd willingly take the journey with him, if only she could have him back.

"I know I don't have to explain," she spoke. "I want to."

"Okay, well, talk." Gunz stood back, unfazed.

"Look, I apologize. That night when you came over, I should've listened. It's just that I was really looking forward to you being there."

"I understand that, but you wasn't even tryin' to hear me. I mean,"—he took a deep breath— "you gotta understand, Gray. I got a lot of shit going on. When I tell you something, take my word for it. Ain't nobody tryin' to play you. Once you get that shit out ya head, we'll be good."

"I know." She shrugged.

Gunz hated to see her upset. Even more, he loathed the way he couldn't control the beat of his heart whenever she was around. What Gray gave him was no ordinary feeling. All he wanted to do was take her back to his crib and lay her body down.

"Wipe the sad look off your face and come on." He reached for her hand.

"Where are we going?"

Gunz smiled his infamous crooked grin. "Home."

For a split second, Gray wondered was she jumping back into things with Gunz too quick. She had a perfectly nice man a few feet away from her that seemed to be genuinely interested in her, but Ra'Shawn would never have the hold on her heart that Gunz did.

Placing her hand in his, Gray followed Gunz out the side door and counted down the seconds until they were back at her place and Gunz could find his way home.

Welcome 2 the jungle . . .

Guns N' Roses, "Welcome to the Jungle"

Chapter Ten

Thanksgiving was right around the corner, and the holiday spirit lived in everyone. The leaves had changed from green to gorgeous shades of orange, red, and yellow. The sun was in hiding, but a slight glimmer of hope shined from the sky. It was forty-seven degrees outside, but Gray and Gunz enjoyed their evening walk through the West End no less. Gray was stylishly cute in a red wool coat that tied around the waist, red gloves, black ribbed tights, and black ankle boots.

Gunz, being the man he was, sported a more thuggish look by wearing a checkerboard black-and-white button-up black hoodie, leather motorcycle jacket, black distressed jeans, and shell toe Adidas. Black aviator shades shielded his eyes, while the hood from his jacket covered his head.

"I love this time of the year." Gray inhaled the crisp fall air.

"I'm more of a summer-type dude."

"I guess I just love winter because of all the holidays and being around your family and friends and stuff."

"Speaking of family, I know you don't know who your old dude is, but what about your moms? Where she at?"

"She moved back to Chonju a few years ago. It's a city in Korea. A lot of our family is there. I only get to visit her once a year, but we talk on the phone at least a million times a week."

"You miss her, don't you?"

"Yeah. I can't wait to see her. I'll be visiting her for Christmas."

"Damn, I'm glad you said something. I thought we was spending Christmas together."

"I'm sorry. I'll be back for New Year's, though. You can have me all to yourself then." She stopped and wrapped her arms around him. "That is unless you wanna come with me."

"Nah, I'm good. I gotta stay back and chill wit' my own people. We can kick it when you get back."

"Okay, don't say I didn't try. Now give me a kiss."

"Man, please, I ain't tryin' to kiss you." He screwed up his face.

"Oh, word? That's how we doing it now?"

"Yep." Gunz slightly smiled.

"Okay, that's what's up." Gray let him go.

"Get yo' ass back over here." He forcefully pulled her back into his embrace.

"Nah, you ain't wanna kiss me, remember?"

"Gray, don't make me fuck you up in front of all these people."

"Oooooh, I'm shaking in my boots." She shook her legs while giggling.

"A'ight, think it's a game."

"So be honest wit' me, Gunz," she stated as they began to walk again. "Do you love me?"

"You tell me."

"Sometimes I think you do."

"Hmm," Gunz replied, looking ahead.

"So do you?"

"Why yo' ol' soft ass always talkin' about love?" he joked.

"I take that as a no."

"Whateva. C'mon, crazy ass." Gunz took her by the hand so they could continue their walk.

"Oh my God, babe, look." Gray pointed to a parade of people.

It was an entire wedding party coming down the street. Everyone was so happy. The bride looked absolutely stunning in a white strapless taffeta ball gown. Her bouquet was made of lilies and blush-colored roses. The groom didn't look too bad himself. He donned a very traditional Carey Grant–inspired tuxedo. There were only four bridesmaids and groomsmen. The bridesmaid's dresses were a deep, sensual shade of purple.

"I can't wait to get married."

"Is that right?"

"Ever since I was a little girl I dreamed of my wedding. It's going to be absolutely fabulous."

"I just bet it is," Gunz said sarcastically.

"Don't tell me you don't want to get married."

"I never really thought about it."

"Well, if you stick wit' me, we gettin' married."

"How you just gon' tell me what I'm gon' do?" He chuckled.

"I'm just lettin' you know. Marriage is in the cards for me. Whether I'm with you or someone else, I'm getting married."

"So what do you wanna do when we leave here?" Gunz changed the subject.

"Ummm, we can grab a bite to eat. I am a little hungry."

"How about Sub Zero?"

"Yes! I have been *dying* for their shrimp tempura salad."

"Well, come on then." He placed his hand around her waist. "I ain't tryin' to be wit' you all day."

"I ain't tryin' to be wit' you either. I just want a meal, *ya dig*." She laughed.

"Gray, don't play wit' me."

"Who said I was playin'?" she countered.

"A'ight, that's enough."

Unbeknownst to Gunz and Gray, across town in a dark, vacant room, chaos ensued. Four hired henchmen dressed in all black dragged a severely beaten man across a cold concrete floor and placed him into a metal folding chair. He'd survived their kicks, punches, and hits with bats, and never once did he cry, scream, or beg for help. This man was a soldier, and if need be, he'd die like one.

With his hands tied behind his back, he took a couple of deep breaths in and out as blood trickled down the center of his face. Thoughts of his wife, three daughters, and unborn son tormented his mind. He hadn't left home on good terms with his wife, Keisha. She'd begged him to stay, but lady luck was calling his name. Bishop had to hit the casino. He promised to only be gone an hour, but Keisha wasn't trying to hear it.

"You are so selfish! All you do is think about yourself! I ask you to stay at home one time, and you can't even do that! Fuck you! The streets can have yo' ass!"

Bishop didn't even respond. He simply grabbed his coat from out the closet and left without saying a word. Keisha stood behind him with tears streaming from her eyes because she knew she and the kids would always play third to his life allegiance with MCM and the streets. Now here Bishop was, regretting his decision and wishing he could turn back the hands of time.

In the corner of the room stood a man he had never seen before. The devil resided in his soul; it was evident by the ominous look in his oval-shaped eyes. Bishop didn't know who he was or what his beef could be. All he knew was that this man was out to kill.

"Jason . . . Bishop . . . Cruz, you've made this entirely too easy for me, my friend." The man stepped up closer. His voice reminded Bishop of The Joker.

"Tracking you down wasn't as hard as I thought it would be. Every week you follow the same routine. You conduct your business in the streets, on Thursday you go to The Delmar, Fridays you're at Lumier, Saturdays you hit up Larry Flynt, and on Sunday, you spend time with the family. For you to be Gunz's right hand man, I expected more from you."

"Who the fuck are you?" Bishop barked.

"I'm your worst fuckin' nightmare." The man laughed hysterically. "No, seriously, allow me introduce myself." He placed out his hand for a shake.

"My name . . . is Christopher Knight. I believe you, a fella named Watts, and the *infamous* Gunz Marciano had the pleasure of killing my brother Richard, better known as Rich."

Suddenly, everything became clear. This guy was out for revenge.

"Ohhhh how . . . I . . . wish you all hadn't done that. You all have made me very angry, and you see I'm a nice guy. I am." Truth cracked his knuckles. "But you've pushed me too far. See, first . . ." He walked around in a circle. "I was just gonna take your drugs . . . then steal Gray away from Gunz, of course, but then . . . you all had to go and get all high and mighty on me and kill my little puppet, Fortune. Now . . . you know I just can't let that go undone. There are rules to this. I kill one of your people, you kill one of my people, and so on and so forth." He flicked his hand. "You get the picture."

"You're a fuckin' dead man," Bishop spat, heated.

"See,"—Truth shook his head—"that's where you're wrong. You're the dead man."

Before Bishop could utter another word, a gallon of gasoline was being poured over his head. The pungent smell made him want to vomit. This was it. There would be no final good-bye to his family. He'd never get to kiss Keisha's pretty face. Like Fortune, he would never get to see his son grow. Bishop only had himself to blame. This was the life he'd chosen. All the dirt he'd done had finally caught up with him, and there was nothing he could do about it.

"Any last words?"

"Yeah." Bishop looked Truth square in the eyes. "See you in hell, muthafucka!"

Unfazed by his comment, Truth stepped back, lit a match, and tossed it on to Bishop's lap. Seconds later, his body was aflame. The foul smell of burning flesh filled the air, and for the first time since he'd been abducted, Bishop let out a bloodcurdling scream.

Gunz sped down the highway doing eighty. While sharing a nice romantic meal with Gray, he received a frantic phone call from Watts, telling him to meet him on the corner of Acme and West Florissant. Unable to drop Gray off before heading in that direction, he let her ride with him. The whole time, she sat in the passenger seat with a troubled look plastered on her face. Gunz could sense her nervousness, but now wasn't the time to ease Gray's fears. He too was in a state of panic.

Pulling up at the corner of Acme, he spotted Watts and placed the car in park. An eerie quietness surrounded them. No one in the neighborhood seemed to be out, even though it really wasn't that late. The only thing wandering the streets was a black stray cat in search of food and shelter, and a small crew of his men.

"Gunz, you're scaring me. Can you please tell me what's going on?" Gray pleaded.

"I can't right now. Just take the car and drive home," he instructed.

"What do you mean take the car and drive home? What the fuck is going on? Where are you going?"

"Gray . . . please . . ." He took a hold of both of her hands. "Just do as I said. Take the car and go home. I'll be by there later."

"But, Gunz, wait a minute—"

"Gray, just go!" He opened the door.

"But, Gunz!"

"Go!" He stepped out and slammed the door shut.

"My bad. I ain't mean to interrupt your time wit' your lady,"—Watts greeted him with a pound—"but we got trouble."

"What kind of trouble?" Gunz asked as they proceeded to walk around the corner to the alley.

"It's all bad, G. I don't know who did it, but it's fucked up, yo."

Gunz followed Watts into the trash-infested alleyway, and before his eyes, hanging from an electrical pole was Bishop. Gunz was shocked. For the first time in years, tears entered the brims of his eyes. To stop himself from feeling, Gunz took his eyes off the body and looked down.

"They found him an hour ago," Watts confirmed.

"GET HIM DOWN!" Gunz growled, infuriated.

Swallowing hard, he pursed his lips together tightly and allowed a tear to slide down his cheek. This was his fault entirely. He'd brought Bishop into this life, and now because of it, he was dead. Bishop was not only his homey, but his best friend. They'd been through everything together. Since the age of seventeen, they'd held each other down. How was Gunz supposed to go on living when Bishop would no longer be right there by his side? Things were now better than ever. They were financially back on top and both happy in their personal lives; but now he had to tell Keisha that the love of her life, her husband, and the father of her kids was dead and gone. Unwilling to show any sign of weakness, Gunz wiped his face.

As he turned around to face Watts and his crew, he saw Gray turning the corner. The look on her face said it all. The reality of what he did for a living was no longer just a figment of her imagination or something she could just sweep under the rug. It was screaming in her face, loud and clear. Gunz was a monster. He killed people on an everyday basis. Lies, deceit, and mayhem were all a part of his world, and somehow she'd infused herself in it without even a care or a bat of the eye. Gunz knew from that day forward she would look at him differently. The man she'd gotten to know would just be a shadow and imagery of the man he really was underneath the surface, but his eyes still begged for her to understand.

"What are you doing here? I thought I told you to go home."

"I . . . CAN'T . . . DRIVE!" Gray screamed before throwing his keys at him and running off.

Hours later, as rain poured from the sky, Gunz stood outside of Bishop's door, unprepared to do the worst. Reluctantly, he rang the doorbell. Gunz could hear the sound of Keisha coming down the steps.

"Who is it?" she asked nervously.

"It's me, Keish. Gunz."

Perplexed by why he was at her house so late, Keisha tightened the knot on her pink robe and quickly unlocked the door.

"Hey, Gunz." She smiled warmly.

"What's up, Keish? I'm sorry to be stopping by so late."

"It's okay, but I was gon' say if you're looking for Bishop, he's not here. The last I know he was at the casino."

"Oh, I know. I actually came to speak to you."

"Is there something wrong?" She placed her hand on her protruding belly.

Gunz knew that he should just spit it out, but for a minute, he got caught up in the reality of the situation. On any given day, Keisha was due to pop, and what should have been a joyous occasion would now be filled with loss and regret. He couldn't do it to her. Everything in him wanted to give her a little bit more peace.

"Gunz, are you okay?" she asked softly, taking him by the hand.

"Keish, I got something I need to tell you."

"Uh-uh." She shook her head, fully knowing what he was about to say. "No."

"I'm sorry." Gunz held her hand tight.

Unable to digest it all, Keisha stood frozen stiff. Her forehead was scrunched together, causing her eyes to squint as tears flowed like rivers from her eyes. At that moment, she was willing to give up her heart, her home, anything she owned, just to be with Bishop again. He was her rock, her shoulder to lean on. She was part of him, and he was a part of her, so now that he was gone, a part of her had died too.

Gunz pulled Keisha into him and wrapped his arms around her. It didn't matter that rain was dropping heavily onto them at a rapid pace. They needed each other like they both needed air to breathe. Under the midnight sky and cloud-covered moon, they mourned the loss of the person neither of them wanted to let go.

Soaking wet, Gunz buzzed Gray's loft for the fifth time. He had to see her. At that moment, he needed her more than ever before.

"Will you just go home," she pleaded through the intercom.

"Not until you come talk to me."

"That's the problem. I don't have anything to say."

"Please," he begged, placing his forehead on the metal gate.

Gray ran her hands down her face and sighed. "All right."

Minutes later, she exited the building with her hands in her pockets. Gunz swallowed hard. By the look on her face, it seemed as if she'd had enough. Gray entered her code and walked through the gate.

"What is it, Gunz?"

"Come here." He reached out his hand for her.

"No." Gray shook her head.

"Are you okay?"

"Does it look like I'm okay? I just saw your best friend hanging from a pole. This shit is crazy. I can't do this. More importantly, I can't believe that I tricked myself into believing that I could be with a man like you."

"A man like me?"

"You sell drugs for a living, Gunz. You kill people," she stressed.

"You don't think I see how my life affects people?" he questioned, angry. "This whole thing is my fault!" He pounded his fist against his chest. "Bishop wasn't supposed to sell dope. I forced this life on him. He was supposed to go to college and play ball, but one night, we got pulled over by the police. I had some weed and coke stashed in the ride, so I ran. Bishop didn't get out fast enough and got caught, but guess what? My nigga didn't snitch or nothing. He took the bid for me. Now look . . ." Gunz's bottom lip trembled. "My nigga dead and I gotta carry around the burden of knowing it's my fault." He broke down and cried.

Seeing Gunz in such a state caused the ice around Gray's heart to melt. Gunz wasn't the type of man to show emotion, so to see him cry only told her that their relationship was growing, not fading away. Gray took her hands out of her pockets and wrapped her arms lovingly around Gunz. Yes, his life was dangerous and she should back away now while she had the chance, but there was no way she could turn her back on him now.

Go on and take a bow . . .

Rihanna, "Take a Bow"

Chapter Eleven

Gray sat at her desk. She silently thanked God that it was Wednesday. Only two more days to go until the weekend and Gunz's birthday. She'd been working her ass off to prove to everyone that she deserved her new title. When everyone went home, Gray stayed late. Even on her off time, she would think of new ideas to pitch.

Working for *Haute Couture* was a chance of a lifetime, and she cherished every second. Gray loved living the life of a jetsetter. One day she could be on a set styling a shoot, and the next, sipping mimosas with Donatella Versace. She wouldn't trade her life for the world.

Gray looked down at her wrist and admired the gold Rolex watch Gunz had given her. The watch previously belonged to Bishop. After his funeral, Keisha decided to give Gunz a couple of his things, the watch being one. It took Gray a while to get over Bishop's death and the realization of the danger that consumed Gunz's career choice, but she loved him. Besides, what kind of person would she be if she left him when he needed her most?

"Excuse me, Gray," her assistant, Breann, buzzed in.

"Yes," she buzzed her back.

"I just received a call from Kema. Sienna wants you in her office a.s.a.p."

"Okay."

For a second she sat puzzled. She hoped she wasn't in trouble. Gray ran through a list of things in her mind and wondered what she could've possibly done wrong. Nothing came to mind, but it was still odd that Sienna wanted to see her.

Gray checked herself in the mirror she had placed in her office. Once she saw that her outfit and hair were intact, she hopped on the elevator and went up to the twenty-fifth floor.

Kema was standing behind her desk, frantically going through papers and talking on the phone. She looked cute in crisp white fitted shirt, wide black leather belt, gray pencil skirt and heels. Pausing, she stopped what she was doing and said, "Sienna wants to see you now!"

"For what? Did I do something wrong?" Gray whispered so no one else could hear.

"I don't know, but she did seem upset."

"Shit."

"Sienna, Gray is here to see you," Kema buzzed her office.

"Send her in," Sienna replied back.

Gray inhaled deeply, pushed the glass doors open to her office, and entered. To her surprise, Sienna wasn't alone. Jean-Pierre, her right hand man and go-to guy, was seated across from her with his legs crossed.

"Have a seat, Gray." Sienna pointed to the empty seat next to Jean-Pierre.

Gray nervously sat down. She prayed to God she wasn't being fired.

"We've been watching you performance closely," Jean-Pierre began.

Gray looked back and forth between him and Sienna.

"And we feel . . . that you have been doing an excellent job."

"Thank God." Gray placed her hand over her chest and smiled.

"Yes," Sienna chimed in. "The shoot that you styled for the wedding issue was fabulous. I especially loved the Monique Lhuillier gown."

"That one was my favorite too," Gray gushed.

"Well, to congratulate you, we have decided to send you to Paris."

"We want you to do an article on how women in Paris style themselves versus women in the U.S.," Jean-Pierre added.

"This is a once in a lifetime opportunity, Gray. There are a lot of people in this building who would kill to be in your position, so please don't take this offer lightly."

"How could I? I'm honored. It's always been a dream of mine to go to Paris, let alone for a week."

"Good. You'll be flying out tomorrow morning."

"Tomorrow," Gray repeated, remembering Gunz's birthday.

"Yes. Is that a problem?" Sienna questioned.

"No, no," she assured. "Everything's fine."

*   *   *

Gray gazed blankly at her plate while picking at her food. All night she'd been dreading telling Gunz her good news. For weeks, he'd gone on and on about his birthday party and how we wanted her to be there to share it with him. Once she told him about her unexpected trip, she was sure he would flip.

Gray hated letting her loved ones down, especially Gunz. Any second of the day she could spend with him, she did. She, too, had been excited about his birthday party. She couldn't wait to be that chick on his arm. She didn't want there to be an opportunity where some other broad could come and take her place. She hoped and prayed Gunz would understand.

"What's wrong wit' you? Why you not eating?" Gunz took a sip of wine.

"I guess I must've lost my appetite." She looked up from her plate.

"You straight?"

"I wanna talk to you about something." Gray leaned her elbows on the table and leaned forward.

"Go 'head."

"Today at work I got some good news."

"Don't tell me you got another promotion."

"Nah, not yet." She laughed some. "I've been given the opportunity to go to Paris for a week."

"That's what's up, ma. I'm proud of you. Have you ever been before?"

"No."

"You gon' love it. I've been twice. As a matter of fact, while you out there, I might come fuck wit' you for a couple days."

"Really? You would do that?" She got excited.

"Yeah, why not? When you leave?"

"See, that's the thing. They want me to leave to-morrow."

"Tomorrow, as in Thursday, the day before my birthday?"

"Yeah."

"Umm." Gunz was noticeably upset.

"Please don't tell me you're mad."

"I mean, what you want me to say? Don't get me wrong." He toyed with his napkin. "I'm happy for you. It's just some fucked-up-ass timing. So are you gon' go?"

"I want to, but I also wanna be here for you."

"I want you to be here, too, but I guess you gotta do what's best for you," Gunz spat in a sarcastic tone.

"What's that supposed to mean?" Gray shot back, offended.

"Look, do what you gotta do." He stood up and threw down his napkin.

"Where you going?"

"Outside. I need a smoke."

Shanell's techno-inspired jam "Substitute Lover" was on full blast as Gray raced frantically around the house like a mad woman. It was almost 6:00 PM. Gunz would be there in an hour, and she was nowhere near being ready. A part of her regretted choosing not to go on the trip to Paris, but knowing she was about to see Gunz's face lifted her spirits. Gray had it all planned out. Before they went out to The Loft, where his birthday party was being held, she was going to surprise Gunz with his favorite Latin meal, Caribbean seafood parrillada.

Gray had been studying the recipe all week. She couldn't wait to see the expression on his face, but first she had to pack her overnight bag that she would take to Gunz's house and get dressed. There was a lot to do in so little time. She still had to get her clothes together, as well as all of the ingredients that went into making the parrillada.

Before she could even start, there was an impromptu buzz at the door. Gray prayed that it wasn't Gunz arriving early as she allowed the visitor up.

"Tyra Mail!" Tee-Tee threw his hands up in the air as she opened the door.

"What in the hell is yo' ass doing here? I thought you and Raymon were going out."

"We were," he said in passing. "But at the last minute, when I'm on my way to the restaurant, this sorry-ass negro ups and call me and says he can't make it. So I said the next time you wanna bend me over and pop my asshole open like it's a cherry, I won't be able to make it either."

"I often ask myself why are we friends." Gray stopped and looked at the ceiling, perplexed.

"Fuck that." He playfully pushed her as she continued walking. "You better get down like me, girl. These men out here got to be put on restriction. That's the only way they asses gon' act right. I'm tellin' you."

"I guess," she replied as they entered her second bedroom, which had been turned into a storage room for all of her clothes and shoes.

"You can guess all you want to, but it ain't gon'

get you nowhere but somewhere cryin' wit' ya feelings hurt. Now, what is going on wit' you? Why is this house lookin' like a scene from *The Crying Game*?" Tee-Tee looked around, disgusted. Gray had clothes and shoes thrown everywhere.

"I'm gettin' ready to go over Gunz's house."

"I forgot you were going over there this weekend."

"Yeah, bitch, get it together," Gray quipped, going through her clothes.

"Gray, don't let the fake eyelashes and big boobs fool you. I will cut you the fuck up," he declared, pulling out a pocket knife.

"Man, please. If you don't put that shit up."

"Okay, think I'm playin'. Now, what time you supposed to be leaving?"

"He's supposed to be here in an hour." Gray tried on a pair of black skinny leg jeans.

"Although I shouldn't, since I'm here . . ." Tee-Tee threw his head back and inhaled deeply. "I guess . . . I could drop you off since I'm going that way."

"Thank you, wit' yo' dramatic ass. That'll save Gunz the trip, so let me call him."

"You do that, while I pick you out some sexy lingerie that'll light his dick on fire."

Gray left the room and pretended as if she hadn't heard Tee-Tee. Once she located the cordless phone, she dialed Gunz's number. Five rings and no answer later, she hung up. Gray tried calling him again, but there was still no answer. Unwilling to give up, she tried once more, but he still wouldn't pick up. Gray decided this time to leave a message.

"Hey, babe, this me. I just wanted to tell you that instead of you coming to get me, Tee-Tee will drop me off. Call me back."

After pressing the pound button, she hung up and went back into the room.

"What he say?" Tee-Tee asked, trying on one of her backless tops.

"Nothing. He didn't answer."

"Don't worry. He'll call back."

Thirty minutes later, Gray still hadn't heard from Gunz. She found it quite odd that after talking non-stop earlier in the day, he was now not answering his phone. A bad feeling stung her gut. Gray was about to call him once more when her phone started to ring. She didn't even have to look at the screen. By the ringtone she knew it was Gunz. Gray left the room and answered the phone.

"Hello?"

"What's up?" he asked, sounding impatient.

Gray could hear loud music and a bunch of people talking in the background.

"Where you at?" she questioned, already agitated.

"Why?"

" 'Cause I wanna know, that's why."

"Man, do you work for the police?"

"Anyway, why you ain't been answering your phone?"

"I ain't hear that muthafucka ring. Why? What's up wit' all the questions?"

"So I guess you didn't get my message either. I was callin' to tell you that Tee-Tee can bring me down to your house instead of you coming all the way over here to get me."

"Well, I ain't at home right now."

"When will you be?"

"I don't know." He chuckled. "Why is you twenty-one questioning me? I thought we agreed that I was coming to get you, so why don't we just leave it like that, 'cause I'm in the middle of something right now."

"In the middle of what?" she countered back. "It don't sound like you too busy to me."

"Man, go 'head wit' that. I told you about always assuming shit."

"Whateva, Gunz. Are you still coming to get me or what?"

"I said I was. Calm down," he snapped. "Look, let me call you back."

Gray didn't even give him a chance to say goodbye before she hung up. *Fed up* weren't the words to describe how she felt. Once again Gunz was on some bullshit. She was so sick of being number ten on his to-do list.

"What's the deal, ma-ma?" Tee-Tee asked as soon as she came back into the room.

"I don't know." Gray tried not to show how upset she was. "He said he was gon' call me back."

Two hours and six unanswered phone calls later, Gray and Tee-Tee had watched two episodes of *Keeping up with the Kardashians*, ate pizza, and looked up clothes on the Internet. Gray attempted to act as if she wasn't in turmoil, but each second that passed without Gunz calling was like walking on glass. Her stomach felt like it had dropped to her knees. They'd been planning for her to come over all week, so what was the hold-up now?

"Look, girl." Tee-Tee turned and looked at her

as they sat at the computer. "Where is yo' man at? 'Cause I gots to go."

"I don't know. Let me try and call him again."

Gray picked up the phone and called Gunz. This time her call was immediately sent to voicemail. She was pissed. Here he was playing games again.

"You can go 'head. He not answering the phone." She snapped her phone shut.

"What's that about? Don't make me call the homies and have somebody whoop his ass. And please don't sleep, 'cause my niggas in the Get It Gurl Mafia don't play."

"I'm sure they don't. Thanks, Tee, but that will not be necessary."

"Well, I'm about to go have a drink. You wanna roll?" He placed on his coat.

"Yeah, 'cause right about now a bitter bitch like me needs one." She put on her shoes and grabbed her purse.

"I know you not going nowhere wit' me lookin' like a tomboy." He looked her up and down.

"What?" She examined her outfit. She thought she looked casually cute. Gray rocked a vintage AC/DC T-shirt, skin tight dirty wash jeans, and checkerboard Nike Blazers. Her hair was filled with loose, messy curls. A pair of diamond studs and the gold wristwatch Gunz gave her was the only jewelry she cared to sport.

"Boy, boo." She waved him off, knowing she was the shit. "Let's roll."

The infamous words "It's Britney, bitch" rang through the air as Gray sipped on cranberry and

Absolut. Tee-Tee snapped his fingers and popped his booty to the beat. The Complex, St. Louis' largest gay nightclub was packed. Being around a lot of people lifted Gray's spirits some, but thoughts of Gunz still invaded her mental space. The fact that he still hadn't called spoke volumes. Maybe they would never get past the drama. Maybe this was how their relationship was destined to be, one unfulfilled promise after another.

"Peep game." Tee-Tee nudged her arm. "Li'l Daddy over there by the bar is jockin' me."

Gray looked in the direction he was pointing. It was dark, so she could barely see.

"All right, from what I can see, he look kinda cute. I'm glad I know now he playin' for yo' team."

"Don't sleep, girl. Most niggas these days like gettin' it in they dookey chute."

"C'mon, Tee-Tee, that is revolting. You done made my stomach hurt. I don't even want the last of my drink."

"Shit, I'll take it." He took her glass and gulped down the last of what she had left. "Uh-oh, code ten! This is my shit." he twirled around in a circle like a disco queen.

"Buttons" by The Pussycat Dolls was playing. Like Gray, Tee-Tee loved to do his thing on the dance floor. Just like in the video, he slowly sauntered over to his prey while mouthing the words to the song. Tee-Tee ran his hands across his chest, popped open his shirt and sang, "You've been sayin' all the right things all night long, but I can't seem to get you over here to help take this off."

Gray didn't know if she should try to stop him, or let him continue on with his striptease. No matter what she did, it wasn't gonna stop him. Tee-Tee was completely in the zone. With his focus on the guy, he tossed his hair wildly then bent down. On his way back up, he grabbed his right leg and placed it in the air. After that, he found a chair and took a seat, but Tee-Tee wasn't done.

Spreading his legs wide, he rolled his torso then crossed his legs. Gray was speechless. Just as she was trying to recover from Tee-Tee's antics, her cell phone began to vibrate. Every fiber of her being prayed that it was Gunz so she could light his ass up. Her prayers were answered when his name popped onto the screen.

"What?" she answered with an attitude as she made her way outside.

"Where you at?"

"No, the question is where are you, and why haven't you been answering your phone?"

"One question at a time, ma," he joked.

"I'm not playin' wit' you. Where are you? You were supposed to be picking me up hours ago."

"I know, I know. Shit just got hectic, ma."

"Yeah, okay, tell me anything." Gray rolled her eyes. "So when are you coming?"

"It's already late. Why don't I just come get you in the morning?"

"Are you fuckin' kidding me? I just turned down a muthafuckin' trip to Paris to be here wit' you and you got the nerve to ask me can you come get me in the morning? I don't think so. You said you was coming to get me tonight, so that's what you're going to do."

"Gray, it's already going on ten, and I got to go to the crib and get dressed."

"That sound like a personal problem to me. Besides, I'm down here by your house anyway, so I'll just have Tee-Tee drop me off."

"You hard-headed. What I just tell you? I told you we'll get up in the morning, so what's the fuckin' problem?"

"You the one making it a fuckin' problem," Gray snapped, having had enough. "If you don't want me there, just say so."

"When have I ever not wanted you there?"

"Exactly, so what's the fuckin' problem today?"

"I'm about to get off this phone, 'cause you trippin', and I'm not about to argue wit' you."

"I'm trippin'," Gray repeated, offended.

"Did I stutter? And besides, why you sweatin' me?"

"Sweatin' you?"

"Don't act stupid. You been blowin' up my phone all night."

"The only reason I called yo' ol' raggedy-ass phone so many times is because you wouldn't answer the phone!"

"And that didn't tell you something?" Gunz barked.

"You know what? Fuck you! You don't ever have to worry about me callin' that muthafucka again!"

"This conversation is a wrap. I'll holla at you tomorrow." He hung up.

Gray held the phone, stunned. Gunz had never spoken to her that way. Unwilling to let him get the last word, she called back, only for him to send her straight to voicemail. Gunz had her fucked up if he thought shit was about to go down like that. Amped as hell, she went back into the club and found Tee-Tee on the dance floor, bumping and grinding with the tender from the bar.

"I looooove your tattoos," Tee-Tee confirmed, running his index finger down his arm.

"I got a whole lot of 'em too. My favorite one is the one I got above my ass that say B-A-N."

"B-A-N?" Tee-Tee twisted up his face, confused. "What does that mean?"

"C'mon, ma, don't tell me you ain't never met a bad-ass nigga before."

"Okay, that's enough." Gray broke up their banter. "Look-a here, Dance Fevah. We gots to go." She pulled on Tee-Tee's sleeve.

"Uh-uh, girl. I think I might've found the man of my dreams. Gray, meet my new boo, Death Row. Ain't he fine? I bet you any money he and Gunz cousins."

"What it do, Dim Sum?" He stuck out his hand for a pound and smiled.

Gray looked around to make sure he was talking to her. When she realized he was, she tried to figure out whether she should laugh or get mad. Death Row was a hot mess up close. Souljah Boy Tell'em's song "Yahh Bitch Yahh" kept on playing in her mind as she looked him up and down. His mouth was filled with gold teeth, but what made it worse was that the top row spelled out *Death* and the bottom spelled out *Row*. Covering his eyes were a pair of white Ray-Ban shades.

His outfit consisted of a red handkerchief tied around his neck, white T-shirt that reached all the way down to his knees, and too big MFG jeans. Instead of rocking one chain, this fool wore not only a gold herringbone necklace, but a silver one too.

His choice of shoes made Gray even more furious. Death Row had the nerve to rock a pair of white K-Swiss with red stripes on the side. The icing on the cake was the homemade prison tattoos that covered his arms. Any part of her that thought he was attractive went away with a quickness.

"Not a damn thing," she replied dryly.

"Now wait a minute, Crab Rangoon. I know you jealous and all 'cause Teyana got at me first, but you can save the attitude, big girl."

"Excuse you?"

"You're excused. Lookin' like yo' name Me So Horny."

"I'm not even about to go there wit' you. Tee-Tee, bring yo' ass on!"

Is it a crime . . . . that I still luv u?

Sade, "Is It a Crime"

Chapter Twelve

"Where in the hell are we going?" Tee-Tee slapped his hand across the steering wheel, pissed. "I'm supposed to be at The Complex right now making love in the club, but noooooooooooo, I'm in the car wit' no heat, stuck wit' yo' depressed ass," he rambled on, "I swear this is some bullllll shit. It never fails. Er'time we go out, y'all bitches wanna cock block! Er'time I go to get me a li'l taste, here one of you lonely hoes go. 'Tee-Tee, I'm tired. I wanna go home. My feet hurt.' And don't think I didn't see you giving Bernard the eye. I'm tellin' you now, Gray, I will go Kung Fu Panda on yo' ass. Don't fuck wit' me. I will stomp a bitch over him."

"Who the fuck is Bernard?"

"That's my B.D. government name. Ain't it cute, girl?" Tee-Tee smiled.

"This is too much muthafuckin' playin'. And by the way, don't nobody want that Peabody reject but you. Up there lookin' like Flava Flav illegitimate son," Gray snapped back, staring out the window.

"Okay, that is what the fuck is up. See, I was gon'

make you my maid of honor, but fuck that! Yo' ass ain't gon' be nowhere near the church. Now, where are we going?"

"To The Loft."

"What's at The Loft?"

"Gunz."

"What? You told him I would drop you off or something?"

"No. I wanna see who he's there with."

"Oh heeeeeeeeeeeeell no! No you don't got me on no *Fatal Attraction* shit. Where is the white rabbit, Glenn Close? Huh? In the trunk?" He shot her a look.

"Negro, please. You the last one to talk. Remember that night you had me get out my sleep so I could be the lookout for you while you put sugar in Derek tank?"

"You sho' right. You always was a ride or die chick. So let a bitch know the deal. Do I got to call the goon squad or what? 'Cause please believe Delicious number is on speed dial. One clap of the hand and a *kooo-kooo!* the Mafia will attack, no questions asked."

"Tee-Tee, I appreciate the help, but Gunz will kill all of y'all asses on sight."

"Oh, you must think this is a game. I ain't no punk, Gray. I goes hard for mine." He reached under the seat and pulled out a nickel-plated .22.

"If you don't put that shit up . . ." Gray scooted close to the door, nervous. "What are you doing wit' a gun?"

"Ride or die, fool. Ride . . . or . . . die."

"I am so over this conversation. Here I am thinking I need to be scared around Gunz, and the whole time you the real thug. This is some bullshit. Pull over right here." She pointed.

As always, The Loft was jumpin'. Gray could hear the sound of Li'l Wayne's "A Millie" all the way across the street. Unconsciously she began to dance in her seat. Gray almost wanted to say fuck Gunz and go in and do her thing, but she couldn't. She had to stay focused on the task at hand, and that was catching his lying ass in the act.

Gray scanned the front entrance of the club. The line to get in stretched all the way around the corner. She could hear some of the women complaining about their feet hurting. One girl even went so far as to take her heels off and stand barefoot on the cement. A slight grin formed on Gray's face. Seeing the girl in pain reminded her of the night she first met Gunz.

Who would've thought nine months later she would be sitting outside a club on some crazy woman shit. What fucked Gray up was that she knew she was trippin'. She was acting like a psycho but couldn't stop herself. An intense need to find out the truth had taken over, although deep down inside she already knew what the deal was. Gray knew Gunz was up to no good, but a part of her still wanted to believe that everything he said was true. Her female intuition was screaming that he was with another woman. The question was, who?

"Do you see his car anywhere?" Tee-Tee interrupted her thoughts.

Gray examined the row of cars that lined the street in front of the club. If Gunz was there, he would most definitely be parked near the door. Sure enough, his Aston Martin was right up front.

"Yeah, I see it." Her nostrils flared.

"Text him and see if he'll reply back," Tee-Tee suggested.

Gray pulled out her iPhone and texted: **So you really not gon' answer none of my calls? It's like that now? After everything we said.**

For the next couple of minutes, she sat and waited with bated breath, hoping that Gunz would realize how much his sudden change in demeanor was hurting her and call back. If things were a wrap, he could just say that. There was no need for him to hold up traffic. If he wanted to step, Gray was more than willing to give him the green light so his ass could go. She could easily find someone else.

Gray was so into her feelings that she didn't even realize that Tee-Tee had been calling her name.

"Gray?" He nudged her.

"Huh," she answered, coming back to reality.

"It's about to be a 'code ten, man down' situation. Ain't that him over there?" He pointed.

Gray's heart stopped mid-beat. Tears welled in her eyes to the point she couldn't see. What she saw couldn't be happening. It all had to be an illusion. Gunz wasn't walking with a huge smile on his face, hand in hand with Devin. And he most definitely wasn't opening the door for her ass. He said she was old news, a thing of the past, so why in the fuck were they together?

Gray was the one who listened about his hopes and dreams. She stayed up with him when he couldn't sleep at night. She sucked his dick until her jaw hurt. She cooked, cleaned, and washed his clothes when he wasn't even technically her man. She bent over backwards to make sure he was happy. She put him before everything, including her career, so why at that moment, instead of being with Gray, was he with her?

She couldn't understand it. Had she been getting on his nerves? Did she demand too much of his time? Was the pressure of knowing she wanted him as her man and not her friend too much stress? Gray came to the conclusion that what she was envisioning was all an evil dream; any minute she was gonna wake up. But time kept on ticking away and the pain in her chest was spreading like wildfire. A part of her wasn't surprised by his actions, but the part of her that believed he cared felt betrayed.

"All I got to say is you bet not cry. You better not let a muthafuckin' tear drop. You feel me? Fuck him!" Tee-Tee wagged his index finger in the air.

For once Tee-Tee was right. There would be no crying, at least not yet.

"Fuck this." She unlocked and opened the door.

"That's right, girl! Go shut that shit down! Represent yo' clique!"

With each step Gray took, it was a struggle for her to breathe. The closer she got to Gunz, the more faint she felt. She didn't know what she was gonna say or how she was gonna say it. Maybe she wouldn't have to say anything at all. Maybe the distressed expression on her face would say everything.

"Gunz," she called out as he gave a pound to one of his homeboys.

Shocked to hear her voice, he spun around.

"So this why you couldn't come get me tonight?" She pointed in the car at Devin.

"What you doing here?" He looked bewildered and confused.

"What you mean, what am I doing here? I came to see what yo' lying ass was up to."

"So you following me now?"

"Nigga, please. Don't flatter ya'self. But it's good. Now I know what's up."

"You don't know shit."

"I know I gave up a trip to Paris to be here with you, but instead you wit' another chick."

"Baby, you ready?" Devin asked, opening the passenger side door.

"Chill out," he spoke sternly, closing the door in her face.

"Don't be actin' brand new now. You ain't got to be rude to her on my account. Just a minute ago y'all was hand in hand, all lovey-dovey and shit."

"Quit actin' fuckin' stupid." He grabbed Gray by the arms and pushed her away from the crowd.

"Let me go! We ain't got shit to talk about. Everything I needed to know is right in front of my face, so like I said, it's good. Go 'head! Take her home, fuck until her pussy gets sore! As a matter of fact, cum for me twice! I don't give a fuck!"

"You don't mean that," Gunz said, fearful that he might've lost her for good.

"What the fuck you think this is, a game? *I'm done fuckin' wit' you.*"

"Look, man, just go home. I'll be there in a minute, a'ight."

"You'll be there in a minute? Nigga, have you lost your fuckin' mind? Are you clueless? You come anywhere near my house and I'ma call the police!

Get it through your head: I'm ... through ... fuckin' ... wit' ... you." Gray tried to break loose.

"Will you let me explain?"

"No. Let me go!" She snatched her arms away.

"Man, calm the fuck down." He yanked her by the arm.

"Uh-uh, nigga, don't get stupid." Tee-Tee jumped out of the car.

"I ain't tryin' to disrespect yo' peoples, but you better tell this muthafucka to fall back."

"Muthafucka? I ain't no muthafucka! It's Miss T if ya nasty!" Tee-Tee waved his index finger in the air.

"Real talk, get yo' boy."

"I ain't got to get shit! Now let me go," Gray screamed, breaking loose from him again. This time, she swung her arm so forcefully that Bishop's watch slipped off and fell to the ground, causing the face to crack. For a second, they both looked at it in awe.

"That was an accident."

"Don't say shit to me." He picked up the watch and placed it in his pocket.

"You know good and well I didn't do that on purpose."

"What the fuck I just say? Don't say shit to me." His chest heaved up and down.

"So now you got an attitude?" Gray shot him a look.

"What the fuck ever, Gray." Gunz was heated. So much anger consumed him that he couldn't see straight. He wanted to choke the shit out of her. Gunz could literally see her face turning blue. If he didn't leave at that very second, he was sure to kill her. Swallowing the desire, Gunz walked over to his car and got in without uttering another word.

Death loomed around Gray. She could feel it. A part of her had died. The whole ride home, she'd suppressed her tears, even though they begged to fall. She felt like a fool. How could she be so stupid to think Gunz wouldn't be like all the rest? She was so dumb to think they could be more than what they were. And how silly of her to think he could be everything she needed.

It seemed like it took forever to get home, but as soon as her key entered the lock and she stepped across the threshold, the tears that choked her throat spilled out through her eyes. The ache in her chest was torturing. Gray just wanted it all to go away. If she could rewind time, she would go back to the day they met and walk away.

She detested the fact that her friends were right about him. Why hadn't she listened? Was she so blinded by his good looks and big dick that nothing else mattered? Had all of Gray's common sense gone out of the window? Before him, she stood tall. She had a mind all her own. Now, here she was once again, torn into pieces. Gray was sick of being led on and let down. All of her life, men had swallowed her up then spit her out at their own convenience, and she sat back and took it.

Before Gunz, she vowed to never be another man's doormat. The first sign of bullshit and she was out. With him, she ignored every sign. She should've known he was trifling when his word didn't live up to his actions, but no, Gray being the love-sick puppy she was, looked past it. The hell with that. She deserved better, and better was what she was gonna get. Being with someone should never be as difficult as it was being with Gunz.

Little by little, Gray picked herself up off the floor. Nothing would improve her situation but lying in her bed underneath the covers. Just as she was about to make her way upstairs, her bell rang. It was Gunz. He was never gonna let things end the way they had. Whether he was right or wrong, if he thought something else needed to be said, it would be. Gray reluctantly went over to the door and let him up.

Gunz had rehearsed every word down to "baby, I'm sorry" down to a T, but as soon as he came face to face with Gray's tear-stained face, all of that went out the window. There were no more games to play. Now was the time to lay everything on the line.

"What do you want?" she asked, holding on to the doorknob. Gray couldn't even look him in the face.

"I just wanna explain."

"There ain't nothing to explain. All that shit you said was a fuckin' lie. You said you wasn't gon' lie to me, you wasn't gon' hurt me, and that you was gon' be honest wit' me, but you's a fuckin' fake! I told you if you wanted to see other people let me know, and you looked me dead in the eye and said you would. But nah, fuck that. My feelings don't count." She finally glared at him. "What was all that shit about? I mean . . . did you even fuckin' care for me at all?"

"Of course I did. I do. You know that."

"How the fuck am I supposed to know that when you constantly hurtin' me? From day one you been playin' games."

"It ain't like that. I care about you. You know that."

"You care about me?" Gray looked at him, disgusted. "Well, isn't that original."

"Can I come in?"

"Why not?" She stepped back so he could enter. Gray closed the door behind them.

"Listen, baby." Gunz took her hands.

"Uh-uh. Get ya hands off me." She snatched her hands away and gave him a warning glare.

"I'm sorry."

"No, you're not. You're only sorry you got caught."

"Look, I know what I did was fucked up, but you gotta understand where I'm coming from. All this shit is new to me. Yeah, I done been in relationships in the past, but none of them were serious—at least not to me. But then here you come. I ain't never met nobody like you. And yeah, it may sound like some sucka shit, but sometimes I get scared too," he finally admitted. "There. I said it."

"I ain't tryin' to lose you, ma. If we can work this shit out, I swear to God, I'ma do better."

Like anyone would be, Gray was flattered by Gunz's fascination with her. Like most single black women, all of her life she'd wanted someone to crave. Gunz was like uncharted territory, greatly intriguing. But now that she'd seen what lay behind his smile, like his constant lies, cheating, and unfulfilled promises, she needed a moment to deliberate whether he was even worth her time.

"I don't know, Gunz."

"So you don't love me no more?"

"That's not even relevant right now." She shook her head.

"I'm askin' you a question."

"Yes, I still love you. That shit ain't gon' go away in a matter of seconds, but loving you is not enough. You're not gonna continue to play around wit' my heart. I'm tired of tryin' to be wit' you. I'm tired of tryin' to get you to see what I see so fuckin' clearly."

"And what's that?"

"The fact that you would even have to ask says everything." Gray began to walk away.

"Where you going?"

"I'm done talkin'."

"What is it that you see so clearly? Tell me."

"That we're supposed to be together," she yelled, spinning around on her heels.

Gunz knew Gray's answer before she said it. He'd known from the start that she was the one. The fear of loving her and losing her like he'd lost his sister and best friend was just too much for him to ever consider. But now that he was forced to swallow that bitter pill, he recognized that loving Gray was the best decision he'd made in life so far.

Gray, on the other hand, was unfazed by his too little too late apology.

"Okay, well, let us be together."

"No. I'm done. I'm not going back this time," she cried.

"C'mon, ma, you don't mean that." He caressed her face.

"Yes, I do." Her lips trembled. "I can't do this no more."

"So that's it? It's that easy for you to walk away?"

"No, it's not easy, but that's what I gotta do for me."

"If that's how you want it then . . ." Gunz nodded his head, disappointed.

Gray held the door open for him, but opted not to look at his face. If she did, she knew she would go back on every word she'd just hit him with. Gunz swallowed the tears in his throat and headed out the door. Nothing he had to say would make up for the way Gray felt. The damage had already been done, and at this point, he deserved to get everything she dished out.

Gray walked at a steady, but brisk pace. Snowflakes the size of nickels fell rapidly from the sky onto her bare hands as she tried her best to shield herself from the wind. Starbucks was only a few more feet away. Gray couldn't wait to get inside and get a hot cup of joe.

The aroma of fresh brewed coffee danced through the air and up Gray's nose as soon as she entered. Rubbing her frozen hands together, she stepped into the line. It wouldn't be long until it was time for her to be back to work. Normally she would've eaten in the cafeteria, but on that chilly November afternoon, Gray felt like being alone with her thoughts.

After ordering the house blend, she made her way

over to an empty table for two by the store window. Gray took off her cashmere coat and placed it on the back of the chair. For a second she imagined that Gunz was the one doing it. She'd been doing a lot of that lately. Gray never imagined that getting used to the idea of being alone would be so difficult.

Often, she second guessed herself and wondered if she had made the right decision by saying good-bye. Maybe she shouldn't have said they could never go back. Coping with the fact that he was gone and they were over was cruelty in its worst form. Each day became more difficult. Gray's days weren't long enough, and her nights seemed to go on for an eternity. And yes, he'd hurt her in the worst way imaginable, but for weeks she hadn't eaten or slept. Her favorite color to wear had become black. Every five seconds she checked her phone to see if it had rung. Everybody but him seemed to call.

Missing him wasn't a surprise, but she needed to know that he missed her too. Her friends all said that she should get over him and move on, but was it such a crime that key parts of her longed to be with him? And yes, she should fall back and let the chips land where they may, but Gray couldn't risk her heart being on the losing end of the stick and them not being together for good.

She was a complete and utter mess. Any and everything made her cry. It was as if her life was stuck on pause, and everything else around her was continuing on as normal. Being alone couldn't be her reality. God knew her heart and how she longed to be with a man. Gunz had to have been brought into her life for a reason. Maybe he was the one she'd been praying for. Nobody was perfect, and relationships weren't easy.

Taking a sip from her cup, she stared out the window. A young couple was crossing the street hand in hand. The guy led the way. When they entered the coffee house, he unraveled the woman's scarf and took off her coat. She laughed as he picked snowflakes out of her hair. They seemed so carefree and in love. At the table, he took a hold of each of her hands and gazed lovingly into her eyes.

Jealous, Gray focused her attention elsewhere. Unfortunately for her, the sight of love was everywhere she turned. If rewinding time was something she could do, she would in a heartbeat. She needed her lifeline back, but even if they got back together, things would never be the same. And yes, she could see through all of his lies. Yet and still, something in her wanted to try again. The nauseating feeling in the pit of her stomach had to end. She couldn't cope with it one more day.

For Gunz, being without Gray was like moving mountains—damn near impossible. She was his life support, his stairway to heaven. Unknowingly, she'd become a part of him. Often, he'd find himself staring blankly out into space with thoughts of her on his mind. If only he could turn back the hands of time. He'd hold her body so tenderly, as if it were made of glass. He'd treat every precious kiss as if it were the last. In the next lifetime, he'd promise to find her sooner.

And no, he wasn't perfect, but without Gray, he was left with nothing. She was the yellow to his blue. Forever with her seemed like the perfect ending to his story, but his immature, selfish ways had finally caught up with him. Gunz knew while he was out in the streets tricking off, he should've been home with her. Gray was a good girl. He should've never had her thinking she was the only one.

Yet and still, the mere thought of her being with someone else caused his stomach to churn. From the moment they met, she was his. Fucking around with Devin wasn't worth seeing her cry, but a part of him recognized that he couldn't love her right. The vibe between them was all wrong; yet and still, he wasn't willing to let go. He wanted to escape from the unexpected feelings that inflicted his heart, but Gray had him hook, line, and sinker.

It seemed like no matter how hard he tried, he couldn't get her out of his system. He tried to be on some "fuck her, whateva" type shit, but his heart wouldn't let him fall back. He wished and prayed for her to call, but she never did. Gunz had even gone so far as to kick it with other chicks, but no other woman could take the place of Gray.

At night, he rode past her place just to feel close to her. He missed everything from her kiss to the touch of her hand. Surely she missed him too. She was his angel sent from up above. She shone brighter than any star. They'd come too far to end things now.

Before long, Gray had unknowingly begun a routine of going to work, coming home, showering, and then lying on the couch under Gunz's favorite mint green throw cover. The smell of his Jean

Paul Gautier cologne still lingered in the fabric. Gray placed the cover up to her nose, closed her eyes, inhaled deep, and then sang along to Tamia's "Officially Missing You."

"Just a week ago you were . . . my baby. Now I don't even know you at all. I don't know you at all. Well, I wish that you would call me right now."

Holding her chest, Gray allowed tears of regret to roll down her face. She should've followed her first mind and backed out gracefully a long time ago. Gunz was everything she prayed for, but nothing like he could've been. He was the only man she'd love not to forgive. Gray wished that she was strong enough to say love me or leave me, but the fear of Gunz not being there at the end of the day was too excruciating to put up with.

And yes, it fucked her up how he would say no one came before her, but over and over he scarred her heart with his cheating ways. Hate for him lingered in her limbs, but in the same instance, to take a breath without him was like fighting the wind— impossible. Gray didn't want to love him. She desperately wanted to see past him, but thoughts of was he missing her too devoured her mind.

As the track changed to John Legend's "I Love, You Love," Gray's phone began to ring. Gray glanced at the screen. In a split second, her heart dropped to the pit of her stomach. It was Gunz. Should she answer? Tears filled every crevice of her face as she reached to pick up the phone. Choking back the tears, she pressed the ANSWER button.

"Hello," she spoke just above a whisper.

"I need to talk to you."

"Okay."

"I'm outside. Can I come in?"

"Yeah."

"A'ight, here I come," he replied before hanging up.

Unprepared for their confrontation, Gray slowly got up from the couch, walked to the door, and opened it. Gunz towered above her. The smell of his cologne melted her senses. He wasn't fighting fair. He looked sexier than ever in a white tee, blood red cardigan, dark denim jeans, and red-and-white Cre8tive Recs. His signature aviator shades shielded his eyes, while a TAG Heuer watch shone from his wrist.

Gunz was like a decadent piece of chocolate, rich and delectable. Being in his presence was like staring into the face of danger. The question was, was she ready to pull the trigger? To see him broke her heart because she knew what he was there for. He'd come back to reclaim the piece of her heart that he'd left splattered on the floor.

"So how you been?" he asked as he took a seat on the couch.

"As well as can be, I guess." Gray stood across from him with her arms folded across her chest.

"Why you got my cover out?" He pointed over his shoulder.

"Gunz, you didn't come over here to talk about that cover. What do you want?"

"You," he stated bluntly.

"Yeah, right," she replied dryly.

"So what, you don't believe me?"

"No," she said, trying to avoid his eyes.

"Gray . . . you know me. I don't play about how I feel."

"Gunz, when you had me, you didn't know how to treat me."

"I understand that, but all I know is . . . somehow, some way, you snuck into my heart, and no matter how hard I try to fight it . . . the shit just won't go away."

"Okay, so what am I supposed to do about that?"

"Let me come home," he said sincerely.

"No. I can't keep doing this shit wit' you." She threw her hands down to her sides. " 'Cause you know what? For a while it'll be all good, and right when I get comfortable, you'll go and do something that'll break my fuckin' heart all over again. No." She tried to convince herself. "I won't do it. I love you, Gunz, I do, but this shit is crazy," she yelled, trying to regain her composure despite the tears that trickled down her cheeks.

"So what you want me to do? Just walk away?"

"Yes! Please do that for me, 'cause I have tried to walk away from you . . . but I can't," Gray stressed. "My heart won't let me. I love you and I always will, and you know it. And you use it every time to pull me back in, and that's what you're doing now. You have this hold on me and I can't break it no matter how hard I try. And it scares me to death 'cause I know that you could push your way out of my life if you wanted to, so I'm asking you to let me go."

"Nah, I can't do that." He shook his head, unwilling to let her go.

"Why not?"

" 'CAUSE I FUCKIN' LOVE YOU, THAT'S WHY!" Gunz jumped up from the couch and got into her face. "You my fuckin' wife! I ain't giving up on you that easy! Look . . . yo, I know I did some fucked-up shit in the past, but I'm here and I'm ready."

For a minute, Gray stood speechless. For almost a year, she'd died to hear those words escape from Gunz's lips. Now, here they were, floating in space, waiting for a response. It was obvious that she still loved him, but was her heart willing to admit the truth and risk being broken in half again?

"Ready for what?" she finally asked.

"To be the man you need."

Gray was astounded. She'd never heard Gunz speak so passionately, and about her, no less. Should she let the wall she'd built fall down? She loved Gunz too much to let him hurt her again. If she let him back in her life, he was sure to hurt her ten times worse the second time around. But then he took her into his arms and placed his soft lips upon hers. All the doubts she had dissolved like snow on a warm day. And yes, she should tell him to go so she could wean herself off of him for good, but Gunz was her drug of choice. And like most addicts, it may cost her a lot in the end, but Gray was willing to give him one more chance.

"Where are we going?" Gray asked as she and Gunz drove out to the middle of nowhere.

"To my crib." He took a long pull from the blunt in his hand and exhaled slowly.

Gray knew that she had a follow-up question, but unknowingly, she became caught up in Gunz's swagger. He was the true definition of sexy. The way the smoke from the blunt escaped through his lips and into the air turned her on to the fullest. Gray wanted him to put it on her in the worst way imaginable. She wished for nothing more than for him to pull over, ease the seat back, push her knees up to her chest, and kiss her pussy until she screamed out, "Wait a minute, muthafucka!"

He looked good as hell in a black Yankees cap, red-and-black lumberjack flannel, Monarchy jeans, and high top Vans. Gunz took his eyes off the rode and looked at her out of the corner of his eye. Gray didn't have to say a word; he already knew what was on her mind. He simply hit her with his infamous crooked grin and refocused on the road.

"What are you talkin' about?" she finally questioned, coming back to reality. "Your place is in the city."

"I got more than one spot where I lay my head, Gray."

"Why you just now tellin' me about it?"

" 'Cause I don't tell many people about it."

Gray didn't know if she should feel honored or put off.

Ten minutes later, they pulled up to a secluded gated community. Gray was amazed by how immaculate and beautiful the area was. Gunz's house—better yet, mansion—was by far the flyest on the block. It was 6300 square feet and worth $3.5 million. There was a Spanish appeal to the exterior.

Gunz hopped out and opened her door. With her hand in his, he led her up the steps. Gorgeous bushes and white flowers lined the walkway.

Gunz unlocked the front door and escorted Gray inside. Striking brunette hardwood paneling and floors filled the interior of the home. An appearance of awe was plastered onto Gray's face as Gunz gave her a tour of the quarters. The mansion held five bedrooms, six bathrooms, a gourmet kitchen, vaulted cathedral ceilings, French doors, a den, an office, a foyer with massive skylights, a pool with a waterfall, an outdoor cooking area, and a guest/maid quarters.

Although Gunz's place was gorgeous, it looked barely lived in. There was hardly any furniture or knick-knacks.

"I take it you don't come here too often." She turned and faced him.

"Nah, not really." He leaned up against the built-in kitchen island.

"Why not?"

"I just don't."

"I think the reason is because you get lonely. I mean, this is just too much house for one person."

"Maybe you're right." Gunz smiled.

"Is this one of the paintings you were talkin' about in Chicago?" Gray pointed to a self-portrait of the famed artist Salvador Dali.

"Yeah."

"It's beautiful in a sort of demented way."

"C'mon. I got a surprise for you." He took her hand.

"What kind of surprise?" Her face lit up.

"Come wit' me and you'll find out."

Gunz led Gray downstairs to the basement. She was shocked to find a bowling alley and arcade room, but what took the cake was when Gunz revealed his movie room. It wasn't fully finished, but a huge projector hung from the ceiling. Instead of sitting on custom made seats, he had a pallet on the floor. On top of the satin covers were beautiful handcrafted Indian pillows. In front of each of their pillows were popcorn buckets filled with an assortment of snacks. A popcorn machine and soda fountain were off to the side of the room.

"I can't believe you did all of this," she gushed.

"It's cool. Anything for you." He kissed her gently on the forehead. "C'mon. The movie about to start."

"What are we watching?" Gray asked as she took a seat on the floor.

"Since I know you like all them girlie flicks, I asked my man out in New York to get me a copy of that new Sarah Jessica Parker film."

"Oh my God. Thank you so much, Gunz. Nobody has ever done anything like this for me."

"A'ight, don't get all sentimental on me," he joked.

"No, for real, this is really sweet." Gray became quiet as tears filled the brims of her eyes.

"Come here." She leaned forward and placed her hands on both sides of his face.

Gunz closed his eyes as Gray lovingly kissed his lips. Whatever in life she wanted, he was willing to provide. He loved to see Gray happy. As long as she was satisfied, he was good. He just hoped they could get past all the drama. Gray was still very insecure and sensitive about everything that had gone down. And yes, he was the cause of it. Gunz knew at times he could be arrogant and all about self, but loving someone outside of himself and his family was new to him.

For as long as he could remember, he'd only had his own feelings to be concerned with. Sometimes, he looked at Gray and wondered, *Why does she stay?*

From day one, all she'd ever wanted was him. She always put him before herself. He never spent as much time with her as he could. Gunz knew deep down that he was unworthy of her love. He often questioned, could he be the man she needed him to be? Hopefully, if given the time, he would be able to figure it all out before it was too late.

Melt my heart to stone . . .

Adele, "Melt My Heart to Stone"

Chapter Thirteen

Gray never looked more beautiful. Everyone she encountered that night told her so. Her hair was perfectly styled and coiffed into a side bun. Chanel makeup adorned her face. The dusty pink kimono-sleeve Thayer mini-dress she rocked cost $300. On her feet were the black Givenchy ankle boots Gunz bought for her. As always, her eyebrows, nails, and feet were done to perfection, but none of that changed the fact that she felt miserable on the inside.

The man she adored stood before her, texting on his cell phone as if she were invisible. Half the night had passed, and they'd barely said two full sentences to each other. Kema and King were over to the side, laughing, drinking, and having a good time. No one seemed to notice or care about the torture she was going through. But Gray only had herself to blame. She'd wanted Gunz no matter the cost, and now she had him.

For years, she'd prayed to be in a relationship. She grew weary of spending all her weekends alone. She hated when the phone rang and it wasn't that special someone on the other end. It hadn't been fair that she didn't have someone to hold on to during the still of the night. Why couldn't she have a man to kiss all of her pain away? At last Gunz came into the picture.

On paper, he was everything she wanted: fine, wit' a pretty smile, fat pockets, and a big dick. You couldn't tell her in the beginning he wasn't sent from Jehovah himself. Gray never expected all of the bullshit that came along with him. None of that was a part of her fantasy. They were supposed to fall in love and ride off into the sunset. Never was she supposed to put his needs before her own not to get the same in return.

There were to be no tears. Her heart wasn't supposed to mend itself only to be let down time and time again. Maybe this was how all relationships were and someone forgot to give her the memo, or maybe Gunz just wasn't the man she wanted him to be. Either way, Gray was tired of teeter-tottering on the crossroads of disappointment.

"You okay?" Kema asked, taking a seat across from her.

"Uh-huh." Gray absentmindedly nodded her head.

"You sure? 'Cause you've been quiet all night."

"I'm fine." Gray forced herself to smile.

"Okay, let me know if you need something." Kema rubbed her knee then went back to dancing.

Gray sat back and folded her arms across her chest. She was past ready to end the night and go home. She just wasn't in the mood for being in a club around a bunch of drunken fools, especially when her man wasn't paying her any attention.

Feeling her eyes on him, Gunz stopped texting and looked over his shoulder.

Gray was staring directly at him with a fed up expression on her face. He was so sick of seeing her look like that. He understood that she was still hurt over the Devin situation, but damn, how long did he have to suffer behind it? Every time he turned around, she wanted to talk about how she felt and how he'd hurt her. If his phone rang and he didn't answer, she immediately assumed it was a chick. If he didn't come over like promised, he was fuckin' another chick. Gray had become the insecure woman he'd never wanted her to be. Gunz had bigger things to worry about than the made-up shit that was running through her brain. And no, he wasn't making light of her feelings; he just felt that if they were going to make it work, it was time for her to get past the drama and move on.

"What's wrong wit' you?" he said dryly, pulling up a chair.

"Nothing," she lied.

"You ready to go or something?"

"No. I mean, if you wanna leave, we can."

Gunz leaned his head back and exhaled. It was obvious to anyone with two eyes that Gray was ready to go. Why she wouldn't just admit it was beyond him. Gunz simply chalked it up to silly shit women do.

"Well, look, we can leave after I finish my drink."

"Okay."

Gray looked out the corner of her eye and watched as Gunz checked his phone. He'd received a new text message. She couldn't see what the message said, but she did recognize the name Devin on the screen. Gray felt as if she'd been stabbed one hundred times in the chest. The first question that came to her head was why she was still contacting him when he said they'd broken things off. *Maybe he did and she just won't get a clue*, Gray tried to convince herself, even though her gut was screaming out *Bitch, please*!

"You ready?" Gunz asked, bringing her back to reality.

"Yeah," she replied, grabbing her coat and clutch purse.

Gray gave Kema a hug and air kiss good-bye then followed silently behind Gunz back to his car.

"What is wrong wit' you?" he questioned, fed up.

Gray stopped dead in her tracks and looked up from the concrete.

"Why is Devin still textin' you?"

"What are you talkin' about?"

"You know exactly what I'm talkin' about. I saw her name on your screen."

"What was you doing lookin' at my phone?"

"I wasn't," she lied. "I just happened to look over and saw her name."

Pissed, Gunz opened the passenger door and let her inside without saying another word. Gray wanted an explanation, but he wasn't about to give her one. He didn't have to, because he wasn't doing shit. Once he too was in the car, he started the engine and hit the highway.

"So you not gon' answer my question?" She turned in her seat to face him.

"What you want me to say? She text me. You see I ain't reply back."

"But why is she still callin' you?"

"That's a good question. Why don't you call her back and ask her?"

Gray was speechless. A snarl formed on her face. *I can't stand his punk ass,* she thought.

"This is some bullshit," she whispered underneath her breath, turning back around straight.

"What you say?" Gunz took his eyes off the road.

"You heard me. I didn't stutter. This . . . is . . . some . . . bullshit." She bobbed her head.

"If it's so much some bullshit, then why you still fuckin' wit' me?" he shot.

"That's a good question," she quipped as they pulled up to his spot.

Gunz got out and slammed the door. Gray sat inside the car, fuming, thinking, *What the fuck am I doing? This nigga is so full of shit, and my dumb ass just keep on steppin' in it like a fool.*

Gunz popped the trunk and grabbed her overnight bag.

"Are you coming or are you gon' sit yo' ass in the car?" he shot, standing by the entrance door of the building.

Without uttering a response, she got out. An unsettling quietness swept through Gunz's condo as they stepped inside. Gray felt unwelcome and out of place. Gunz acted as if he didn't even want her there. Instead of making her feel at home, he proceeded with taking off his clothes and going to bed. Not knowing what else to do, Gray followed suit. Gunz pretended not to watch as she stripped down to only her black lace Agent Provocateur panty and bra set.

Since he was mad at her, he was happy that the comforter over him concealed the hard-on he had growing inside his boxers. He didn't want Gray to have the satisfaction of knowing her body alone made his dick hard.

Unable to rest, she sat up underneath the covers. Too much was on her mind, and she wasn't about to leave any of it unsaid.

"What are we doing?"

"Going to sleep," Gunz answered with his face buried in the pillow.

"You don't even sleep, and you know that's not what I'm talkin' about. What are we doing? Better yet, what am I doing? This is not how it's supposed to be."

"What are you talkin' about now, Gray?" he huffed.

"This is not the relationship I envisioned for myself. You are not giving me what I need."

"What the fuck you mean, I ain't giving you what you need? Don't I take care of you?"

"Yeah, but it's about more than that. You don't love me. Hell, you not even my man. All we doing is fuckin', so technically all I am is a high-price ho."

"Are you fuckin' conscious? Are you even listening to yourself right now?" he asked as his cell phone began to ring.

Gunz picked up his phone from off the nightstand and checked the screen, but opted not to answer it.

"Hmm, must be a bitch," Gray scoffed.

"Real talk, you need to chill out," he warned, fed up.

"Whateva, Gunz. Since when you don't answer yo' phone?"

Before he could reply with a smart comeback, his phone rang again.

"Answer it!"

"How can I answer the phone when I'm 'sleep?" He laughed.

"I'm glad you think this shit a game."

The words weren't even all the way out of Gray's mouth when there was a buzz at his door. An ache resonated through Gray's body so strong that the air in her lungs ceased. It was apparent that whoever had just called Gunz was now at his door. Gray checked her watch. It was 3:00 AM. She'd grown to know Gunz well enough that if it were a business call, he would've answered. The fact that he didn't confirmed her female intuition that the caller and person at the door was a chick. The only person that came to mind was Devin. It had to be her. Gray would've bet her last dollar that it was.

"Let me guess; you not gon' answer the door either?"

"Nope. Whoever that is will get the hint." Gunz folded his arms underneath his head, unfazed.

If he didn't play it cool, Gray would see the worry in his eyes. Devin was really on some immature shit. Ever since he'd broken things off with her, she'd begun to bug the fuck out of him. If she wasn't calling, she was texting or stopping by unannounced. She insisted that they should be together and that the bond they'd built throughout the years was unbreakable. Gunz didn't know what it was going to take for her to see that he wasn't feeling her like that.

"I ain't got time for this shit." Gray snatched the covers from off her body and shot up.

"Where you going?" He sat up.

"Home!" She started to put on her dress.

"Quit trippin', man. Calm down and get back in the bed."

"I wish I would. Fuck that. You ain't about to sit up here and disrespect me."

"So I'm tryin' to disrespect you 'cause I don't feel like answering the door?" he questioned, perplexed.

"Whateva, Gunz. You play too many games." Gray waved him off.

"Now I play too many games. Which one is it? 'Cause I can't possibly be doing both," he joked.

Gray ignored him and placed on her heels. Whoever was at the door had stopped buzzing the bell and left.

"So you really about to leave?" he asked as she picked up her purse.

Gray continued to give him the silent treatment as she grabbed her overnight bag. *I should've never brought my ass over here in the first place*, she thought, heading toward the door.

"Gray." Gunz jumped out of the bed and followed her. He caught up with her and took her hand.

"Don't touch me." She jerked her hand away.

"What the fuck is your problem?"

"You're my problem! I can't keep on doing this shit wit' you!"

"What shit? You the one that's trippin'!"

"Gunz, you got a a fuckin' bitch at your door at

three o'clock in the morning and I ain't supposed to say shit? Like, you really got me fucked up," she stressed, shooting him a look that could kill.

"I got you fucked up? Really?" he stated sarcastically. "Gray, I swear to God, sometimes you be on some bullshit."

"You know what? I ain't even for all the back and forth bullshit. Do you want to be wit' me or not? 'Cause I ain't the one for holding on to a muthafucka that don't wanna be kept."

"If I didn't want to be wit' you, do you think I would be tryin' this hard?"

"Hard," she repeated in disbelief. "Gunz, you haven't tried to do shit! What, you think 'cause you call me every now and then and spend a little time with me that you trying? Nigga, please." She looked him up and down.

"So that's honestly how you feel?" Gunz questioned, crushed.

"It's always something wit' you. If you not standing me up, you lying to me or fuckin' wit' another female. You not gon' do me like that."

"I thought we was tryin' to get past all that."

"How can we when shit like this keep on happening? Just be a man about it and admit that you still fuckin' around."

"See, you hardheaded." He pointed his finger in her face. "How many times I gotta tell you that I ain't fuckin' wit' nobody else? I know I was on some fucked-up shit at first, but since we've been back together, I've been good. I ain't tryin' to be wit' no one but you, Gray, and you know that." He stepped closer. "I need you."

Hearing him say the words *I need you* caused Gray's heart to skip a beat, but that didn't stop the growing suspicions that plagued her mind.

"I don't know, Gunz."

"You mean to tell me after everything we've been through you, gon' leave me now?" he spoke softly in her ear.

"Maybe we should just let each other go now before one of us gets hurts," she suggested, really not wanting to.

"How can I let you go when your heart's where I lay my head?"

Gray rubbed her forehead, overwhelmed. Her gut was telling her to walk away, but her heart couldn't bear the notion. Gunz had a hold on her that was unbreakable.

"Just come lay down." He lovingly caressed the side of her face.

Before Gray could react, his lips were on hers. She felt smothered yet wanted at the same time. Gunz's hands roamed up her thighs. Seconds later, her hands were gripping the sheets. The freakiness she and Gunz created was sinfully orgasmic. She'd cum numerous times, but the thought still lingered: *Why do I feel so empty?*

It was morning. The dim light from the sky shone across Gray's face. For hours, she'd been in between sleep and consciousness. She wished that the events from the night before had all been in a dream, but the harsh reality of the dried-up wet spot next to her forced the painful memory to resurface. With each second that passed, she felt less and less like herself. Nothing was as it should be. She knew she was more than just a toy for Gunz's satisfaction.

It wasn't fair that he was getting his cake and eating it too, while she was being force fed bullshit on a daily basis. Gray could hear the sound of the shower running in the distance. She swallowed the lump in her throat and focused on a line in the hardwood floor. It seemed to go on for days. As she followed it, the line led her to the bathroom and straight to Gunz.

Gray shook her head and sat up. The cold sensation from the floor chilled her feet. One of Gunz's old Biggie T-shirts was lying in a chair across the room. She grabbed it and put it on. The shirt was two times too big, but the smell of his Jean Paul Gautier cologne made up for the fit.

Gray was just about to head downstairs to the kitchen when she heard the all too familiar sound of Gunz's cell phone ringing. He'd received a text message. Gray wondered if she should check it. The shower was still running. Maybe she had enough time.

Her heart was racing. The palms of her hands became clammy with sticky sweat. She knew it was wrong to invade his privacy, but the nagging thoughts in her head had to be silenced once and for all.

Gray looked over her shoulder and tiptoed quickly over to the nightstand. Quietly, she picked up the phone. Once more before opening it, she glanced over her shoulder. The coast was clear. Gray flipped open the phone. The message was from Devin. It read: Who is it gon' be? Her or me?

Gray's hands trembled. All of that time he'd been lying to her face. She'd asked him time and time again if he was still seeing Devin, and each time, the reply was no. Why was he doing her like that? Was he intentionally trying to hurt her? Did he enjoy seeing her cry? Maybe his intentions were to drive her insane. Whichever one it was, Gray had had enough.

"What you doing wit' my phone?"

Startled, she jumped and turned around. Gunz stood in the doorway with a menacing scowl on his face. Beads of water cascaded down his chiseled physique and to the floor. The only thing that covered him was the blue, tan, and white cotton towel wrapped around his defined waist.

"Answer me!" he shouted.

"I needed to know the truth," she answered nervously.

"What the fuck you mean, you needed to know the truth? I gave you the truth last night!"

"Gunz, I don't know what to believe anymore when it comes to you."

"So instead of coming to me you go through my phone? You really thought that was okay?"

"I didn't say it was okay." She tried to explain, but Gunz wouldn't allow it.

"Get the fuck out."

"What?" Gray looked at him, confused.

"You heard me. Get . . . the . . . fuck . . . out!"

"How the fuck you gon' tell me to leave when you the one caught up? And what the hell does she mean, is it gon' be her or me?" She held up his phone.

"Man, fuck all that bullshit!" His nostrils flared;

he was so angry. "How would you feel if I went through yo' shit?" He picked up her purse and emptied the contents.

All of Gray's personal belongings, like her lip gloss, tampons, and wallet fell to the floor. Gunz located her phone.

"Let's see . . ." He scrolled through her address book. "Who the fuck is Allen? Huh? Who the fuck is Chad Dickerson from GEICO Insurance? You fuckin' him, Gray?"

"Fuck you!"

"No, fuck you!" He threw her phone at her. Gray quickly caught it.

"This is too much." Gunz shook his head. "I can't do it. Nah, fuck that. I *won't* do it. I love you, Gray, but we need to chill out for a second."

"What?" She froze in place, astonished by his words.

"This right here," he said, pointing his finger back and forth between them, "ain't gon' work."

"Let me get this straight. You leaving me alone?"

"For right now, yeah."

Gray was astonished. She never imagined things between them would end with him being the one to say good-bye. Maybe it was all her fault. For the past year, she'd done nothing but make excuses for his intentions and pretend that he was the man she'd wanted him to be. The truth of the matter was that Gray was the only one in love. He hadn't even recognized that she'd been wearing her heart on her sleeve, waiting day by day for him to open up his too.

"So that's it? It's just over?" She looked at him. "After all the bullshit you've put me through, it's over now 'cause I went through your phone? Really, Gunz?"

"Look, man, I'm tryin' not to hurt yo' feelings, but I ain't feelin' this." Gunz couldn't even look her in the eyes as the words slipped from his mouth.

Gray simply nodded her head. "It's cool. You know what? Fuck you! I should've left yo' tired ass alone a long time ago," she spat, beyond pissed.

This time, there would be no compromising or long, drawn out conversations. There weren't any words to make him want her anyway. She was tired of seeing the look in his eyes that shot her dead each and every time. Bitter beyond words, Gray swallowed her pride, grabbed her things, and left without expressing another word.

My eyes are green 'cause I eat a lot of vegetables. It don't have nothin' to do wit' your new friend . . .

Erykah Badu, "Green Eyes"

Chapter Fourteen

"Smoke" by Mary J. Blige was stuck on repeat. Gray sat on her butt with her knees up to her chest, singing the words as tears slid out the corners of her eyes and under her chin. "Why you're gone, the reason is supposed to make sense, but it don't, but it don't, it don't, it don't . . . ohhhhh, it don't." Almost a week had gone by and she hadn't left her room. Gray knew it was wrong to call off of work, but she just couldn't handle the pressure of having to concentrate on work and deal with a broken heart.

It seemed like the only time she moved was when the smell from her body got to be too much to bear. Food had become a foreign object, and sleep was a concept she for some reason, couldn't grasp. Every time she moved, Gray could sense that her stomach had caved in, but she didn't care. It didn't matter that she was so weak and feeble she could barely walk. The only thing that mattered was that Gunz was gone. He'd tried calling to apologize for the way things went down, but all they would end up doing was arguing.

Gray stressed how he lied and cheated, but none

of that was of his concern anymore. She'd gone through his phone and betrayed his trust, so now things were over, finito, finished, done. It fucked Gray up that out of all the bullshit he'd put her through, this was how their so-called relationship ended. There were numerous times she could've told him to step, but she didn't. Maybe that was her fault for looking past all the warning signs.

Since she'd known Gunz, he'd done nothing but shower her with lies. And yes, it was wrong, but she wished him nothing but antagonizing pain and loneliness. She hoped his nights were cold and filled with remorseful memories of her. Like Jazmine Sullivan, she wanted to bust the windows out of his car. It wouldn't mend her broken heart, but Gunz couldn't go around playing with people's feelings, especially hers.

As Gray grabbed a tissue to blow her nose, she heard a loud knock on the front door. She wondered who could've gotten past the gate. Wiping her face, she walked briskly down the steps.

"Who is it?" Her voice cracked.

"Us, girl. Open up the goddamn door," Tee-Tee responded.

Gray loved her friends, but she really wasn't in the mood for a bunch of "I told you so." Inhaling deeply, she wiped the disappointed look off her face and opened the door. The whole squad was there: Tee-Tee, Kema, and Heidi. They'd even brought her favorite guilty pleasure, McDonald's.

"Guuuurl, you look a hot mess." Tee-Tee tuned up his lips, almost not wanting to come in.

"Fuck you." Gray turned around, leaving them standing there.

"No, fuck you, lookin' like who did it and what . . . the . . . fuck . . . fo'." He and the girls came in and began taking off their coats and boots.

Gray was a wreck. Dried tears traced her face. She hadn't combed her hair in weeks, and her body and water hadn't spoken in days.

"Bitch, you know I'm over here going through something." Gray plopped down onto her zebra print chaise lounge.

"You over here smellin' like something too. What, you and Jarrod been talkin', comparing notes and shit about who funk smell the best?"

"Nigga, don't be talkin' about my man," Heidi jumped in.

"Now he yo' man? I swear y'all bitches is crazy! Ain't got not one bit of damn sense! You up here shacking up wit' a goddamn dirt ball." He pointed to Heidi. "You over here ten seconds away from a nut house behind a man that *told you* . . . from *day one* he ain't want a relationship! And you,"—he looked at Kema—"you'll open up yo' legs for anybody wit' a dollar bill!"

"You goddamn right." Kema lifted her legs in the air. "All money is good money."

"That's a goddamn shame." Tee-Tee pursed his lips, shaking his head.

"Anyway, I know yo' ass ain't talkin'," Heidi snapped. "It wasn't too long ago when we had to have a "fuck 'em, girl" meeting for yo' ass."

"See, you always bringing up old shit," he snarled. "But this ain't about me. I gots me a dime piece. This about this depressed ho. You better get yo' mind together. Fuck Gunz. He ain't nobody.

We told you not to fuck wit' his ol' lying, sexy ass in the first place."

"Okay, now, how is that helping me any? And GIVE ME MY GODDAMN FOOD!" Gray snatched the bag from his hands.

"Oh, see, yo' hungry ass done lost yo' mind. Gray, don't make me dropkick you."

"Whateva," she replied, munching on a hot crispy fry.

"For real, Gray, you do gotta get up." Heidi rubbed the outside of her hand. "And I'm not saying it's not okay to cry, but cry, wipe your eyes, and get something accomplished. Your life has not stopped because that nigga ain't around no more. He wanna step, let him go, 'cause at the end of the day, you can't make somebody want to be wit' you. It's either they do or they don't. If a nigga tellin' you he don't want to be in a relationship, then you gotta respect that and play your position or move on."

"I mean, I understand that, but we had an understanding that we weren't supposed to be seeing other people. He promised that if he started fuckin' wit' somebody else that he would let me know," Gray tried to explain.

"Gray, are you listening to yourself right now?" Kema looked at her like she was retarded. "What man in they right mind gon' tell you that he fuckin' wit' somebody else? Ain't no nigga gon' do that shit, especially if they like you. That nigga was gon' keep on fuckin' you and whoever else he was fuckin'."

"Personally, I blame you." Tee-Tee sat back in his seat and crossed his legs.

"Excuse me?" Gray arched her right eyebrow in surprise.

"You're excused. Gunz has remained who he is since the beginning. He told you 'I like you, I enjoy spending time with you, and I wanna keep you in my life, but I'm . . . not . . . the man for . . . you.' You the one that tried to make y'all li'l relationship more than what it was. You tried to make Gunz be this prince charming, riding in on a white horse, when really, from the start, all y'all shoulda been was fuck buddies."

It hurt like hell to hear it, but Gray knew her friends were right.

"I mean, do you even think that he loved you?" Heidi asked.

"Honestly, I do. I just think that things got to be way too much too soon for him, and that I wanted him to be more than what he was."

"Well, I just hope you don't go back to him," Kema proclaimed.

"You do not have to worry about that. Me and Gunz are over for good."

Gunz zoned out and bobbed his head to the mellow '70s classic, "Sunshine," by Roy Ayers. Lying back with his feet propped up, he inhaled smoke from a Garcia Vega. It was rolled so tight it could barely hit. Gunz was on a mission to get as high as the sky. His heart missed Gray too much to deal with the fact that she was gone. Maybe he'd over-reacted by saying they needed a break, but things between them had to change.

She didn't trust him, and maybe that was his

fault; but from the moment he stepped to her door promising he was a changed man, he had been. Gunz had finally set all the bullshit aside and aligned his heart with hers. He just hated that once again he was to blame for her pain, but he'd warned her from the start that he wasn't ready for a relationship. Somehow, all of that got lost in the wind and he was branded the bad guy. Now shit was all fucked up. He'd ended their relationship on an immature impulse, and Gray wasn't trying to hear a word he had to say.

That didn't stop Gunz from wanting her back. He was a man with pride, but some nights, his body ached to be near her so bad it made him sick. He longed to hear the sound of her sweet voice. Gunz just wished he could talk to her.

His wish came true when his phone started to ring. He didn't even bother to look at the screen.

"Hello?"

"We need to talk," a female voice said.

"Who is this?"

"Devin."

"Do the Naomi Campbell walk, Naomi Campbell walk. Walk across the room like Naomi Campbell!" All the girls sang the words to Beyoncé's song as Tee-Tee strutted down the hallway of his condo with his hand on his hip.

"You . . . better . . . work," Kema yelled, clapping.

Gray cracked up laughing. This was what her life had been missing—fun. For months, all she had was one drama-filled moment after another, but no more. It was New Year's Eve and she was gonna start the new year off right. Taking center stage, Gray snapped for the kids.

"Okay, bitch," Heidi shrilled in delight as Gray did her thing.

"That is my shit," Gray stated, plopping down on the floor after the song went off.

"Right. I still bump that in the car," Kema agreed.

"My big ass need a drink. Who else need their glass filled?" Tee-Tee asked, going into the kitchen.

"Me," all three women yelled.

"Drunk asses!"

"Whateva. I need to drink," Heidi confessed. "Jarrod ol' dirty ass is driving me crazy."

"Yo' ass is insane. One minute he's ya boo, and the next y'all broke up. Which one is it?" Gray quizzed.

"Right now we're broke up, but his retarded ass just won't get the hint."

"What he be doing, girl?"

"He calls my phone every five minutes wanting something. It has gotten to the point where half the time I don't even answer my phone 'cause I'm afraid it's him. At first I kind of felt bad for letting him go, but I can't deal with a muthafucka who can't read and don't wash his ass. I mean, I could've bought that nigga Hooked on Phonics, but not taking baths? Uh-uh." She twisted her face in disgust.

"I didn't know the nigga couldn't read," Tee-Tee said, coming back into the room.

"I was too embarrassed to tell anybody. This muthafucka always tryin' to take somebody to a nice restaurant knowing he can't read shit on the menu. One night we went to Lucas Park and Grille to eat. This dumb coon pronounces it *grillay*."

"Hell to the naw."

"Then he pronounces *café*, *calf*."

"Wow."

"He gets on my damn nerves. I swear to God. But anyway, what's going on wit' you and King?" Heidi turned her attention to Kema.

"He cool. I mean, you know I'm still doing me, but he a cool li'l daddy. I just talked to him the other day. By the way, I ain't know Gunz got a baby on the way."

"Wit' who?" Gray scrunched up her face and placed down her glass.

"The chick that he cheated on you with. I thought you knew."

"By the way she looking, evidently not," Tee-Tee barked. "You okay, mama?"

"I guess," she replied, stunned.

"Girl, fuck him," Kema retorted. "Don't be sittin' up there getting all depressed again over that shit. You was too good for his ass anyway."

"Her feelings are still hurt, Kema." Tee-Tee rolled his eyes.

"Fuck that! You think he over there trippin' off her? No! 'Cause guess what? He a nigga. The same day they broke up, I bet you he ate, put on some clothes, went out, and came back home and went to sleep while her ass"—she pointed at Gray—"was sittin' at home, cryin' her eyes out."

"I'll be back." Gray got up from the floor.

"Look what you did." Tee-Tee pushed Kema in

the arm. "If she start cryin', I swear to God it's gon' be a 'code ten, man down' situation."

Gray stepped outside onto the balcony. The sky was as dark as Gunz's skin. There was no way it could be true. Devin couldn't be pregnant. If she was, that meant he was fucking them both without a condom. She had to get confirmation.

Gray pulled out her cell phone and dialed his number. He picked up on the second ring. It was almost like he'd been waiting on her phone call.

"You busy?" she asked.

"Nah, you good."

Gray could tell from the tone of his voice that he was smoking.

"I called to ask you a question."

"What's up?" He exhaled the smoke.

"And please just tell me the truth. Do you and Devin have a baby on the way?"

Gunz sucked in his bottom lip and closed his eyes. Everything in him wanted to lie, but lying had gotten them in the position they were in now. He just knew if he told the truth, things between them would be over for good.

"Yeah, man," he finally answered.

If Gray had a gun, she would've shot him. "So you were fuckin' her while you were fuckin' me?"

"It wasn't even nothing like that."

"Well, what was it, Gunz?" Her voice trembled. "Are y'all together?"

"Thanks to you, I ain't wit' nobody."

"I can't believe this shit." She shook her head in disbelief. "This shit is crazy. You got a fuckin' baby on the way."

For a couple of seconds, they sat in silence, un-sure of what to say. Neither wanted to be the one to say good-bye, but the words were inevitable.

"Well . . . that's all I wanted," Gray finally spoke up. "So that's it, huh?"

"I mean, what else do you want me to say?"

"I guess nothing."

"All right then."

"Bye," Gunz replied before hanging up.

Truth held Gray up by the waist and led her into her loft. They'd just left Brennan's in the Central West End. Gray was wasted. All night she'd gone on and on about Gunz, and although Truth would've rather discussed dog feces, he played the role of supportive friend and listened. He hadn't even tripped off the fact that she'd drunk too much. By the end of the night, Gray's words had started to slur. When she went to stand up, her legs gave out and he had to catch her. That's when he knew she'd had enough. Truth picked her up and carried her into her bedroom.

"I need to go pee." She tapped him in the chest.

"No, you don't, Gray."

"How you gon' tell me what I gotta do?" she yelled.

" 'Cause you just got done peeing two minutes ago in the lobby restroom."

"Oh . . . I sure did." She giggled. "Arggggggh, excuse me." She burped then cracked up laughing.

"Come on and lay down." Truth placed her down onto the bed.

Gray was so out of it that she couldn't even take off her own clothes.

"Gunz, take off my shoe."

"What did you say?" Truth asked, standing in front of the bed.

"You heard me. Take off my shoe." She propped her right leg up in the air.

The bottom of her dress fell up above her waist. Truth could see the white silk lining of her panties. Her body had changed since back in high school. Gray's thighs and legs were succulent and firm.

"Baby, what you waiting on?" she whined, running her fingers through her hair.

Truth realized in his heart that what he was about to do was wrong, but he couldn't hold back the urge to kiss Gray. If she thought he was Gunz, he'd happily play along.

With her foot in his hand, he slowly undid the strap on her heel. Gray had the prettiest feet. She always kept them polished and pedicured. Truth took her pinky toe in his mouth and sucked.

"Oooooh, Gunz," she moaned.

"You like that, baby?"

"Yes."

Truth lovingly placed a trail of kisses from her feet down to the inner part of her thigh. The print of her pussy was staring him right in the face. He had to get a taste. Truth set the seat of her panties aside. Closing his eyes, he placed his nose up to the lips of her pussy and inhaled. He would forever cherish the scent. Truth swirled his tongue around the bud of her clit. It instantly hardened, letting him know she was aroused.

"Gunz, I love you." She rubbed the top of Truth's head.

"I love you too."

"Ahhhhhh," Gray groaned when she woke up the next morning.

She could hear the sound of bacon crackling downstairs. The smell made her sick. The question was, who was at her house cooking breakfast? Covering her mouth, she tried to prevent herself from throwing up. Unable to suppress the chunks of food in the back of her throat, she ran to the master bathroom. She barely made it to the toilet before pink vomit spewed from her mouth and slid down her chin.

Gray placed her hands on the toilet to balance herself. The cold tile from the marble floor caused a chill to run up her spine. After throwing up once more, she wiped her mouth with the back of her hand. Nauseated beyond belief, she slowly got up from the floor and made her way over to the sink. Gray turned on the faucet. A mixture of cold and hot water poured into her hands. Bending over, she splashed her face. The warm water soothed her skin.

"I didn't know you were up," she heard a voice say from behind.

Scared out of her mind, Gray jumped and turned around.

"I'm sorry. I didn't mean to scare you." Truth grabbed a fresh towel from the rack.

"What are you doing here?" she asked, confused by his presence.

"What do you mean, silly?" He took the towel and patted her face.

Gray grabbed his hands and stopped him. "No, for real. What are you doing here?" This time she asked in a tone that let him know she wasn't playing.

"You don't remember, do you?" he asked with a quizzical expression on his face.

"Remember what?"

"I spent the night. We slept together, Gray."

"What you mean, like slept in the bed wit' each other?"

"No, *slept together*, slept together," he stressed.

"No, we didn't." She laughed.

Truth stood frozen with a deranged look on his face. "What's so funny?"

"You." Gray turned back to face the mirror. "You know damn well we didn't sleep together."

"Why would I lie to you about something like that?"

"You're serious?" She turned back around.

"Yes, you told me you loved me."

Gray was mortified. Had she really slept with Truth? For the first time since she woke up, she looked down at herself. She was still in the dress from the night before, except the airy sensation between her legs let her know her panties were missing. Gray rushed past Truth and into her room. The bed was a mess. The white Victoria's Secret panties she wore had been thrown in the middle of the floor. Truth's clothes were too.

"Are you gonna be okay?" Truth questioned as she sat on the edge of her bed.

"Yeah, I'm just in shock. I don't remember a thing."

"Well, that makes me feel good," he stated in a sarcastic tone.

"Oh no, I'm sorry. I didn't mean it like that." She patted his hand.

"It's cool. You enjoyed yourself last night; I promise."

"That's good to know," she stated mockingly. "Did we use a condom?"

"No. You said you didn't want me to," Truth lied.

"Really?" Gray asked, unsure.

"Gray, why would I lie to you?"

"It's just all so weird." She massaged her temples.

"Look, everything is going to be okay." He bent down and caressed her face. "Trust me. Now, I cooked breakfast, so once you get cleaned up, come downstairs and eat."

"Truth, we need to talk."

"Shhhh." He placed his index finger up to her lips. "Not right now. Let's just enjoy the moment."

Gray could see how happy he was. She didn't want to hurt him, but eventually it would have to be done. She would never see him in a romantic way. She hoped when the time was right for her to tell him, he'd understand.

It was one of those days where everything seemed to go wrong. From the minute Gunz woke up, it had been one bad thing after another. Watts called and said that a shipment was lost; then Devin called and said she didn't feel good and was too afraid to be alone, so Gunz got out of bed and went to get her. Since then, he'd regretted his decision. If she wasn't nagging him, she was complaining.

Gunz didn't know how he would be able to put up with her for eighteen more years. On top of that, his mother called with news that his father was in the hospital. She wouldn't tell him what for, though, over the phone. Gunz pulled up to Barnes-Jewish Hospital with Devin in tow. She refused to stay back at his house. After stopping at the receptionist's desk, they hopped on an elevator to the triage center. Gunz's mother, grandmother, and uncles were already there.

"Gavin." His grandmother rushed over to him.

"What's going on?"

"Uh-uh, who is this?" She stepped in front of him and stared Devin up and down.

"Hi. I'm Devin." She stuck out her hand for a shake.

"Hi. . . . Where is Gray?"

"At home, I guess. Can we talk about that later?" Gunz spoke, aggravated.

"Sorry. Look, sweetie, I'm not tryin' to be rude, but this is a family matter. Do you mind stepping outside?"

"No problem." Devin faked a smile.

Once she was out of the room, Gunz's grandmother sat him down. He stared over at his father. He was asleep, with tubes in his nose and arms. He looked completely different from the last time he'd seen him at the barbecue. His skin was dry and ashy. He looked like he'd lost over fifteen pounds. For the first time, Gunz allowed himself to feel sorry for him.

"What's wrong wit' him? Why he look like that?" he asked.

"Gavin, your father is dying."

"What?" He turned with a bewildered look on his face.

"You father has full blown AIDS."

"I wanted to tell you, sweetie." His mother placed her hand on his shoulder.

Gunz didn't know what to say. Was he supposed to cry, or show some type of emotion? He'd just gotten used to the idea of his father being back around, and now he was about to taken away again, this time for good.

"Why you ain't tell me?"

"He didn't want us to."

"So that's what we do now in this family—keep secrets?"

"Don't be mad at them, Gavin," his father spoke in a raspy voice.

"Joseph, you need to rest." His mother stroked his hand.

"I know, ma."

"I'm sorry it took me so long to get here." Gray rushed into the room.

Gunz spun around in his seat and looked in her direction. He couldn't have been more surprised to see her. It had been over a month since their last encounter. It felt good to see her face; being around her made him feel relaxed.

For Gray, all of the feelings she'd been trying to

suppress came flooding back. She quickly looked the other way.

"Gray, it's so good to see you." His mother hugged her.

"What is she doing here?" Gunz asked.

"Uh-uh, rudeness." Vivian wagged her finger at him.

"What?"

"I told them to invite her," Joseph spoke up.

"How are you feeling, Mr. Marciano?" Gray asked, ignoring Gunz.

"Okay, I guess."

"Gunz, can I talk to you for a second?" Devin asked, reentering the room.

For some reason, Gray was shocked to see her. Her eyes immediately darted to her stomach. She wasn't showing yet.

"Uh, yeah." He got up to leave.

He was almost happy to. The tension in the room was so thick you could cut it with a knife.

"What is it?"

"I just wanted to know was everything all right?" she asked, sincerely worried.

"No . . . look here." He went into his pocket. "Why don't you go on home?"

"Why, 'cause she's here?" she shot, ready to go off.

"No, because I'm askin' you to. Besides, you said you wasn't feeling good. Don't you think you need to go home and rest?" Gunz tried to reason.

Devin wanted to object, but she couldn't argue his point.

"All right." She took the money. "Will you at least call me when you get home?"

"I can't make you no promises. I'll see what I can do."

Devin looked into his troubled eyes and attempted to kiss his lips, but Gunz wasn't feeling it, so instead he turned his face and gave her his cheek. Devin was devastated. If only Gunz could see how much she adored him. Instead of reacting negatively to his dismissal of her kiss, she simply gave him a slight smile and pressed the DOWN button on the elevator.

Once she was gone, Gunz went back into the room.

"Can you all give me and Gavin a minute alone?" Joseph requested.

Everybody obliged his wish and stepped out into the hallway. Gunz pulled up a seat next to his bed.

"You know Gray is sure sweet on you." Joseph tried to smile.

"How you know?"

" 'Cause every time you walk out of the room her eyes turn gray. And when you return, they turn blue again."

"That's impossible." Gunz waved him off.

"How do you know, smart guy? You ever seen the color of her eyes when you're not in the room?"

"Hmm." He rubbed his chin.

"You know, I know we haven't had the best relationship, but I really want the best for you. I don't want you to be like me, Gavin. My life has been a mess. I didn't have anybody and it was my entire fault. I pushed everyone away."

"Now, I don't know what's going on wit' you and Gray, but I seen how happy you were with her. Don't let your pride hinder you, son. You'll regret it in the end. Believe me; I know. Every time I see you and your mother, I regret my decisions. You all mean the world to me. And I know it might not mean much to you, but I was at Adriana's funeral."

Gunz looked at his father, shocked.

"I attended the burial. I saw you holding your mother."

Tears slipped from his eyes as he thought back on the day.

"Why didn't you let us know you were there?" Gunz asked, confused.

"Y'all were going through enough and I didn't want to make it worse. Besides, you didn't need to see me like that. I was a mess."

"And here I was thinking all these years that you didn't care."

"I've always loved you, son. I love you more than you know. The problem was that I didn't know how to love myself."

Whenever you look at me . . .

Chapter Fifteen

For the past three months, Gray had been feeling nauseated and fatigued. Every ten minutes she had to pee, and her breasts had even been tender and swollen, but she didn't pay it any mind because her period was still coming; however, during the third month of her symptoms, her period didn't make its monthly visit. That's when Gray became worried.

Now she sat alone in a state of shock. Her mind couldn't comprehend what she was seeing. There she was, sitting on top of the toilet seat with a white stick in her hand. The pregnancy test confirmed that she was indeed pregnant. Truth would be ecstatic to learn the news. They'd been spending a lot of time together.

The problem was Gray didn't know how she felt about it. She'd always envisioned herself being a mother; she just never pictured the father being Truth. They weren't even a couple.

"What am I gonna do?" she spoke out loud to herself as she stood up and faced the mirror.

Gray was the epitome of grace and beauty. Her

hair, makeup, and clothes were flawless as usual. People around her thought her life was picture perfect and that she had it going on. If only they knew that she felt sad and worn out on the inside. Plus, thoughts of what Gunz would think when he found out tormented her mind.

Why the fuck do you even care? He got a baby on the way too, her conscience screamed.

Gray felt stupid and confused. The only thing she could do was gaze off into space and shake her head; that was, until her assistant, Breann, buzzed her office. Gray quickly pulled herself together, washed her hands, and rushed over to her desk.

She cleared her throat before speaking. "Yes."

"Sorry to bother you, Gray, but can you come out to my desk? I think you need to take a second look at the Perfect Proposal article before I send it over to Sienna."

"Sure, Breann, I'll be right there."

Gray wondered what the problem could be as she walked over to the door. She'd gone over the article a million times. It was perfect.

"So what's the problem?" she asked.

"Right here." Breann turned the paper around to face Gray. "Look at this."

To Gray's surprise, written in bold print letters were: GRAY, WILL YOU MARRY ME?

"What?" she whispered.

"Behind you." Breann pointed and giggled.

Gray swiftly spun around and found Truth, along with Sienna and all of her other coworkers, smiling. Truth was charmingly handsome in a classic black Hugo Boss suit. The lapel of the jacket was unbuttoned, revealing a crisp white shirt. On his feet were a pair of patent leather lace-up Salvatore Ferragamo dress shoes. A robust bouquet of pink peonies and a small black velvet box completed the picture perfect moment.

"Are you okay?" he asked, handing her the flowers and taking her hand.

"Uhhhh, I guess," Gray answered, flabbergasted.

"Look, I know you're in shock." Truth got down on one knee. "But, Gray, I love you. I've loved you from the day we met, and I know that if you give us a chance, I can make you happy. You're the one for me. Please tell me I'm the one for you and say yes."

Gray stood shell shocked as everyone looked on, awaiting her answer. She couldn't believe Truth was proposing. Yes, they'd been hanging out a lot, but she hadn't made any real commitment to him.

Maybe it's a sign, she thought. Gray was carrying his baby. Maybe they were supposed to be together. She and Gunz didn't have a future. He was building a life with Devin. Why should she deprive herself of some happiness too?

"Yes, I'll marry you."

The smile on Truth's face lit up the entire room. Everyone clapped and cheered as he placed a Martin Flyer platinum-beaded round diamond engagement ring onto her finger. Truth stood up and took her into his arms.

"You are making me so happy," he spoke softly into her ear.

"Uh-huh." Gray hugged him back, all the while thinking, *What am I doing?*

*   *   *

Gunz sped down 1-70 blasting "Live Your Life" by T.I. and Rihanna. Bobbing his head to the beat, he mashed his foot on the gas. The speedometer raced up to eighty miles per hour. Thoughts of his father swarmed his mental museum. He'd spent the last three hours at the hospital with him. Watching his father die was a tiring and agonizing experience.

Each day, his father grew more weak and exhausted. He'd lost so much weight that he was barely recognizable. The one good part of it all was the many long conversations he and Gunz shared. Joseph called it droppin' jewels. During their daily chats, he relayed many life lessons he'd learned throughout the years.

Gunz listened with an open heart and mind to each story. He'd learned that although his father wasn't a perfect man and had made many mistakes, he was very smart and insightful. He realized that in life you needed two things: your family and the love of a good woman. Gunz already had his family by his side; the only thing missing was Gray. Pushing her away was the worst decision he'd made in life thus far.

Gunz was just getting off the exit when he received a call from his mother.

"What up, Ma?" he asked, excited to hear her voice.

"Gavin . . ."

"Yeah."

"I don't know how to tell you this, but . . . your father just passed."

* * *

"You got it smelling good in here." Gray stepped into the kitchen and watched as Truth cut up pieces of chicken into cubes. He was preparing her favorite meal, chicken and shrimp alfredo with broccoli.

"Thanks, Future." He leaned over and kissed her cheek.

A flashback of Gunz uttering the same words instantly entered her mind.

"Can you please not call me that?" She turned and opened the fridge.

"Why not? You are my future wife."

"I know. I just . . . don't like the term, that's all." Gray poured herself a glass of cranberry apple juice.

"A'ight," Truth replied, slightly put off.

It bothered him that since his proposal, Gray hadn't been able to look him in the eye. When she did, it was almost like she was seeing through him. It was obvious that her heart wasn't his. It still belonged to Gunz. Truth was nothing more than her rebound guy, but with time, after they were married and the baby was born, she'd feel differently.

"Ay, can you turn the stereo on for me?" he asked.

"Sure. What do you wanna hear?"

"I don't know. Something good."

After taking a sip of her drink, Gray placed down her cup and went into the living room. She still couldn't get over the fact that she was engaged—and pregnant, at that. Truth had responded just like she knew he would when she told him the news of her pregnancy. He was overjoyed. He couldn't wait to call his mother and give her the exciting information.

Gray sat on the floor and went through her CD case. After a moment of deliberation, she decided to put in Eric Roberson's first disk, *Presents: The Vault, Vol 1*. She loved his velvety voice.

As she eased her way up from the floor, there was a knock on the door. Not expecting any guests, Gray wondered who could've gotten past the gate.

"I'll get it, babe. You sit down and rest," Truth suggested.

"No, I'll get it." She waved him back into the kitchen.

Gray unlocked the door, and to her amazement, standing there as clear as day was Gunz. He was no longer a mere memory and a man from her past. He was there, close enough to touch. Gray quickly closed the door behind her and stepped out into the hallway.

"My bad. I ain't mean to stop by announced. I just needed to holla at you for a second," he spoke while looking everywhere else but her face.

"What's wrong?"

"My ol' dude just passed."

"Gunz, I am so sorry to hear that." She reached out and caressed his arm.

She had only witnessed it once before, but it looked as if Gunz had tears in his eyes.

"I wish there was something I could do."

"This shit is fucked up, yo." His voice trembled as he finally became able to stare into her slanted blue eyes.

"I'm so sorry, Gunz." Gray lovingly placed her arms around his waist.

Gunz, without hesitation, wrapped his arms around her as well. Everything in that moment made sense. Their bodies molded together like clay and they became one. Gray never wanted to leave his side. Gunz felt the same way. She would forever hold his heart in her hands.

"Babe, are you okay?" Truth opened the door.

"Yeah." She abruptly let Gunz go and stepped back.

Truth tried to hide the fury that was raging inside of him, but hate for Gunz flooded his eyes.

"Umm . . . Gunz's father just died." Gray tried to explain.

"No need to explain, sweetheart." Truth looked at Gunz and kissed the outside of her left hand.

Gray's engagement ring gleamed like the sun. Gunz didn't know how he hadn't recognized it before. Gray focused her attention on the floor. She couldn't bear seeing the throbbing look of pain in Gunz's eyes.

"Did you tell him, sweetheart?" Truth smirked.

"Truth, stop." Gray shot him a look that could kill.

"What? I think the man needs to know we're getting married and you're having my baby."

"Gunz . . ." Gray tried to explain.

"It's good, ma." He sucked in his bottom lip and massaged his chin. "Like I said, my bad for just poppin' up. Y'all have a good night."

The Waffle House was filled to the brim with people. It was a Sunday morning in April. Kema, Heidi, Tee-Tee, and Gray shared a booth, awaiting their food. Gray could barely fit in the seat; her stomach was so big. She was four months pregnant and showing a lot. That didn't stop her from ordering the All-Star Special Breakfast, which consisted of a waffle, eggs, hash browns, toast, sausage, bacon, and orange juice. On top of that, she added on a side of grits.

"Girl, yo' ass gon' be as big as a house you keep on eating like that," Tee-Tee commented.

"Leave my pooh-pooh alone." Heidi hugged Gray. "She looks beautiful, and I can't wait till my god-baby get here."

"Yo' god-baby?" Tee-Tee scrunched up his forehead. "I think you got it confused, miss. That is my god-baby."

"Both y'all bitches got it twisted," Kema confirmed. "I'ma be the god-mama. Ain't that right, Gray?"

"First of all, all three of y'all are crazy. Tee-Tee, you're the god-mama."

"Boo-yah!" He clapped his hands then snapped his fingers. "Told you! Now, take that in ya ass!"

"Heidi and Kema, you are too."

"What?" Tee-Tee curled his lips.

"You all are my best friends, so all of y'all will be godparents."

"Whaaateva." He twisted up his lip and rolled his eyes. "So have you started planning the wedding?"

"Nope. I'm going to wait until the baby is born."

"I think you should call it off," Kema retorted, rolling her eyes.

"Why?" Heidi said, astonished. "Truth loves her."

"Exactly. Truth loves her. She don't love him.

And besides that, his ass is two screws away from being crazy."

"Truth is not crazy."

"Shiiiiit."

"Okay, can you quit talkin' about the father of my child like that, please?" Gray cocked her neck to the side.

"I'm just sayin'." Kema threw up her hands in defeat.

"He do be having that *Hand That Rocks the Cradle* look in his eye sometimes," Tee-Tee agreed.

"Don't he?" Kema laughed, giving him a high five.

"Fuck the both of ya's, all right," Gray shot.

"Girl, forget them," Heidi jumped in. "Now, why aren't we planning our wedding?"

"Did this bitch not get the memo? She . . . don't . . . love . . . Truth," Tee-Tee announced.

"Okay, can you be any more louder?" Gray looked around the restaurant, embarrassed.

"So you really don't love him?" Heidi questioned.

"I mean, I want to love him, but I just don't see him that way."

"Well, why are you marrying him then?"

" 'Cause her retarded ass don't want to be alone," Tee-Tee declared.

"And because Gunz is wit' Devin," Kema added.

"Are they serious?" Heidi asked, sincerely worried.

"No, that is not the reason." Gray gave Tee-Tee and Kema the finger. "I'm marrying him because it's the right thing to do."

"You sound like one of them dumb-ass bitches

on *Desperate Housewives*." Tee-Tee couldn't help but laugh.

"Keep on making fun of me and I'm gon' leave."

"Yo' ass ain't going nowhere. Don't be mad at us 'cause we know the truth. You still in love wit' Gunz, and I dare you to say that you ain't." He pointed his fork in her face.

"If you don't get that fork out my face, I'ma stick it up yo' loose ass," she warned.

"You ain't know? I likes it rough." Tee-Tee rolled his chest and danced.

"Ughh, you get on my nerves."

"Do you still love him, Gray?" Heidi asked, dying to know.

"Yeah, I do. So what?"

"Then you gotta break this engagement off. That ain't right, Gray."

"Look, I know that it's fucked up to be engaged to one person but in love with another, but what am I supposed to do? Gunz has moved on with Devin. They have a baby on the way, and so do I. Truth loves me, and I know that he'll make a great father and a good husband. And eventually, my feelings will change. Who knows? The baby might bring us closer together."

"I just hope you're doing the right thing."

"Me too, friend. Me too."

Silence filled the room. The stark white walls and sheets that covered the furniture in Gunz's condo reminded him of death. Everything in his life that he loved was gone. He had no one to turn to or lean on. Gunz had ended up just like his father said he would be—alone. There he was, isolated from the world.

His elbows rested on the back of the couch while a pair of shades concealed his eyes. In one more hour, his condo would no longer be his. He'd sold it for a quarter of a million dollars, but the money didn't mean a thing to him. Gunz just wanted his life back. He needed to feel whole again. He needed his lifeline back. He needed Gray. Without her, nothing was as it should be. The time they'd spent apart had made him a better man. All the games he'd played had been thrown away. He wanted nothing more than to give her his all. He didn't care that she belonged to someone else. She was his, and that would always remain the same.

What they shared couldn't even be compared to a summer's day. If he could have one wish in the world, it would be to wake up to the sound of her breath on his neck, or to feel the touch of her hands on his skin. There was no corner or dark place her love couldn't fill, but so much stuff stood in between them. Gunz didn't know if they could ever make their way back to one another again.

"Gunz, are you here?" Devin asked, peeking her head in the door.

"Yeah," he answered, unsure of why she was there.

"How are you?" she asked, taking a seat next to him.

"I'm good. You?"

"I'm fine. I just stopped by to check on you."

"I thought you had a doctor's appointment today at one." Gunz checked his watch. It was 1:30 PM.

"Oh, I forgot to tell you I rescheduled it," she answered nervously.

Gunz eyed her suspiciously. From the minute Devin told him she was pregnant, he'd had doubts, but her increasingly odd behavior made him doubt her even more. The fact that she was six months pregnant and not showing also alarmed him.

"So what day you reschedule it for?"

"Uhh . . . next Tuesday."

"Well, I'm going wit' you this time."

"No! You don't have to. My mama gon' go wit' me."

"Well, we'll all go then," Gunz confirmed. "Ain't you supposed to be having an ultrasound done?"

"Yeah, but I'm tellin' you it's fine. You don't have to be there," she declared, feeling suffocated.

"Why every time I try to go to the doctor wit' you, you got an excuse?" he said with a menacing stare.

"What are you talkin' about? Ain't nobody got no excuse. I just know how busy you are." Devin shot up, offended, her back now facing him.

"What doctor do you be going to anyway?"

"I go to a clinic. Why you askin' me so many questions? What, you think I'm lyin'?" she asked, agitated.

"I mean, that's what it seems like. I'm tryin' to be involved, but you don't want me to."

"I want you to be involved, but don't treat me like a liar."

"Okay, if you ain't lyin', then what clinic you go to and what's your doctor's name? As a matter of fact, when the last time you went to the doctor and what the doctor say?" Gunz quizzed.

"Why?" Devin snapped.

" 'Cause we supposed to be having a muthafuckin' baby together and I don't know shit! I got a muthafuckin' seed coming into this world and I don't even know when my baby due. When the baby due, Devin?"

"August, I guess." She shrugged.

"You guessing, Devin. This ain't no muthafuckin' game to me. This real life."

"Why you treating me like this?" She began to cry.

"What the fuck you cryin' for? You cryin' 'cause I'm askin' you questions about what's mine? This shit I need to know. I ain't sign up for this. You sittin' up here tellin' me the baby due in August, but if you six months pregnant, the baby supposed to be here in July. A three-year-old could've calculated that."

"You ain't gon' never love me, are you?" Devin's bottom lip trembled.

"What the fuck are you talkin' about? You know me and you not together."

"I thought that tellin' you that I was pregnant would bring us closer together, but whenever you look at me . . . I wish that I was her."

"So that's how you thought you would get my attention? Do you realize how fuckin' stupid that is? How somebody gon' lie for six months sayin' they pregnant? Bitch, are you insane?" Gunz's blood pressure rose.

"I just wanted to be wit' you," she cried.

"Man, if you don't get yo' crazy ass out my house!"

"Gunz, I'm sorry."

"Yeah, you sorry all right. Just get the fuck out my house!"

"Will you please let me explain?" she begged.

"Don't make me have to tell you to leave one more time. Just g'on and burn out, real talk."

Devin contemplated pleading her case, but the killer look in Gunz's eyes told her to think otherwise. Swallowing her pride and the feelings she'd harbored for him, Devin held her head up as best as she could and walked out knowing she'd fucked up for real this time.

I just wondered . . .

do you ever think of me?

Ne-Yo, "Do you"

Chapter Sixteen

Six months had gone by. Spring and summer came and went like the wind. It was fall once again. October clouds crammed the sky. Gunz gazed absently out of the window of his Rolls Royce as Lorenzo drove him to his next destination. It was sure to rain later on that day. Gunz welcomed a downpour. The sound of rain rushing from the heavens gave him a sense of solace.

He needed something to keep him sane. Life for him consisted of one mundane scenario after another. His only joy came from his family. They'd become his center of gravity. Gray, on the other hand, was his universe. There wasn't a minute out of the day that he didn't think of her. He just wondered, did she think of him too?

Gunz missed her so much, he even went as far as to send her a letter. Gray received it on a sunny day. She, Truth, and the baby were sharing a quiet afternoon at her home. She stood in the kitchen against the island, going through her mail. Suddenly, she came across an envelope addressed to her but with no return address. Perplexed as to whom the sender could be, she ripped it open. Gray unfolded the note. It read:

Gray,

    If you're reading this, it means I worked up the courage to mail it. Good for me, I guess. Look, I'm not tryin' to interrupt your life, but there are a few things that I need to get off my chest. I know that at times you have felt that I'm arrogant, selfish, and immature. All this may be true (LOL) but there are a few things about me that you have yet to learn. On Sunday mornings, I like to chill and watch the Food Network. Tyler Florence and Bobby Flay are my mans, no homo. I dig Basquiat paintings, I don't clean up behind myself, and I often leave weed ashes all over the floor.

    But I digress. Let's move on. I've met this girl, right. It was an accident. I wasn't looking for it, but she's kinda special. You see, she said one thing, I said another. And in that very instant, I found myself wanting to spend the rest of my life in the middle of that conversation. I got this feelin' in my gut that she's the one. She's crazy as hell, but in a cute way that makes me smile, and a great deal of maintenance.

    She is you, Gray. The only problem is I don't know how to be with you, and knowing that scares the shit outta me. 'Cause if I'm not wit' you, I got this feeling that we'll get lost. And I can't tell you why you should take a leap of faith on a nigga like me, but damn, you smell good, like home. You make a mean Kimchi too.

That's gotta count for something, right? Call
me.

> *Loving you still,*
> *Gunz*

Unfortunately for Gunz, he never received the
phone call he'd so desperately wanted. It kind of
fucked him up 'cause love was no longer a mirage
of the mind for him. His days and nights were spent
reeling in self-indulgent wishes of her kisses. Pangs
of guilt consumed his soul. If only he'd treated her
right. There were many times when Gunz held the
phone in search of her voice. He needed his heartbeat back.

Unbeknownst to him, his wish was about to come
true.

He was in the Delmar Loop. Lorenzo had just
pulled up to the light when the silhouette of her
figure appeared. Time stood still as she crossed the
street in slow motion. Everything about her had
changed for the better. Gray's hair was jet black and
flat-ironed straight, with Chinese-cut bangs. The
hairstyle enhanced her Korean features. She'd
slimmed down a bit, but all the curves she used to
possess were still in the right places.

Gunz couldn't help but to admire her swagger.
Gray was rocking the hell out of a white oversized
men's button-up. The sleeves were rolled up, while
the first five buttons were undone, revealing her
caramel-colored skin and the fact that she wore no
bra. Over her shirt and around her waist was a
brown-and-gold skinny belt. The rest of the ensemble consisted of dark blue skin tight skinny jeans,

five-inch Alberta Ferretti heels, brown Gucci shades, her engagement ring, and Bishop's gold watch.

"Yo, let me out," Gunz demanded, not wanting to waste another minute.

"Is everything okay, sir?" Lorenzo questioned, concerned.

"Just park the car. I'll be right back," Gunz replied, jumping out into traffic.

Gray was already across the street. She was just about to head into a boutique called Zeizo when he caught up with her.

"Gray," he called out.

The sound of Gunz's voice sent chills up her spine. For a second Gray wondered if she was hallucinating; that was, until Gunz called out her name again. Gray looked over her shoulder and spotted him coming toward her.

"Goddamn," she whispered underneath her breath. Gunz was finer than a muthafucka. His hair was freshly lined and cut. The black cashmere cardigan he donned draped over his muscles like silk. Underneath, he sported a white V-neck. Dark jeans, old school Air Jordans, shades, a gold rosary, and a Nixon watch completed the look. Gray could hardly compose herself.

"What's up wit' you?" he asked.

"Nothing. How you been?" she asked, unsure of what to say or do.

"I been a'ight. I heard you had a li'l girl."

"Yeah, about a month ago."

"That's what's up. I bet she look just like you."

"Yeah, everybody says so. She's in the store with Tee-Tee right now. I have a picture of her on my phone if you wanna see it."

"You can show me."

Gray went into her back pocket and pulled out her phone. "I took this picture of her last week after I gave her a bath." She handed Gunz her phone.

"Damn, she look just like you. What you name her?"

"Aoki."

Gunz couldn't help but smile. Gray's daughter was the prettiest baby he'd ever seen. She lay on her back above a pink blanket, dressed in all pink. Her hair was jet black, while her eyes were shaped like diamonds. Aoki's cheeks were a rosy shade of pink, and her lips were full and pouty, just like her mother's.

"Congratulations." Gunz handed her back the phone. "I'm happy for you."

"Thanks."

"So have you gone and got married on me yet?"

"Nope, still engaged." She flashed her ring.

"When's the wedding date?"

"I haven't planned one yet."

"What you waiting on? What, you scared or something? Don't tell me you having second thoughts."

"Okay then, I won't."

"If you having second thoughts, then that'll be all bad for ol' boy."

"Humph." Gray put her head down and laughed some. Gunz hadn't changed one bit. "So how is Devin and the baby doing?"

"Devin wild as hell, man. I don't know what's going on wit' her."

"Well, what about the baby?"

"Man, it ain't no baby. We ain't even gotta get off into all that right now. What you doing later? Why don't we go and have dinner or something?"

"I don't know if that's a good idea."

"It's cool," Gunz responded, crushed. "I just wanted to see what was up wit' you. Catch up on old times."

"I mean, I wish I could, but—"

"Ma . . . it's good. You ain't gotta explain. It was good seeing you, though, for real."

"It was good seeing you too." She smiled slightly.

"Be good, a'ight." He softly kissed her cheek.

"You too," she replied as she watched him walk away.

"Girl, you need to quit playin'," Tee-Tee said, coming out of the store with the baby.

"Boy, what are you talkin' about?"

"The chemistry between you two is so thick you can cut it wit' a knife. I don't know why you still lyin' to ya'self."

"Tee-Tee, what Gunz and I shared is in the past, where it should be."

"Bitch, please. I ain't Kema and Heidi. You can't fool me."

Hail and rain tapped against the window. The familiar sound of thunder echoed through the air. The soothing humming sound from the heat roamed throughout the house. Gray lay curled up on her side, snuggled underneath covers. It had been a long, tiring day, so a good night's sleep was overdue. She'd gone to bed early to ensure she'd get enough rest. The next day was gonna be hectic. In her living room were racks of designer samples. *Haute Couture*'s holiday must-have issue was about to hit newsstands, and Gray had to come up with ideas for new trends to present to Sienna the following Monday.

Gray was running herself ragged, but she'd much rather excel in her career and as a mother then mourn the death of her relationship with Gunz. That didn't stop her from thinking about him every second of the day or dreaming of him, though. That night, she dreamt they were strolling on the beach hand in hand in Mexico. Waves from the ocean splashed against her feet.

Gunz lifted her left hand and kissed her palm. A diamond ring the size of a nickel shimmered in the afternoon sunlight. They were married and happily in love. A smile graced the corners of her lips as she lay still asleep.

She never wanted the moment to end, but just as she was about to turn over, there was a sudden ring at the door. Startled by the noise, Gray's eyes shot open.

The first thing she did was look at the clock. It was a couple minutes to four. Gray wondered who could be at her house that time of the morning. As she sat up and grabbed her robe, there was another ring. Pissed off by the visitor's impatience, she stomped down the steps and to the door.

"Who is it?" she asked with an attitude.

"Me."

Gray's heart skipped what seemed to be a million beats. The voice on the other side of the door belonged to one person and one person only—Gunz. Gray squashed her fears and opened the door slowly. Her eyes traveled up to his. He looked sexier than ever, but the sadness in his brown eyes was more evident.

Gunz knew he should say something, but fuck it; they'd done enough talking in the past. Never taking his focus off her, he gently took a hold of the sash on her robe and untied it. The sides of it flew open, exposing her satin negligee. The imprint of her hard nipples poked through the fabric. Gunz pushed her robe off.

Gray felt like she was in a whirlwind. Her body craved him. She watched closely as his index fingers pulled the straps of her gown down. Gray allowed it to fall into a heap on the floor. Gunz admired her gorgeous physique. Her body was like a work of art. Every dip, curve, and fold was magnificent. Hungry for her touch, he picked her up.

Gray eagerly wrapped her arms and legs around him. It seemed like a decade had passed since they last kissed. Every flick of his tongue felt like heaven. Gunz sucked the side of Gray's neck, but not without taking a delicious bite.

"Ahhhhh," she moaned in delight.

With each of her butt cheeks in his hand, he led her over to the nearest wall. His dick was so hard it was about to bust through his pants. The rough surface of the wall scratched against Gray's back. She enjoyed the pain.

"Baby, I missed you."

"I missed you too," he groaned as she got down and dropped to her knees.

Gray swiftly undid his pants. His big, black dick sprung to attention. If she were a veteran, she would've saluted. With ease she took him inch by inch into her mouth. The veins in his dick throbbed against the taste buds of her tongue. He tasted like Godiva chocolate.

Gunz tilted his head back in agony. He wanted to cum so bad. Gray was sucking his dick like it was the last thing on earth she'd get to taste.

Not ready to cum, he pulled her up and made her face the wall. The arch in her back was perfect. Gunz spread her ample butt cheeks apart and inserted himself deep within her valley. All the blood in his body rushed to the tip of his penis. Gray was wetter than wet. With his hands on her hips, he grinded in and out of her at a feverish pace. Sounds of his shaft slapping against her butt echoed around them.

"Ohhhhh, baby," Gray wailed as he hit her spot.

Her face was pressed up against the wall. There was no place for her to run or hide. Gunz had her right where he wanted. She was trapped in his web.

He wanted to ensure that she came over and over again. Using his hand, he reached around and began massaging her clit. Grays's thighs began to shake uncontrollably as she came. Sweet, sticky cream saturated his dick.

Gunz could feel himself about to cum too. Squeezing his eyes shut, he rotated his hips in a circular motion. An electric spark rushed through his body as he came. Spent, he placed sloppy, erotic kisses down the center of her back.

Hours later, Gray lay drained in Gunz's arms. He'd taken her body to forbidden places of ecstasy. The orgasms she experienced were earth shattering.

Gunz lightly caressed the side of her arm. This was where he belonged. For a while he'd resisted arrest, but Gray had handcuffed his heart. No matter the obstacle, she stuck by his side. She proved that love could be patient and kind. She made him want to be better, not only for her, but for himself.

"Marry me," he spoke barely above a whisper while massaging her forehead with his fingertips.

"What?" she asked, shocked.

"You heard me."

"Gunz, don't play wit' me."

"I'm for real. Don't marry him. Marry me."

"Where is all this coming from?"

"My heart. I tried, but I don't work without you."

"So you really wanna marry me?" She faced him.

"Yeah, I mean, I know I fucked up. We fucked up. But we can make this shit work."

"I don't know what to say. I mean, have you forgotten that I'm engaged?"

"You don't love that man."

"But we have a child together."

"I understand that, but you can't sit up here and tell me that yo' heart don't belong to me."

"Oh my God." Gray ran her fingers through her hair and shook her head. "This shit is crazy."

"Nah, you make me crazy," Gunz joked.

"That's good to know," she replied in a sarcastic tone.

"Straight up. You fuck me up how you try to pretend that the past don't count, but I know it does."

"That's the problem, though. In the past, all I ever wanted was to be a part of your heart, but you wouldn't let me. Now I've moved on. I got a child with that man. I promised to be his wife. I can't just up and leave like that."

"So you tellin' me no?" he countered.

"I don't know what I'm sayin'."

"If you can look me in my eye and tell me that you don't wanna be wit' me then I'll leave and never bother you again."

Gray stared Gunz square in the eyes, but the words she so desperately wanted to say were too hard to form. She needed Gunz as bad as she needed a heartbeat.

"I promise I got you. I swear to God everything gon' be a'ight. I'ma give you my all, and I'ma love Aoki as if she was my own."

"Like, I wanna say yes, but I honestly don't think we're ready for all of that."

"And you're sure about that? No is your final answer?"

"Yeah, I just think we should wait. If we're going to do this again, then I need to make decisions with my head and not my heart."

"I can dig that," Gunz replied. He was hurt, but deep down inside, he knew that she was right.

"I just don't want you to hurt me again."

"Trust me; I won't." He took her into his arms and kissed her forehead.

"I can't believe you are playin' that mess," Gray said, sitting Indian-style on the living room floor as Gunz played Grand Theft Auto.

"Quit hatin'."

"I'm far from a hater, sweetie."

"Yeah, yeah, yeah, that's what your mouth say."

"Whateva." Gray laughed, focusing back on her work.

"Baby, you mind getting me a beer?"

"Gunz, you see I'm working."

"Please." He looked at her and winked his eye.

"Ooh, you get on my nerves." She smiled as her cell phone began to ring.

By the ringtone, she knew it was Truth. She'd been dodging his calls all day.

"Hello?"

"What you doing? Why you ain't been answering your phone? What, you got a nigga over there or something?" he joked.

"No. You know I told you I had work to do today." She halfway told the truth. "What's up wit' you?"

"Shit, I was tryin' to come see you. Ain't Aoki coming home today?"

"Uhhhhh . . ." She stalled. "Actually, I asked Tee-Tee to watch her until tomorrow. I thought you had to work tonight."

"They told me I ain't have to come in."

"Oh."

"Are you all right?" he questioned, sensing her nervousness.

"Baby, what's taking you so long?" Gunz yelled, interrupting her conversation.

"Who the fuck was that?" Truth questioned, heated. "Don't tell me it's some nigga over there for real."

"Truth, just let me—"

"Yo, you *wild* than a muthafucka! You straight up got some cat over there like I ain't yo' fuckin' fiancé! Who the fuck was that?" he asked, heated.

"Gunz."

"Gunz! So you back fuckin' wit' him?"

"Truth, it just happened. I was going to tell you."

"When? When were you gon' tell me, Gray, huh? On our wedding day, or the fuckin' honeymoon?"

"Can you please calm down?"

"Fuck nah! Here I am tryin' to be the man you need, and this is how you do me? You know how much bullshit I had to go through to be wit' you! You got life fucked up if you think you just gon' ride off into the sunset wit' that nigga and I'ma just fade into the background like ain't nothin' happened. Bitch, please."

"Excuse me?"

"You heard me. You just like all these other hoes out here. Any nigga wit' a li'l dough can get it." He tried his best to hurt her.

"Okay, I know your feelings are hurt, but you buggin'."

"Nah, you the one trippin', and if you think I'ma let you have my fuckin' daughter around that nigga, you got another thing coming!"

"Truth, I understand that you're upset, but you need to calm down. Holla at me when we can talk like adults," she spoke before hanging up.

Gray knew it would never be an easy way or a good time to break Truth's heart, but it had to be done sooner or later. She just hoped that ultimately, they could maintain a friendship for the sake of the baby.

Gray popped open the fridge and pulled out a cold Boulevard Wheat Beer. Back in the living room, she handed Gunz his drink.

"Who was that on the phone?" he asked, seeing that she was upset.

"Truth."

"Everything good?"

"I hope so," she answered, praying that it would be.

The next day, Truth rang Gray's doorbell with a bouquet of yellow roses in his hand. Nervous energy resonated through his system as he shifted from side to side. Gray wasn't expecting him, so he wasn't sure how she would react.

"Who is it?" she asked.

"Truth."

For the first time since they'd known one another, Gray was uncertain about his presence. Checking herself, she opened the door. At the end of the day, Truth was still one of her very good friends.

"Hi," she spoke.

"Hi. These are for you." He kissed her cheek.

"Thanks." Gray took the flowers and inhaled the fragrant scent.

"Can I come in?"

"Sure." She stepped aside.

Truth came in, and Gray closed the door behind them. They both sat on the couch.

Gray tried to be as normal as possible and asked, "So how are you?"

"As good as I can be, I guess. Where's Aoki?"

"Upstairs asleep. Look, Truth, I am so sorry about the other day. I never meant to hurt you. I just wish we could've talked about it face to face."

"I know." Truth reached out and touched her hand. "You gotta understand how I feel, Gray. I love you. I always have, and I know we could be great together. You just have to give me the chance to show you."

"Truth, I love you too."

"So what's the problem?" he asked, hopeful.

"Just not in that way. You're one of my best friends, and that's all I can ever really see you being. I hope you understand, 'cause I don't want to lose you as a friend."

"But you just said you loved me." He held her hands tight.

"I do."

"Stop lying to me," he shouted. Truth took her arms and shook her.

"Have you lost your mind? Let me go," Gray screamed, trying to pull away.

"Tell me you love me!"

"Are you fuckin' crazy?"

"Just let me make you feel good." He kissed her roughly.

"Get off of me!"

"C'mon, Gray. I know you want me!" His tongue slithered from her ear, across her cheek and to her mouth.

"I said get the fuck off of me!" She yanked her arm away.

Before Truth knew it, Gray had slapped him with so much force that her handprint was left on his face. Truth reacted quickly with a backhand slap of his own. His hit sent Gray flying backward off the couch.

"You think you can treat me any way you want and get away with it, bitch?" He towered over her.

Truth kicked Gray in the stomach. Off in the distance, she could hear Aoki begin to cry.

"Well, guess what?" He took a fistful of her hair in his hand and yanked her head back. "If I can't have you, no one else will either!"

Truth threw her head back. It hit the floor with a loud thud. Just like in the cartoons, Gray saw stars. She couldn't believe this was happening. Where was the man she'd known the last eleven years? Maybe she never knew him at all.

"I loved you, bitch." Truth paced the room. "And this is how you do me? I can't believe you gon' choose that punk-ass nigga over me! He killed my fuckin' brother! I'll be damned if he take you and my daughter away from me too!" A sadistic thought crept into his mind. He ran into the kitchen and grabbed a butcher knife.

Tears streamed down Gray's face. What had she done to deserve this? Using her hands and feet, she stood up. Truth wasn't about to kill her without a fight. Gray ran around the couch with him hot on her tail. Spotting a glass vase, she picked it up and threw it at him. Truth blocked the throw by placing his hands in front of his face, but pieces of glass still became lodged in his arms.

"Fuckin' bitch!"

Gray was more scared than ever. As she continued to dodge his attempts to grab her, she heard the sound of someone buzzing her door. If she could just get to the door and press the button . . . Gray held her side and tried making it to the door, but Truth had caught up to her. Swinging the knife, he slit her back.

"Awwww!" she screamed out in agony as she fell to the floor.

The exposed skin burned, and blood began to spurt out and drench the back of her shirt. Determined not to give up, she struggled with all her might to crawl, but Truth had grabbed her leg.

"Get off of me, you sick fuck!" She kicked and screamed.

"Oh yeah, I'm sick all right! You know that night we fucked and you told me you loved me? You thought I was Gunz! You still love me now, Gray?"

"You raped me?" she shrieked, shocked by his confession.

"Bitch, you enjoyed it! Just like I enjoyed killing Bishop!"

"Oh my God, you are fuckin' crazy!" Gray used her free leg and kicked him.

The force of the kick caused Truth to drop the knife. Always a quick thinker, Gray raced over to grab it. Truth quickly took a hold of her hair once again. The pain was excruciating. She could feel strands of her hair being ripped from her scalp, but Gray wasn't going to let that deter her. With her arm stretched forward, her fingertips touched the handle of the knife.

Gray used all the strength she had and slid the knife into her hand. Truth swiftly clutched Gray's hand in a desperate attempt to take the knife from her. Unwilling to die, Gray flung her head back and butted Truth in the face. Natural reflexes caused him to place his hands onto his face, giving Gray enough time to turn onto her back and plunge the knife into the center of his chest.

The universe stopped. Time stood still. Gray's and Truth's eyes connected. Regret and sadness swept over them like a winter's breeze. This was how their story would end—fatally. They would be forever bonded by the little girl that lay crying in her bassinet, but the friendship they'd built over the years would be buried along with Truth and his deceitful ways.

Gray's lips trembled as she sat up. Both of Truth's hands were on the handle of the knife. His soul was breaking right in front of her eyes. Blood trickled out of the corner of his mouth. He could hardly breathe. Gray sobbed hysterically as he pulled the butcher knife from his chest.

"I love you," he whispered before closing his eyes. Seconds later, he fell onto his side, dead.

Gray raced to the door. Without hesitation, she ran out, screaming for help. Down in the lobby, she came face to face with Gunz.

"What's wrong?" he asked, visibly worried.

"Truth just tried to kill me!"

Epilogue

Three years later, Gray sat at her desk with her legs crossed, gazing out the window. Finally everything was as it should be. All of her hard work and determination had paid off. She now had a corner office on the twenty-fifth floor, right next to Sienna. Gray was the editor-at-large of *Haute Couture* magazine and Sienna's new right hand. After Jean-Pierre retired, she was a shoo-in for the job.

Gray had come a long way. She was no longer the little mixed girl with homemade clothes. She proved to everyone that dreams really do come true; you just have to reach out and grab them one at a time.

She now knew that to love someone, you have to be comfortable with yourself. When she first met Gunz, she wasn't. She was lonely and desperate for companionship. Instead of letting things go as they may, she latched on, determined to make him be the man she wanted. But what Gray had to learn was that love shouldn't be forced. It should come naturally, and eventually, in its own time, it did.

Sometimes nightmares of the day Truth tried to

kill her invaded her mind, but Gray wasn't going to let the negative experience take over her life.

A scar from the cut on her back still existed, but she'd forgiven Truth and moved on. She even attended his funeral. Gray knew that no one was perfect. She'd made her fair share of mistakes too. Gray recognized that she hadn't been the best friend to Truth at times. It didn't excuse what he'd done to her, though.

At peace with her life, Gray took a much needed breath and spun around in her chair. A photo on her desk caught her attention. It was a picture of her three-year-old daughter. Aoki was her world, her inspiration, and the love of her life wrapped up in one.

"Gray," her loyal secretary, Breann, buzzed her office.

"Yes."

"You have a call on line one."

Gray pressed the button.

"Gray Rose speaking."

"You miss me?" Gunz asked.

It took him a minute, but after seeing how his choices affected the people around him, he backed out of the life and went legit. Gray couldn't have been happier. Their relationship was more solid now than ever.

"Of course I do." She lit up and smiled.

"What time you gettin' home?"

"I'll be there no later than four."

"A'ight, well, I was just callin' to see what was up wit' you."

"How did the meeting go?"

"Good. I signed the contract. My fifth restaurant will be open in the fall."

"I'm so happy for you, babe."

"Thanks."

"Love you."

"I love you too."

Gray hung up the phone and took a glance at the ring on her left hand. After dating exclusively for almost three years, Gray finally felt that they were ready for marriage. She wasn't willing to say yes until Gunz had proven himself worthy of a lifelong commitment, but surprisingly enough, Gunz had gone above and beyond proving himself worthy.

With his actions, he showed that he was the man for Gray. He lived up to his words and loved her unconditionally. He loved Aoki just like he said he would. She was his daughter, and he was the only father she knew. And no, getting to the point they were at hadn't been easy; but kinda like the old saying goes, if you love it, then you should let it out of its cage, and if it comes back, then you know it's there to stay.

Coming Soon

Material Girls 2: Labels and Love

By Keisha Ervin

1

In a years time, life for Dylan Monroe had changed drastically. She'd gone from trips around the world, designer dresses straight from the runway, and A-List soirees to weekly runs to Wal-Mart, clearance rack clothes, and catering the parties she once used to attend. She'd found the love of her life heavy weight champion of the world Angel Carter, but after having a torrid affair with her newly married, ex fiancée State, she lost him.

After nearly a year apart they rekindled their romance at her best friend and his sister Billie's wedding. Dylan hoped that night would be their chance for a new beginning, but still unable to forgive and forget, Angel made it clear that what they once shared was a thing of the past. Heartbroken, Dylan accepted their fate but still held out hope for them in her heart. All the signs to their relationship pointed to over, but unforeseen circumstances stepped in and two months after the wedding Dylan learned that she was pregnant.

Now she was more confused than ever. Desperately needing the help of her two best girls, Dylan met up with them at The City Diner for breakfast. Dylan loved going to The City Diner. Despite their wide variety of comfort foods, she thoroughly enjoyed the whimsical way in which it was designed. The diner was filled with old movie and music memorabilia, 50's style booths, tables and a jukebox. Adjusting the strap of her purse on her shoulder she made her way over to table where Billie and Tee-Tee were waiting.

"Okay, now I know you ain't doing it like you used to but just 'cause you a one step away from being in the welfare line don't mean we have to starve to death," her cousin Tee-Tee complained as soon as she sat down.

"Tee-Tee shut up. I got enough going on to be dealing wit you and your nonsense. It's too damn early."

"Uh, ah, did slumdog just read me?" He looked at Billie appalled.

"Yeah honey, you just got served," Billie nodded tryin' to be hip. "Does anybody still say that?"

"No." Dylan shook her head.

"Anyway." He flicked his wrist. "Miss Unfashionably Late I know you're a recessionista now but I know you not shoppin' in the Miley Cyrus collection at Wal-Mart?" He curled up his lip and looked Dylan up and down.

"What?" She gazed over her outfit which she thought was cute.

Dylan wore a black fitted fake leather jacket from Forever 21, wife beater, white jeans and motorcycle boots. Her accessories consisted of a green scarf, gold watch, skull ring and a black hobo style purse.

"You are such a hater, but anyway, how are you my love?" Dylan turned her attention to Billie and patted her on the arm.

"Good," she cooed. "I am so excited for my honeymoon," Billie clapped enthusiastically.

"I know you are. Where are ya'll going again?"

"India, Italy, Japan and Rome. We'll be gone a month."

"Can I come too?" Dylan half joked.

"Nigga no," Billie laughed. "I have been married to my husband for two months and we have yet to spend a moment alone. I can't wait to get the hell up outta here."

"Them li'l critters you call kids gon' have a fit. You know they can't live without they mama," Tee-Tee took a sip from his glass.

"They will be alright." Billie crossed her legs. "Their father is watching them and say something else about my kids and see don't I reach across this table and stab you in the neck with this fork."

"And I thought marriage would soften you," he chuckled.

"Actually it has," Billie smiled. "Guess who I invited over for New Year's Eve."

"Fantasia brother Tiny?" Tee-Tee exclaimed over the moon.

"No." Billie looked at him as if he were crazy.

"Don't be lookin' at me like that. If I wasn't married, Tiny could get it."

"Oh my god, I can't it's too early," Billie hung her head and laughed.

"Well who is it?" Dylan asked.

"Cain and Becky."

"What the fuck was on yo' mind?" Tee-Tee drew back. "Bitch was you high? We don't like them."

"I know but the kids want they daddy there so I couldn't just invite him and not her," she explained.

"Shit, why not? I would've."

"That's 'cause you're ignorant," Dylan chimed in.

"You damn right I am. That skank wouldn't be up in my house."

"Well Cain and I have children together so I have to learn to tolerate her," Billie added.

"Yous a good one honey 'cause er'time I see ha we'll be fightin'," Tee-Tee bobbed his head like a ghetto girl.

"Me and you gon' be fightin' if you don't leave my friend alone," Dylan warned.

"Well ain't you feisty this morning." Tee-Tee gave her a sly grin.

"I swear to God I can't stand you," Dylan laughed.

"Well you know ya'll are invited," Billie said.

"We better," Tee-Tee shot. "If Pam and Tommy Lee can come I know we invited."

"You are a damn coon."

"I'm pregnant!" Dylan blurted out unable to keep it bottled in anymore.

"Oh my goodness," Tee-Tee placed his hands in front of him as if to say freeze. "Oh my goooooood-ness. We having a baby!"

"You have to got to be kidding me." Billie rolled her neck and folded her arms across her chest.

"What?" Dylan looked at her perplexed.

"You know you really had me fooled. I'm up here thinking you have changed and you pregnant by State."

Dylan covered her mouth and laughed.

"And you think it's funny? Bitch you must have me fucked up. Let me go before I have to choke the shit outta this hoe." Billie grabbed her purse and stood up

"Billie sit yo' ass down," Dylan demanded pulling her arm. "I am not pregnant by State."

"Well who then?" She retook her seat.

Dylan licked her lips nervously and swallowed.

"Angel."

"Oh hell to the no!" Tee-Tee wagged his finger. "You done stole my man and you gettin' ready to have a baby by him. Just shoot me now!"

"You are so dramatic."

"Hold up," Billie jumped in. "So you mean to tell me you pregnant by my brother, Angel?"

"Yes."

"And can't nobody else be the daddy?" Billie questioned still skeptical.

"No."

"Nobody?"

"No!" Dylan shrieked.

"Okay," she placed her hands up. "I believe you."

"Damn was I that much of a ho?" Dylan looked at both Billie and Tee-Tee.

"YES!" They both said in unison.

"Ya'll ass ain't shit." She shot them both an angry look.

"No we speaks the truth," Tee-Tee objected. "Shit yo' ass was about to be the female Wilt Chamberlin."

"Fuck you." Dylan gave him the middle finger.

"No thanks my man already did this morning." He batted his eyes.

"Ugh, don't make me throw up again. I already have twice this morning." Dylan rolled her eyes.

"Okay let's get focused here." Billie interjected. "How far a long are you?"

"Two months."

"Whoa." Billie's eyes grew wide. "So that means that you and Angel did the oochie wally oochie bang bang the night of my wedding."

"Yep that's about right."

"Wow." Billie shook her head dazed.

"So the million dollar question is." Tee-Tee placed his right elbow on the table and leaned forward. "Does he know?"

Dylan winced.

"No."

"Ooooooh scandalous," Tee-Tee snapped his fingers.

"Why haven't you told him?" Billie asked.

"'Cause it's already weird between us. I mean after we smashed—"

"Speak English," Billie waved her hand cutting her off.

"Fucked, made love, had sex. He basically told me it was a wrap and that we would never be so what do I do, call him and say hey how you doing? Did you hear ole girl from the Hills had ten surgeries in one day and oh by the way, I'm pregnant?"

"Girl don't she look faaaaaaaaabulous," Tee-Tee added.

"No, more like a hot mess," Dylan disagreed.

"Fuck all of that." Billie waved her hands. "When are you going to tell him?"

"Soon, of course. I'm just tryin' to find the right time."

"Girl you better tell that man. Nothin good ever came from keeping something a secret. Especially not no shit like that." Tee-Tee cautioned.

"Okay . . . you just got really deep," Dylan said in a Valley Girl like tone.

"I know and now I have a headache." He massaged his forehead.

"Look there's no time like the present. The longer you wait the harder it's gonna be," Billie said.

Dylan took a deep breath.

"I guess. I just have never been this scared before in my life." Dylan buried her face in her hands.

"Why?" Billie asked concerned.

"'Cause I'm still in love with your brother and what if he don't want me to have it?" Dylan swallowed the tears that were rising in her throat. "Could you imagine anything worse?"

"Yep," Tee-Tee nodded. "A Coogi sweater with the matching pants."

"Anyway," Billie tuned up her face. "If I know anything I know my brother, he gon' want you to keep it."

"I hope so."

"Look, quit stalling and call him," Billie persisted.

"Okay," Dylan dug into her purse and pulled out her phone. "I'll be back." She pushed her chair back.

Outside the restaurant Dylan stood on the sidewalk. The chilly November air kissed her face as she held her phone in her hand. Nervous as hell she looked over her shoulder to see if Billie and Tee-Tee were watching her. Of course they were. Turning her head, Dylan took a much needed deep breath and found Angel's number in her address book. Reluctantly she pressed send. A second later the phone began to ring.

Damn, why couldn't his line be busy, she thought.

Three rings later her call was sent to voicemail. Knowing she would never build the courage to call him again Dylan decided to give him the news via voicemail.

"Hey . . . it's me Dylan," she spoke softly. "I know we haven't spoken in a while but I really need to talk to you." Dylan paused and tried her best to swallow the baseball like lump in her throat. "Umm . . . I'm pregnant and I'm scared. I just . . . really need to talk you so call me as soon as you get this message."

Dylan took the phone away from her ear and ended the call. She hadn't realized it when she was on the phone, but her entire body was shaking. She prayed that Angel would call back soon because if not she knew that she would be on pins and needle for the rest of the day every time her phone rang.

1,593 miles away in sunny Malibu, California, Angel sat on the side of the bed in nothing but a pair of Armani Exchange boxers. Exhausted, he yawned and rubbed his eyes then picked up the X10 remote control which controlled almost everything in the house. Using the remote he opened the curtains. The view of the Pacific Ocean was right before eyes. Angel sat and watched as the wave's crash onto the shore while reminiscing about the night before. He and his girlfriend of two months Milania had made love in every position imaginable.

She was a little known Victoria's Secret model with no children and no hidden baggage. She was an all around good girl with a heart of gold. He enjoyed her company tremendously, cherished the way she made him laugh and the fact that she was able to take his mind off Dylan was but an added bonus. They'd messed around a year and half before, but nothing serious ever popped off between them due to the fact that Angel couldn't hide his true feelings for Dylan any longer.

But now they were officially a couple and life for Angel was good. He'd finally come to terms that what he and Dylan shared was over. He could no longer dwell on the past and the moments they shared although deep down inside a corner of his heart still ached for her. Angel looked over his shoulder and found Milania who he thought was asleep staring back at him.

She'd been admiring his toned back. Angel was by far one of the sexiest men she'd ever laid her eyes upon and in her industry she'd seen a plenty. But there was something about Angel that set him apart from the pact. Maybe it was his confidence or his cocky swagger that attracted so many women to him. No it was his boy next door charm.

One glimpse at his beautiful smile or one look into his smoldering brown eyes and you were trapped. His skin was a tantalizing shade of warm honey. He was six foot two and 220 pounds of pure muscle. He rocked a bald head and goatee. Across his chest was a tattoo that read Death before Dishonor and along the right side of his body beginning at his shoulder and ending at his ankle was a tribal tattoo.

"What you over there thinkin' about," she asked feeling cream build inside her panties.

"Nothin'," he lied. "Just tryin' to wake up. I'm still tired as hell from last night."

"Really?" She smiled deviously. "Would you like some more?" She removed the covers and revealed her flawless five foot eleven physique.

Angel unconsciously licked his bottom lip. Milania was built like an Egyptian goddess. Her skin was a silky shade of butter pecan. Long ravenous black hair cascaded over her shoulders and down her back. She didn't need a stitch of makeup to enhance her beauty. Her doe shaped eyes, high cheekbones, and Cover Girl smile was all she needed to turn a man on. The winter white lace bra and bikini panties she wore only added to her sex appeal.

"As a matter of fact I do. Come get in the shower wit me." He got up and made his way to the bathroom.

"You ain't said nothin' but a word," Milania beamed getting up too.

As Angel turned on the shower and got in she began to peel off the straps of her bra but as the first strap came down Angel's cell began to vibrate. Milania stopped dead in her tracks wondering should she take a quick peek. For the past two months she'd wondered was she the only woman Angel was seeing. Now was the perfect opportunity to take a glimpse at his contacts and call log and find out. Quietly she crept around the bed and picked up his phone.

Blindsided by the name on the screen Milania had to catch her breath so she wouldn't hyperventilate. *What the fuck does she want,* she thought. Shook, Milania took a quick glance over her shoulder to make sure the coast was clear. Seeing that it was she pressed ignore sending Dylan to voicemail. *This bitch ain't gon' get in my way this time,* she hissed as the icon showing Angel had a voicemail message popped onto the screen.

With the sound of water running in the background she pressed one and listened to Dylan's message. Flabbergasted by the news she stood paralyzed. Her heart was beating a mile a minute. *This can not be happening,* she thought freaking out. *No way can this bitch be pregnant. If Angel finds out he will surely end things with me and go back to her. I can not lose him again. If I do, all of my hard work will go down the drain. The media won't be fascinated with me. The paparazzi won't clamor for my photo. I won't get anymore free swag and most importantly my plans of being Mrs. Angel Carter will no longer exist. Okay Milania think,* she paced back and forth with the phone in her hand. *You just need a lil' more time to solidify your relationship before he learns that she's pregnant.*

"What's takin' you so long? You get lost?" Angel yelled from the shower causing Milania to jump.

"No here I come!" She yelled back.

Milania looked down at the phone realizing she had to make a decision and quick. *Fuck it,* she said to herself. She knew that what she was about to do was fucked up and morally wrong on so many levels but getting put on nowadays wasn't as easy for everybody as it was for Amber Rose. Some chicks had to work a li'l harder, suck a li'l bit more dick, give up a lot more pussy, show even more ass and play a lot more games to be famous.

Now was Milania's time to shine. She would be Hollywood's new "it girl" and Angel Carter was her meal ticket to making all of her dreams come true. Without hesitation or a blink of the eye she erased the message and any evidence that Dylan had called. Pleased with her choice, Milania stripped down to her birthday suit and smiled. Angel was hers and she was willing to do any and everything to make sure things stayed that way.

"I can't believe that muthafucka!" Tee-Tee spat with his hand on his hip.

He and Dylan were inside of Macy's picking out an outfit for her to wear to Billie's New Year's Eve party.

"I mean it's been three weeks since you called him and his ass ain't called and said nothin'?"

"I found it odd too at first but I guess he just doesn't wanna have anything to do with me." Dylan tried to seem nonchalant about the situation as she slipped on a dress.

For the past three weeks she'd put on the illusion that she was this strong, independent woman who didn't need a man meaning Angel by her side. But when no one was around and all she had was herself to be with, she felt sick, like the air God breathed into her lungs had escaped. She felt bamboozled, hurt, pissed off, unwanted, shut out, forgotten and alone.

It wasn't like she had a mother who she could lean on. Her mother Candy couldn't even be put in the classification of a mother. She was like the anti-mother. Candy didn't even teach her her ABC's. One of her many nannies did. Yet and still, crying on her cousin's shoulder was something she wasn't willing to do. Yes the pain in her chest felt like she was being constantly stabbed, but Dylan had to live and stay focused for her baby.

Regrettably with each day that passed that notion became harder and harder. For Dylan, being pregnant only bought on an added stress that she didn't need. She was already dealing with the fact that her bakery, Edible Couture was failing miserably. Everyday it became increasingly hard for her to pay rent on the bakery and her townhouse. Bills were piling up to the ceiling and sooner than later her bakery would have to close.

"It's okay if he don't wanna have nothin' to do with you, but what about the baby?" Tee-Tee continued. "The baby don't have nothin' to do wit ya'll mess. It didn't ask to be brought into this world." Tee-Tee snapped outside the dressing room door.

"Just please give me his number so I can cuss his ass out."

"For the one hundredth time," Dylan stepped out to view herself in the full body mirror. "NO!"

"But why?" Tee-Tee whined. "I'm so good at it. Plus his ass deserve to get a tongue lashing."

"I know he does but it's just not worth it."

Dylan examined herself from head to toe and side to side hoping Tee-Tee would drop the conversation because she was starting to feel claustrophobic.

"Okay, I know that having a baby changes people's views on life but you are not gon' sit up here and pretend that you are not fazed by his behavior."

"Honest to Prada." Dylan raised her hand as if she were giving the Hippocratic Oath. "I'm okay. I mean . . . I'm not okay." She looked off to the side. "You know what I mean. I just have to learn how to deal with having this baby on my own," she swallowed looking down at her feet.

"If you say so." Tee-Tee said fixing the sleeve on her dress. "By the way have you talked to Billie?"

"Yeah like a week and a half ago."

"Has she talked to him?"

"We really weren't able to get off into all of that. She and Knox had to get on their flight to India."

"So is he coming to the party?" Tee-Tee probed.

"As far as I know, no," Dylan said becoming hot. "I gotta sit down."

"You okay," Tee-Tee took her by the hand and led her back into the dressing room.

"No, I feel like I gotta throw up."

"Ughh, just don't do it on me." He scooted back.

"Shut up," Dylan grimaced fanning her face with her purse. "I don't think I wanna go to the party," she pouted.

"Why?"

" 'Cause I look like a fat pig."

"No you don't. You're barely showing and you gotta come. It's gonna be fun and we gon' be the

flyest chicks up in there. Well I know I am 'cause a
bitch like me is about to show her ass while I still
can."

"Oh Tee-Tee I'm so sorry." She rubbed his arm.
"I haven't asked you anything about how the adoption is going."

"It's going. We're now going through the home-
study process now."

"What's that?"

"It's a written report by a social worker were basically the social worker does an intensive background search, finds out our motivation towards
adoption etc-etc-etc. The process goes on for about
six month and afterwards the social worker gives
their summary on us and their recommendation."

"Well if you need my help with anything just let
me know."

"I will and by the way bitch YOU BETTA WORK!
That dress is FIERCE on you!" He snapped his fingers.

Dylan looked down at the dress. It was an all
black sheath dress by Rachel Roy.

"Thanks my love. I like it too, but this is just way
too expensive."

"Girl this dress is a steal!" Tee-Tee looked at her
crazy. "It's only $99.00"

"Yeah, like I just got $99.00 layin' around."

"Well you ain't gon' be coming around me
lookin' crazy so I will buy it for you."

"No, it is not that serious."

"Girl boo, I got you."

"Tee-Tee, thank you." Dylan said hugging him
around the neck.

"And you deserve a phone call from yo' dead beat baby daddy," he eyed her sternly.

"Well we all can't get what we want now can we." She looked down at her stomach somberly and rubbed her belly.